SLOW BURN

breathing hearts series

A.K. MACBRIDE

This one is for you - no matter how broken you think you are, you're still a beautiful, wonderful soul!
Embrace it.
Own it.

This book is a work of fiction. All names, characters, locations, and incidents are products of the authors' imaginations. Any resemblance to actual persons, things, living or dead, locales, or events is entirely coincidental.

Edited by Beth Hale, Magnolia Author Services
Proofread by Magnolia Author Services
Cover by Timeless Designs

1

MADDIE

"Is he naked? Oh, please tell me he's naked."

Even though there was no way for her to see it, I rolled my eyes and pressed the phone closer to my ear. "Yes, Frankie, he is butt naked, working his wood while the midday sun is beating down on him."

Choosing to focus on my words instead of my sarcasm, my best friend slash sister from another mister sighed. Her voice all dreamy when she spoke." Mmm, now that's what I'm talking about. Is he being rough? I like it when they're all caveman." She didn't even give me time to answer before she fired off another round of questions. "Is he ripped? Does he have huge bulging muscles that make you want to hang on for days and days?"

"Frankie," I said into the phone. From my second-floor bedroom window I had the perfect view of the man dominating our conversation, the one I couldn't take my eyes off. "You need help. The professional kind."

She barked out a laugh and I could easily imagine her flicking her inky hair over her shoulder. "You can always send your hot neighbor over, I bet he'll be *real* helpful."

Groaning, I shook my head even though she couldn't see me. "I never said he was hot. Hell, I don't even know if he is; I've only seen the back of him." But if the way his ass was filling out those well-worn jeans was anything to go by, the view would most definitely not be bad. "Before you ask again," I quickly added. "He is not in his birthday suit."

"Ah, boo," she whined, and I could only smile. After Frankie caught her boyfriend of almost five years with his fingers in someone else's cookie jar, she'd completely sworn off men, but that didn't stop her from ogling anything with a stick dangling between its legs.

Looking has never been a crime, she always said.

Good thing too, because I'd sure as hell done a lot of looking since my mysterious neighbor had ventured out of his house for the first time since he'd moved in three weeks ago. Even that had been odd. I'd gone to bed with the house next to me still vacant and had woken up just in time to see a U-Haul truck pull away.

Ever since then, I had been loitering near the windows, hoping to catch a glimpse of the person or family who'd be interested in the rundown house next door.

"Oh my goodness, are you even listening?" Frankie's annoyed voice filtered through the line.

"Nope. What were you saying?" I tore my eyes away from the man furiously sawing thick wooden panels to give my Chinese Crested dog, Sheldon, a stern look. He was dancing around on his hind legs, begging me to pick him up. With a sharp jerk of my head, I mouthed the word *no*. Of course, he didn't care and chose to scratch my leg instead.

Puffing out a breath, I bent down to scoop the little asshole up and was immediately rewarded with a pink tongue attacking my face. When Sheldon had dealt out enough kisses, he swiveled his head toward the window and pressed his wet nose against the glass.

Guess I wasn't the only one who wanted to spy.

"… introduce yourself." I only caught the tail end of Frankie's sentence but felt too bad to ask her to repeat herself…again.

Taking a shot in the dark, I asked, "You think I should?"

"Well, you're neighbors, right? It's the neighborly thing to do." Her tone warned me there was more to come. Sure enough, a second later, she sweetly added, "Plus then you'll know what he looks like and then I'll know if I'm bringing my lawn chair and a pitcher of margaritas."

My mouth was half-open when mystery man next door pulled the baseball cap off his head and dragged his hand over his short light-brown hair. Something caught my eye. Squinting, I leaned closer to get a better look, knocking my forehead against the glass in the process. "Ouch… Oooh! He has a tattoo." Rubbing my forehead, I kept my eyes locked on the ink covering his arm.

"He does?" Frankie sounded just as excited as I felt. Our tastes in men might've been vastly different, but both of us agreed that tattoos instantly took a guy from a 7 to a 9. Especially a full sleeve. "Tell me more?" she cooed in my ear.

"Ugh, I can't see from up here." I narrowed my eyes even more, as if by some miracle that would magnify whatever I was looking at. "But I'm pretty sure it's covering his entire arm."

"Madison Taylor Young, you have to go down there and introduce yourself immediately." As if understanding every word Frankie had just uttered, Sheldon set his tiny paws against the window and scratched furiously.

"You two are horrible," I muttered. My eyes were still stuck on Mr. Tattoo. His cap was back on his head and he was manhandling a piece of wood as if it had offended him. Tugging my lip between my teeth, I mused, "Nothing wrong with a friendly introduction."

"Nothing at all," Frankie agreed.

"Okay, fine. You convinced me. I'm going." Not that I needed coaxing in any way, shape, or form. My neighbor was way too intriguing. I set Sheldon down and after giving myself a quick once over in the mirror, I bounced down the stairs. "Call you later?"

"You better."

When the other end went dead, I set my phone down on the thin table next to the sliding doors that led to my backyard and stepped outside. One long drag of salty air to my lungs had the smile on my face growing wider.

Closing my eyes, I took in the soothing sound of the waves crashing and reveled in the soft breeze blowing over my face. That right there almost made it worth it to be back.

Almost.

I opened my eyes and shook off the melancholy before it had time to sink its claws in. Now was not the time for it, not when I had more pressing matters to attend to. Like getting acquainted with my hot-assed, tattooed neighbor.

My approach to the little wooden fence that separated our yards was deliberately slow and I wasn't sure why. It wasn't like I was a jump in head first kind of girl, but I wasn't overly cautious either.

And yet, I felt an odd nervousness in my bones the closer I got. He was still hunched over his bench; one hand gripping the wood while the other furiously worked a handsaw. Now that only a few feet separated us, I saw he was taller and broader, and his entire right arm was covered in ink—well, the parts peeking out from under his t-shirt sleeve.

I had to swallow down a little sigh as I took in his big shoulders, narrow waist, and absolutely perfect butt.

Wow.

It took me a few seconds to realize that if he turned around right then, I'd probably look like a creeper. Clearing my throat, I spoke loud and clear. "Hi, I'm—"

"Not interested."

What?

Taking a step forward, I rested my arms on the fence. "I just want to introduce myself."

"No."

At least that's what I thought the grumble translated to.

My brows knitted together. I was so confused. Never in my life had an attempted introduction gone like that. And I'd spent a year in New York, so that was saying a lot. I also wasn't one to simply give up. Once I had my mind on something, I had to see it through.

"You're not interested in making a friend?" I tried again, using the sweetest tone I could.

The big man on the other side shifted, keeping his left side completely out of my view. He was still looking down but I could see a glimpse of a sharp jaw peppered with a few days 'growth.

"No."

This time I heard him loud and clear. I also happened to notice that if he wasn't being such a grumpy ass, his voice might've sounded sexy. It was deep and gravelly, the kind that could have goosebumps littering your body with just one word.

Licking my lips, I took another approach. "Okay. How about a friendly neighbor? Surely you don't have a problem with that?"

He let out an audible sigh. Dropping his chin to his chest, he gritted out, "Do your ears not work, woman? Not. Interested." The tool in his hand fell onto the bench with a loud thud before he turned and stomped into his house.

Completely stunned, all I could do was stare at the door he'd just slammed shut. It was the sound of my phone shrieking to life from inside my house that finally pulled me out of my stupor. With a sharp shake of my head, I pivoted and hurried to answer. I didn't even have to look to know it was Frankie.

Swiping the green button, I pressed the device against my ear. "He's an asshole."

2

MADDIE

I held my hand above my eyes and squinted at the bright rays smacking me in the face. As much as I would have liked to complain, it wasn't the sun's fault it was so damn bright. Nope, thanks to Frankie's margarita concoction yesterday, I was feeling the slightest bit fragile.

She'd arrived on my doorstep fifteen minutes after I'd informed her of my neighbor's wonderful personality. And because it wasn't in Frankie's nature to show up empty handed, she'd waltzed into my kitchen with lunch, dessert, and drinks.

Lots and lots of drinks.

Naturally we'd hoped to catch a glimpse of Mr. Personality next door, but his grumpy butt hadn't made an appearance once. In fact, I didn't think I was going to be seeing much of him at all.

He'd made that perfectly clear when he stalked back into his house when I returned from the beach earlier this morning. I hadn't even had a chance to lift my arm to wave before the shadowy figure pushed off his chair and disappeared.

From the tiny bit I could make out, I spotted my sister, Jennah, heading toward our parents 'hardware store. Instead of going in, she turned and waited for me to catch up. Great.

"Fun weekend?" she chirped the moment I reached her.

Jennah had two years on me but anyone who didn't know us could easily mistake us for twins. We had the same blonde hair, we shared the same almond-shaped, hazel-colored eyes. Even our damn noses looked alike.

That's where the similarities stopped, though. Unlike me, Jennah had her act together. She was raising my nephew on her own and doing a damn good job at it too. Her bookkeeping skills were the best. And she had yet to disappoint my parents in any way.

Pushing those thoughts away, I forced a smile to my lips and said, "Frankie brought her trunk of drunk over yesterday." There wasn't a person in Clearwater Bay who didn't know about Frankie's trunk of drunk. Creating delicious boozy drinks was her passion. Well, that and baking.

So much so that her bakery, Sugar Booger, was known for its decadent alcoholic cupcakes two towns over.

Jennah made a noise and pulled on the door. "Come on, let's get some coffee in you."

Eager to get out of the sun, I rushed past her, giving her a grateful smile as I did. She smiled back but something was off. She looked almost sad.

"Is Tommy okay?" I asked over my shoulder.

I could only see her brow pull together before I had to focus on where I was going. I didn't want to accidentally walk into one of the shelves and have a hammer or screwdriver fall on my toes.

"He thinks his life sucks and that I am the worst mom for making him eat his vegetables. So, just another normal day. Why?"

I shook my head and immediately regretted it. "You look…off. Are *you* okay?"

A warm hand landed on my shoulder and squeezed. "I'm just tired. The only one who is not okay here is you and that head of yours." The hairs at my nape stood on end. My sister was lying to me and I didn't like it. Unfortunately, my brain hurt too much for me to even attempt to get to the bottom of it.

Focusing on the delicious coffee smell coming from the small kitchen at the back of the store, I made a mental note to ask her about it later. Way later, when the little guy pounding his hammer against my skull went to sleep.

As I knew we would, we found our mom sitting at the little table; sipping her tea and doing her crossword.

"Don't talk too loud, Maddie has a hangover," Jennah cheerily announced.

Mom looked up; her dark brown eyes boring into me from over the rim of her glasses. She didn't have to say a single word. I felt the weight of her disapproval all the way to the soles of my feet.

Shrugging, I muttered the same words I'd said to Jennah." Frankie came over."

When my mom dragged her glasses off her nose and set them on the table with a sigh, I wanted to turn around and run until my legs couldn't carry me anymore.

"Madison, you know better than that. It's irresponsible."

Working my jaw, I thought of the view from my backyard. Of how I got to dance my heart out on that beach every single morning without judgement. I thought long and hard about that before I answered my mother. Because if I didn't, no one would've liked the words that wanted out.

"It won't affect my work." Turning my gaze to my sister who was looking like she regretted opening her mouth, I said, "I won't be needing that coffee." Without another word, I hurried to the front of the store and took my place behind the counter.

A few minutes later, my sister pushed a steaming mug of caffeine in front of me and simply said, "Sorry", before she stalked off to her office to make sure Dad's books where in tiptop shape.

Fun times.

The morning dragged on and my mood simply went from bad to worse. I needed a distraction from the mess that was my life. Staring out the window at our picturesque little town, an image of Mr. Personality and his very fine ass popped into my head.

Needing the escape, I gave my imagination free reign. I thought back to his ink-covered sculpted arm and big, manly hands. They had to be big if he could hold the wood in place so effortlessly.

I bet his palms were rough and would probably have goosebumps popping up all over as it scraped along my skin. Or when it fisted my hair. Or—

Oh, good heavens. Here I was daydreaming about a man I hadn't even seen yet. A very unpleasant man. Was that what my life had come to? Working in my dad's hardware store because I couldn't cut it in New York and fantasizing about a faceless man because the only action I got was from a battery-operated device that lived in my bedside drawer.

I couldn't decide whether to be embarrassed or just sad.

"Good morning, dearie."

Snapping out of my wallowing, I found Mrs. Christi standing on the other side of the counter. Her smile was warm and friendly as she pushed a shower head and a few hooks toward me.

"Morning, Mrs. Christi." I started scanning the items and placed them in a bag. "Did you have a good weekend?"

Her entire face lit up. "Oh, yes. We visited Sharon in the city, and she took us to the new firm she's working at." Clasping her hands in front of her chest, she let out a little sigh. "It was so fancy. They offered us champagne and tiny morsels of food that looked too pretty too eat."

When the Christi's daughter had left to pursue her law degree in Los Angeles, Mrs. Christi had cried for days. And now she was positively beaming.

"That'll be forty-three fifty, please."

"I hear Sharon is making quite the name for herself." Out of nowhere, my dad sidled in beside me, resting one arm on the countertop. I kept my attention on the money the older woman had handed me rather than listen to her and my father talk about how wonderful Mrs. Christi's daughter was.

Not that I had anything against Sharon; she was quite lovely. My issue came with what happened whenever my father heard success stories like the one Mrs. Christi was happily chattering on about.

"Ah, yes," my father drawled. "If Madison's head hadn't been so full of that dancing nonsense, she too might've had her degree now." Laughing as if he hadn't just broken my heart in two, my dad gripped my shoulder and gave me a playful shake. "Ain't that right?"

I tried to smile; I really did, but my mouth refused to give an inch. "Right," I echoed softly and instantly cursed myself for feeling so small. Yeah, so maybe I didn't have a success story but at least I'd tried.

That had to count for something.

Across from me, Mrs. Christi gave me a sympathetic smile. I swear, I hated that even more. I didn't want people feeling sorry for me. "You two have a good day now." She gave me one last look before snatching her bag off the counter and stepping onto the sidewalk.

Once I was certain she was out of earshot, I twisted and pinned my dad with a stare. "I really wish you'd stop saying things like that."

"Like what?" He studied me as if he had no idea what I was talking about. I looked into those eyes that were the same shade as my own and felt something inside me twist and stab. I'd always been daddy's girl until I came home one day and told him I wanted to dance.

His reaction had been startling to say the least and when he told me that I would go to business school even if he had to drag me there himself, I went.

Until…

The bell above the door dinged, alerting us to a new customer. My dad's wrinkly fingers worked back and forth over his thick, gray eyebrows. "Just do your job, Madison." The words had barely left his mouth before he turned around and ambled away.

That was pretty much how the rest of my day went, and by the time we closed the store, I was too wired to go straight home. Choosing to leave my car where it was, I walked the two blocks to the one place I knew would sooth my restless soul.

All around me people were milling about. Couples hand in hand. Families strolling to their favorite dinner spot. And there I was feeling more alone than ever. Just because my family didn't—or rather refused to—understand that my passion differed from theirs.

Right as the melancholy settled in my chest, the little dance studio I'd practiced at since I was eight came into view. Nestled between Mrs. McDower's bookstore and Mr. Purdy's trinket shop, the glass-paneled space was my own slice of heaven.

I came to a stop in front of the studio and took a moment to take it in. The wall of windows had a slight tint to them, allowing the maximum amount of light to spill inside while keeping the dancers obscured from the outside world.

Anxious to escape, I reached for the handle but before I had a grasp on it, the door flew open and the owner, Lucetta, stepped out. "Maddie. Hi." She immediately pulled me in for a hug that I had no idea I needed. One I greedily took and held on to for a few seconds longer before stepping back.

"Closing up?" I asked, eyeing the purse slung over her shoulder.

"I was supposed to leave an hour ago, but the books took a bit longer than I would have liked."

Nibbling on my lip, I nodded tentatively. As much as I needed to work the day out of my system, I didn't want to hold Lucetta up. Maybe I could take Sheldon for a walk on the beach instead.

I was about to say goodbye when she took my hand and squeezed. "What's bothering you?"

A rueful smile touched my lips. "It's just been one of those days." I didn't need to elaborate; Lucetta knew how my parents felt about me dancing. When I'd still trained with her, I'd arrived at the studio in tears more times than I'd cared to count. Her answer to those tears had always been to tell me to dance through my feelings.

"I'm sorry, honey." Her focus shifted to the keys she was fiddling with. "I wish I could tell you it gets easier, but some people are just too set in their ways." It was her turn to look sad and I knew it had something to do with her mother. She'd never told me specifics and I'd never pried, but from the little I could gather, I knew our stories were similar.

"Here." She jerked her chin toward her hand between us. A small copper key was clutched between her thumb and index finger.

I had a pretty good idea what it was, still, I asked, "What's this?"

"You can use the studio whenever you want. Just be sure to lock up when you're done." She nudged me with the key. "And maybe spread the word about the new fitness classes twice a week?"

"You're sure you don't mind?"

"I offered, didn't I?" Lucetta grabbed my hand and set the key inside my palm and closed my fingers around it. "I've got a bottle of Merlot and a fantastic TV dinner waiting for me, so I have gotta run." Along with the meaningful stare she aimed my way, her warm hand squeezed tight over mine.

No words were needed. She understood how desperately my soul needed this. "Thank you," I breathed on a shaky exhale.

Giving me a gentle tap against the cheek, she smiled sweetly. "You can thank me by never changing your dreams for anyone." With that, she spun around and made her way to her car, each of her impossibly long legs moving with grace and elegance.

With a final wave, she pulled away from the curb and I finally stepped into the studio. I dropped my purse to the floor and toed off my pumps before pulling the polo with

Young's Hardware etched on the breast pocket over my head.

Standing in a pair of black leggings and my sports bra, I scrolled through my phone until *Christina Perri's Human* filtered through the tiny speakers. After setting the device on Lucetta's table in the corner, I moved to the middle of the polished floor.

Closing my eyes, I lowered my chin to my chest and slowly rolled my head first left then right. My shoulders came next. Then I shook out my legs. Eyes still shut, I took a deep breath, letting the lyrics and beat lead me.

I flew through the air; kicked and spun until I was too tired to move another muscle. Because when my body had no energy, I wouldn't be able to wallow in the sad fact that the people I loved most couldn't accept me for who I was.

3

ADAM

So much smoke… and heat. I rubbed at my eyes, but it only worsened the sting. Behind my ribs, my heart was pumping two times too fast. I didn't care, I needed to find her. "Angie!!" I yelled for what felt like the hundredth time. Why the hell wasn't she answering me?

An ear-splitting cracking sounded above my head a second before a beam came crashing to the ground. "Shit! Dammit, Angie, answer me!" Nothing but the popping sound of flames replied.

Where the fuck was she?

I opened my mouth to call for her again; no words came. In their place, a coughing fit that left my lungs as hot as the fire dancing around me. Clutching at my chest with one hand, I used my other arm to shield my eyes.

Still, I couldn't see.

"For shit's sake, Angie. Tell me where you are?" I begged hoarsely. Somewhere in the distance, I heard my name being called. It sounded like my friend, Griffin, but I couldn't be sure. Between the crackling fire and my heart's thundering, my hearing wasn't the best.

"Ang—"

A fierce heavy heat stole my breath as it smashed down on my left shoulder. The pain so severe I cried out in absolute agony. Frantically I grabbed at my chest, trying and failing to get air to my lungs.

"Angie," I whispered her name one last time before my already blurry vision distorted to nothing but cold blackness.

"Fuck!" Gasping, I jolted upright and dragged a shaky palm over my face. "It was just a nightmare," I assured myself as I forced a steady breath from my lungs. I swung my legs around and planted my feet on the ground. The cold tiles a welcome reprieve from the memories so vivid, I could still feel the searing heat of them as if it had just happened.

Over my shoulder, I glanced at the soaked linens. Would there ever come a night where I didn't wake up in a cold sweat? Or was this the price I had to pay for failing? For not saving her?

Pushing to my feet, I welcomed the sting of self-loathing that washed over me. I deserved it, and asking for respite was like giving a pardon to a murderer on death row. With sharp, angry movements, I yanked the sheets from the bed and strode to the laundry room where I deposited them in the washer.

Without fail, that was what every night had looked like for the past three years. Peaceful slumbers were only afforded to those whose souls weren't blotched with big, black spots.

My still-shaking hand came up to trail along the slightly raised, too-smooth skin along the left side of my neck down to my shoulder. *Monster.* I felt like one, and now I looked like one too.

A tortured cry tore from my lungs and I smacked my palm against the wall with so much force, it should've hurt. But fortunately—or unfortunately—for me, the deep-rooted anger I felt wouldn't allow any other feeling to the surface.

And I was okay with that.

I made my way to the kitchen and pulled my old friend, *Jack,* closer. Foregoing a tumbler, I screwed the cap off and swallowed down a decent amount of the amber liquid. Even that did nothing to settle my nerves. I didn't understand how you could feel so alone and yet be so crowded by your own thoughts that you felt suffocated.

Bottle in hand, I dragged my ass into the backyard. I didn't bother with lights; darkness suited me just fine. It was where I belonged.

I had no idea how the harmonious humming of the waves managed to break through the craziness inside my head, but I welcomed it nonetheless. The fifty-pound anvil on my chest eased up slightly, allowing me to take my first real breath since the past had pulled me from my sleep.

Tilting my head skyward, I closed my eyes and dragged another shot of salty air to my lungs. And then did it again and again until the chaos inside of me became less demanding. Less intrusive.

By the time I made my way to the couch in the tv room, my lids felt heavy, my limbs tired. My six-foot-six frame collapsing onto the semi-soft cushioning with zero grace. A long heavy sigh pushed past my lips as I curled onto my side, knees pulled to my chest.

There was only one thing left to do: close my eyes and wait for the nightmare to start all over again.

***

Slowly, I pried my eyes open and immediately let out a breath of relief when I realized my demons hadn't come back to haunt me. I maneuvered myself into a seated position, my body protesting furiously.

It didn't matter that I spent hours a day exercising in my garage; I still felt every one of my thirty-five years. Or maybe it was the shitty position and crappy couch that accounted for the gnawing pain in my lower back.

Pushing to my feet, I reached for the ceiling before twisting first to my right and then my left. My backbone giving a satisfying crunch with each stretch. The dull ache just above my tailbone showed no sign of going away, and I made a mental note to add another set of deadlifts to my workout routine later that day.

But first, coffee.

As I shuffled into the kitchen and began preparing my caffeine fix, my mind tried to focus on a million things at once. The wood supply for the deck I was building was running low and I had to put in an order. The guest bedroom and bathroom needed to be redone from the ground up. The floorboards weren't in the best shape, and the color on the walls an awful shade somewhere between pumpkin and shit.

No one really understood why I'd bought this specific house. Much like me, it wasn't in the best shape. And honestly, I had no real reason other than it felt like something I needed to do. An unmistakable pull to this town. Or maybe it was a sliver of hope that I'd find peace here, as undeserving as it may be.

My thoughts were still a jumbled mess when I grabbed milk from the fridge. As the door slowly closed, a little note stuck under a magnet caught my eye. With a wrinkle of my nose, I tugged it off and stared at the words I'd scribbled down a few days ago.

I needed to check in with my parents.

The move had been hard on them. Especially since they'd packed up their lives in Texas City to take care of me after the accident—even though I'd begged them not to. So when I told them I couldn't live in Sault Point anymore, their disappointment was understandable.

Right up until the day I left, they'd voiced their concerns over and over again until I promised to check in at least once a week and even went as far as to tell them they could drive down here unannounced if I didn't.

They jumped on it because being the bastard I was, I went for weeks without talking to anyone when I was still living in the same town as them. Therefor a once a week face to face—if you could call video calling that—was kind of a big deal.

My mind still stuck on my parents, I poured copious amounts of sugar and milk into my coffee and decided to give them a call as soon as I had enough caffeine in me to deal with their endless ways of asking me if I was okay.

I wasn't and I didn't think I ever would be, but they didn't need to know that.

Steaming mug in hand, I poked my head out of the glass door leading to my back yard to check if the coast was clear. I was in no mood to be approached by my neighbor again.

Hell, if I never had to make niceties with another person—except for my family—again, it would be too soon. Even before things went south, I hadn't been the most social person on the planet.

It became a lot worse after the accident.

Satisfied that there was no one, I slipped outside and sank into the Adirondack chair. Bright orange rays burst from the line where the ocean met the sky, with thin strips of yellow streaking through the blue.

It was beautiful.

If only that beauty had the ability to reach inside and touch the dead parts of me, maybe then—

Before the rest of the thought could fully form, a blur of gray and white came rushing toward me. "What the hell?" I couldn't stop my face from contorting even if I tried. Scratching at my legs had to be the ugliest creature I'd ever laid eyes on.

Its body had no coat while the top of its head was covered in long white strands of fur that looked like a stylist had been in there. "Good heavens, you're ugly."

Fugly dropped onto his or her butt and angled its long nose my way. "Shoo. Go away now!" Paying no mind to my not so nice request, Fugly's head simply tilted all the way to the left.

"Oh crap. I'm so sorry."

Just as it had a few days ago, every cell in my body stilled at the sound of her voice. I dropped my chin to my chest and cursed. That right there was what I'd wanted to avoid. I didn't want to make small talk with my neighbors.

Especially not with one who had a voice sweeter than honey.

"Uhm." She sounded hesitant. Good. "Would you mind handing him over? He's very nice and won't bite, I promise."

Nice or not, the woman had to be deluded if she thought I was touching that thing. My gaze flicked to Fugly, who was still watching me. "Go. Away," I muttered through clenched teeth. Unfortunately, it didn't have the desired effect because the stupid mutt thought it was playtime. Jumping onto its hind legs, Fugly's front paws scratched air. A move that most people would find adorable.

I wasn't most people.

"Uh...yeah, hi." It might've been my imagination, but that sweet voice held the slightest tinge of annoyance. "I realize that you're offended by interaction of any kind, but Sheldon doesn't know that. I'd come over and get him myself, but I don't want to get shot for trespassing."

Head still bowed, my gaze shot to her. Big mistake. If the sunrise I'd witnessed mere moments ago was beautiful, she was whatever trumped that. She looked like she'd just come back from a run. Her blonde hair twisted into a messy knot on top of her head. Cheeks tinged a rosy color and her skin glistening with perspiration.

And still, I couldn't recall a recent time where I'd had the privilege of witnessing such beauty.

There was a fluttering inside my chest, one I hadn't felt in a long, long while. I held my breath trying to hold on to it, but it was gone a second later. Instantly my mood went to shit, and I jumped to my feet.

Without thinking it through, I stalked toward her, vaguely aware of Fugly happily trotting along behind me. By the time I stopped at the hip-high fence separating our properties, my body was vibrating with irritation.

My neighbor was standing on her side with her arms folded in front of her. The only sign that I intimidated her somewhat came in the form of her eyes—eyes the color of whiskey—widening.

She licked her lips and I couldn't help but follow the action. When she tilted her chin upward and narrowed those pretty little eyes at me, I let my gaze roam over her face. She was young, probably a lot younger than me, but there was something shining in her intense stare that called to some messed up part of me.

When her gaze softened, I realized, with a horrible shock, that I was facing her. My left side wasn't hidden, and she was staring right at my ugly. My stomach twisted, the knots working in furious circles until I could feel the bile rise in my throat.

I didn't want pity. Not from her or anyone else.

Bending down, I scooped up the mutt and shoved it at her. Her hand grazed mine as she tried to catch the dog and cradle it to her chest. I swore. "Take your damn rat and go away."

4

MADDIE

What the actual hell just happened?

Hugging Sheldon tighter to my chest, I glared at the big giant of a man stomping away from me. Or rather his broad back. I may have sneaked a peek at his butt too, but only because it would have been a crying shame not to.

"Don't go into the mean man's yard again, okay?" I warned Sheldon as I turned and headed for my house. Not ashamed in the slightest, I tried to catch a glimpse of Mr. Personality before I slipped inside, but he was long gone.

Everything that man lacked in manners, he made up for with his gorgeous looks. To be fair, gorgeous was an enormous understatement. The instant I had my first good look at him, the breath had left my lungs in one fell swoop.

Because... *wow*.

That strong jaw I'd gotten a glimpse of the other day was sharp and covered with dark whiskers that I bet would feel amazing scraping along my skin. He had these beautifully full lips that I envied and hated at the same time. No man should have been allowed to have a mouth like that.

It simply wasn't fair.

Nor was it fair that his nose, that had clearly been broken more than once, only added to his broody appeal. Or that his dark, dark eyes were so intense, I felt the weight of his stare all the way to my toes.

Then there were those scars… they ran from his neck and disappeared into his shirt. I was no expert, but it kind of looked like they might've been burn wounds. Thick gnarly wounds. And I would put my life on it, they had something to do with the downright tormented look in those black as night irises.

My heart twisted a little right then.

I didn't dare think about the kind of situation you needed to be in to get an injury like that.

"What a shame," I mused, setting my pup down on the kitchen floor. "The sexiest man I ever see just has to be the biggest asshole too." As I went about getting my breakfast ready—cereal and milk—Sheldon watched me with curious eyes.

Slipping onto the stool at the breakfast nook, I took in the view beyond the kitchen window. This side of the house didn't have an ocean view but that didn't mean the picture was any less appealing.

Bright morning rays filtered through the leaves of the sycamore tree in my front yard and danced over the sidewalk, the spots where it touched shimmering like little diamonds. The sight instantly pulling a happy memory to the forefront of my mind.

I had been in that awful teenage stage where it felt like it had been me against the world. Or at least my dreams against what my parents thought my dreams should've been. My grandma had convinced me to take an early morning walk with her. Instead of giving me the same lecture my dad given me the night before, she'd put her arm around my shoulders and hugged me tightly to her side.

"Do you see that?" she'd asked, pointing toward the shiny sidewalk.

Naturally my mumbled, "What," hadn't deterred her one bit. She'd simply leaned in close and whispered, "They aren't afraid to shine, and you shouldn't be either."

Her words, her acceptance, had stunned me into complete silence. I hadn't known how to express to her how much it meant. But it didn't matter. She knew. She'd always known.

Just like she'd known I'd need a place to come home to if things didn't work out in New York.

Blinking furiously, I shoved a spoonful of cereal into my mouth and glared at Sheldon still sitting next to his bowl. "This is all your fault, you know?" I mumbled around my breakfast. "Why in the name of Zeus did you dart off like your tail was on fire?"

In answer, his head swiveled from side to side, the goofy look on his face almost melting my heart. Before I turned into a big softie—which always happened around Sheldon since he'd been with me through some of the toughest times of my life—I stabbed my spoon in his direction. "Don't do it again."

Although, I wouldn't mind getting another look at Mr. Personality.

"Ugh!" Annoyed, I pushed to my feet and rinsed my bowl and spoon. I seriously needed a hug from a guy, or rather I needed his bits to hug my bits, so I didn't go around fantasizing about my grumpy ass neighbor and his big hands and stupid mouth.

An annoying ping sounded from my phone, reminding me that I needed to get my ass in gear, or I would be late for work. And the absolute last thing I needed was for my dad to have something else to hold over my head.

Maddie couldn't cut it in New York and now she can't even show up for work on time.

It hadn't always been like that, and I honestly had no doubts that both my parents loved Jennah and me fiercely. They simply didn't understand that their dreams and our dreams didn't have to be the same.

Dropping to my haunches, I raked my fingers through the impossibly soft fur on Sheldon's head before bounding up the stairs to get myself ready for the day. I was back downstairs and putting my pup in his crate twenty minutes later.

I kissed him on the nose and with a quick "Be good," I pushed to my feet and hurried out of the house, taking extra care to leave the sliding doors open just a smidge. I couldn't leave Sheldon outside with no supervision, and it didn't feel right for him to have no fresh air.

Maybe not the safest choice but nothing bad had ever happened in our little town, so didn't worry about it too much.

As I made my way to my light blue Prius, the need to search out Mr. Personality was too strong to ignore. I wish I knew why that idiot of a man intrigued me so. There was this nibbling feeling in my gut that it had to do with way more than his good looks and *impeccable manners*.

Or maybe I really just needed my vagina to hug someone's penis.

Pushing all thoughts of my somewhat tortured and extremely sexy neighbor to the back of my head, I slid behind the wheel of my car and made the ten-minute drive to the hardware store.

Just as I slipped through the door, my back pocket buzzed. With a quick reach behind me, I pulled my phone out and swiped the screen to life. My grin spreading almost immediately.

Frankie: I've decided you need to get laid.

My fingers flew over the little screen.

Me: You decided, huh? Since it's my bits we're talking about here, shouldn't I be the one making the decisions?

Of course, my deprived brain would conjure up an image of my neighbor at the mere mention of a little action between the sheets. And I really, really couldn't help but wonder how all that grumpiness would look on him when he was naked and moving over me.

Clearly, I needed help.

The phone I was still clutching vibrated against my palm, saving me from the twisted path my thoughts had taken.

Frankie: Since you're the one holding her hostage, no.

My thumbs hovered above the screen, ready to fire back a response when I heard my dad's gravelly, "Morning, Madison." Instead of giving her the smartass comeback I had planned, I typed a quick, 'gotta go.'

"Hi, Dad." I slipped my phone back inside my pocket and jerked my chin toward the box he was carrying. "New stock?"

"Yes, it's that acrylic paint your sister insisted we get." He stopped a few feet in front of me, his gaze everywhere except on me. I hated this. Hated how we couldn't be together for even a minute without it being awkward as hell.

Behind my ribs, my heart squeezed violently. Emotion crawled up my throat and I swallowed hard to push it back down. "Do you want me to shelve it?"

"Shelve it?" My dad's thick brows pulled together. Blinking a few times, he shook his head slightly before shoving the box into my hands. "If you can be done before lunch, that would be great."

And then he was gone, leaving me to wonder if I'd ever have a normal relationship with him at all.

A heavy sigh blew over my lips as I hoisted the box higher and shuffled to the aisle where we kept the paint supplies. One by one, I slid the small tubes onto the empty space on the shelf, regretting taking my parents up on this job offer.

Maybe I'd subconsciously believed the hardware store was the best I could do, or maybe there'd been a part of me that in spite of everything had still wanted to make them proud.

Whatever it'd been, I'd grabbed this job they'd created for me with both hands.

And now it was draining me.

Shaking my head, I forced my thoughts in a different direction. Unfortunately for me, my mind was hellbent on torturing me because the first thing that popped into my head was Mr. Personality and those thick scars marring his skin.

Pulling my phone from my pocket, I unlocked the screen and tapped my thumb against the Google icon. Less than a minute later, I was staring at all kinds of burn wounds.

I felt sick.

The more I scrolled, the more my stomach wanted to roll over on itself. My hand shot to my mouth, my heart twisting a little as I tried to imagine how horrible whatever happened to him must've been.

"Oh, my gosh," I whispered.

"What's the matter with you?"

At the suddenness of my sister's voice three things happened at once:

A very unladylike curse fell from my lips.

My entire body jerked.

My phone went flying through the air, landing in front of Jennah's feet with dull thud.

Before I had time to react, she bent down and scooped up the device. It was completely stupid of me to think she wouldn't take a peek at the screen first. "What the heck are you looking at?"

Brows pinched together, her gaze bounced between the phone clutched inside her palm and me.

It made me uncomfortable.

And it wasn't just because of the images on screen; my sister and I weren't close. Hadn't been for years. Not since the day our dad very cruelly started comparing me to her. And to no one's surprise, I was found wanting.

Rationally, I knew it wasn't Jennah's fault. She'd never gloated about it when words like that were thrown around like they weren't live grenades with the ability to destroy wherever they landed.

Even knowing that hadn't stopped me from pulling away from her. From building a wall so high, I didn't even know how to scale it.

Moving fast, I stepped forward and snatched my phone out of her hand and shoved it into my pocket. "It's nothing. Did you need something?"

Her face twisted; the same sadness I saw the previous day shone in her eyes again. She opened her mouth, but instead of saying what was on her mind, she pressed her lips together and let out a heavy breath through her nose.

"Just wanted to see the new stock."

That wasn't the truth but because of the uncrossable bridge between us, I didn't push. Even when deep down, I really wanted to.

"I think these paints are a great addition to this section." My gosh, this couldn't be more awkward. Nibbling on my lip, I scraped my palm over the back of my neck. "You…uh…still need me to watch Tommy on Saturday?"

Wringing her hands together, Jennah nodded. "Yeah, if you don't mind."

"Not one bit." And I really didn't. I might've been biased since he was my nephew, but Tommy was the best kid, and spending time with him was always a priority.

"Great." She took a step backward. "I better get back to it, those books aren't going do themselves." The words were barely out of her mouth before she spun around and hurried away, leaving me to stare at her retreating back.

With a heavy sigh and an even heavier heart, I turned back to the paints and frowned at the colorful tubes. Why were we like this? And more importantly, how could I fix it? I didn't have the answers to those questions, nor did I think I'd get them anytime soon.

That's was why I kept my head down and proceeded with my tasks on autopilot like I'd done every other day before this.

By the time my little Prius rolled to a stop in my driveway, I jumped from the car and all but ran to my backyard where I had an uninterrupted view of the beach and ocean.

The sky above the endless stretch of blue was painted in breathtaking shades of orange and pink, in stark contrast with the white sand.

And because my house was right at the edge of the beach, I had the luxury of witnessing the sight before me every single day. My grandma, who had known me better than anyone else, might've had a hand in it too.

Before she'd passed on, she purchased two houses—this one and a bigger one in the central part of town—without telling a soul about it. Jennah and I had certainly gotten the biggest shocks at the reading of her will eight months prior.

As silly as it may have sounded, I often wondered if the breeze that wrapped around me could somehow be her letting me know that even though she wasn't with us anymore, she was *there*?

The wind picked up again, the strands of my ponytail fluttering beside my face. I was in the middle of bushing the wisps of hair when and odd sensation washed over me. A tingle started at the base of my skull before slithering down my spine.

Is someone watching me?

Twisting, I scanned my surroundings. Mr. Stevenson, a seventy-something-year-old retired teacher, lived to the left of me. We'd been neighbors for as long as I'd lived here, and not once had this feeling come over me.

My gaze shifted to the right. Mr. Personality's house. It was quiet, eerily so. Still, I couldn't shake the feeling that someone's eyes—*his eyes*—were on me. Goosebumps popped up all over my skin, a shiver working its way through my body.

Awareness settled deep in my bones, and I couldn't take it anymore. My feet started moving, hurried steps taking me to the safety of my home. I slammed the door shut behind me and made sure to click the lock in place.

It wasn't that I was afraid of the broody man living next to me but rather the intense feeling that'd washed over me at the mere thought that he'd been watching me. I liked it a lot more than I should have.

Exploring those kinds of feeling usually led to nothing but trouble.

Trouble I definitely didn't need.

5

ADAM

"You're sure you're all right? We can be there by tonight."

I closed my eyes for a brief second to try and compose myself before opening them again. There really was no need for my mom to see my irritation. Plus, I had almost three years 'worth of shit behavior to make up for.

"I'm sure, Mom." My voice was tight. I tried to add a smile for good measure. Because those particular muscles hadn't had a workout for a while, it felt weird. I could only hope I looked mildly happy and not constipated.

My mom's eyes flicked to my dad, who was sitting to her right. He looked as uncomfortable as I felt. We still had a lot to get used to. Before I left Sault Point, our meetings consisted of me either yelling at them or giving them the silent treatment. There hadn't been an in-between.

"So, uh—" My dad dragged a palm along the back of his neck. "How are the renovations coming along?"

My gaze drifted to the unfinished deck beyond the open sliding doors. Just as quick, I shifted my attention back to the computer screen in front of me. "It's slow going, but it's keeping me busy." When I first saw this property, it hadn't been the price or even the view that'd convinced me to buy. It was the sheer amount of work it needed. If I kept busy, I wouldn't have time to wallow in self-pity.

My dad nodded tentatively, his eyes darting back and forth over what I presumed was something in his lap. Our entire exchange was damn awkward, and I had no one to blame but myself.

"I still—"

"Do you—"

My dad and I spoke at the same time. Shifting in my seat, I scratched the scruff on my chin. "You go first."

"Do you think you'll go back?"

Before I could say anything, my mom jabbed my dad's ribs with her bony elbow. His thick, gray brows pulled together while he glared at her. "What the hell was that for, Mildred?"

Her gaze rested on the scars along my neck for a few beats too long before she turned to my dad again. Because I only had a side view of her face, I couldn't see the full extent of her expression as she furiously tried to wordlessly convey something to my dad.

Her eyebrows were jumping about while she twisted and pursed her lips. All the while, my poor father was staring at her with a perplexed look on his face.

"It's okay, Mom," I finally said. "I honestly don't know if I'll ever go back." The words left a thick unwanted lump in my throat. I had to swallow it down before I could speak again. "I miss it. A lot. But I'm no good to anyone in this condition."

"Oh, Adam."

The look on my mom's face was too much. I hated the pity and sadness I saw there. When would they realize that the life I was living was one of my own making?

"I…uh… gotta go." There was no hiding the strain in my voice. "I'll call again next week. Same time?"

Mom's shoulders rose and fell with the deep drag of air she took. Her mouth opened and I held my breath. I knew it was hard for her to see me like this. Hell, it was hard for me too. But this was my reality and it didn't matter how many times she, or anyone else, told me things would get better, I knew different.

However, instead of assuring me that whatever was going on would pass, and that I'd be back to my old self again—like she always did—she simply said, "Sounds good." The hint of sadness in her voice caused another one of those stirrings inside my chest.

"Okay. Bye."

As I reached forward to shut the laptop my mom quickly added, "We love you, Adam." Those four little words felt like a punch to the gut. I had done nothing to deserve the love of those two people. Not in the past three years anyway. I'd pushed them away and shut them out.

I wanted to say those words back. Wanted to tell them I knew how damn fortunate I was to still have them, but the words wouldn't leave my tongue. So instead of voicing my feelings, I nodded tersely before closing the lid.

A heavy sigh pushed past my lips as I scraped both hands over my face. I couldn't blame my dad for asking the one question I thought about every single day. Firefighting had been in my blood for as long as I could remember.

If my mom were to be believed, I'd wanted to be one from the moment I'd uttered my first words. I'd never gone through the phases of wanting to be a doctor, policeman, or astronaut.

Fire had always been my passion. Until it stole everything from me. And in a cruel twist of fate, I couldn't hate it for doing what it had been created to do. Losing Angie was on me. I was the one who—

"No!" I jumped to my feet and stomped to the kitchen. There was no way I was going to give in to those kinds of thoughts. I couldn't afford to. Pulling out the carafe, I topped up my mug and headed outside.

It was a long shot but with any luck, the uninterrupted view of the beach and ocean would calm my fraying nerves. Still holding on to my mug, I balanced it on the armrest. My head fell back against the chair and I screwed my eyes shut.

The sound of the waves gently lapping at the shore filled my ears a moment later. I inhaled deeply, dragging a shot of salty air straight to my lungs. It was exactly what I needed after talking to my parents.

Heaven knew I had a lot to make up for. It was still difficult as hell to shift into this new dynamic. To let them into a place I had sealed off a long time ago—or at least attempt to.

Building bridges wasn't my strong suit.

Slowly, I lifted my head and opened my eyes; the endless stretch of blue shockingly not the first thing to catch my attention. I sat up straighter and leaned forward in my seat. There on the beach was my annoyingly friendly neighbor and she was… dancing.

She kicked up a cloud of sand before dragging her foot to the inside of her opposite thigh. Arms stretched high above her head, she spun around and around before suddenly collapsing into a heap.

I jumped up so abruptly, my coffee tipped over. I was vaguely aware of the mug shattering to pieces when it hit the ground, but I couldn't tear my eyes away from the woman on the beach.

She was on her knees now; slamming her hands into the sand before stretching out onto her front. I needed to see more. Completely mesmerized, I walked to the edge of my property just in time to see her roll onto her back and pull her knees to her chest.

The way she moved caused a stirring inside of me. A flicker of something familiar. Something good. My hand came up, absentmindedly rubbing over a spot on my chest. My gaze never leaving her.

In one fluid motion, she was sitting with her leg bent in front of her and the other stretched out behind her, toes pointing to the sky. Her back arched, the knot on her head almost touching her ass. Reaching behind her, she gripped her foot.

It was a damn shame I didn't have my phone because the picture she painted with the orange-pink sky and bright blue ocean was absolutely breathtaking.

That feeling inside my chest made itself known once more, more urgent this time. It was almost as if a bolt of lightning had zipped through the sky and struck me where I stood.

Intense.

Electrifying.

And scary as shit.

Every cell in my body warned me that there was one hell of a storm coming. One I wasn't even remotely prepared for.

6

MADDIE

My lips twitched as I took in the yellow and pink candy stripe awnings and equally colorful glass windows. It didn't matter what the question was, Sugar Booger was the answer.

With my smile stretching, I pushed through the door and was immediately greeted with the sweet aroma of freshly baked goods. Vanilla, cinnamon, and who knew what else hit me over the head and made my stomach growl.

From behind the fully stacked glass counters, Misty waved me over. Working my way through the lunchtime crowd, I met her at the edge of the donut display. Not the best choice since I that really made me want to buy one. Or maybe two.

"Hey Maddie," she greeted me in the overexcited tone that'd taken me a while to get used to. "Frankie said to send you straight to the back when you get here." She let out a little giggle, her hand shooting to her mouth almost instantly. "Well, you're here, so…"

With a grin and a small tilt of my head I told her, "Thanks, Misty." Then because I simply couldn't help myself, I pulled a few bills from my back pocket and handed them over. "Can you box up two glazed donuts for me? I'll grab them on my way out."

I said goodbye to Misty before slipping through the side door that led to the kitchen. As I knew I would, I found Frankie manhandling a blob of dough.

She hoisted the doughy ball above her head before slamming it back down on the counter, hard. I chuckled under my breath. "Whose face are you envisioning every time you do that?"

Lifting her blue eyes to meet mine, she blew at the few inky strands peeking out from under her hairnet. "You know how my parents wanted me to come over last night because they had amazing news to share with me?"

Her question must've been rhetorical because she just kept on talking, "Apparently, my brother is moving back to Clearwater Bay."

"And why are we mad about this?"

The dough in her hands connected with the bench with a sharp thud. "First of all, Caden the twatwaffle didn't even tell me. I'm his sister for shit's sake! And secondly…" she took a deep breath through her nose, but it did nothing to keep the annoyance from rolling off her tongue alongside her words. "Gage is coming back with him."

This was bad. There wasn't a person alive who Frankie hated more than she did Gage Calloway. Not that I blamed her. The guy did take her v-card before running away like the hounds of hell were snapping at his heels.

Kneading a little harder, she groaned, "This is so satisfying." A smile tugged at the corners of her mouth.

"Maybe you'd like to have a go? You can pretend it's your neighbor."

"Yeah." With a way-too-heavy groan, I flopped down onto the nearest chair. "He's a real peach, that one. I don't even know how it happened, but Sheldon got out and take one guess where he ended up?"

Still attacking the yeasted concoction, she cocked her eyebrow. "And how did that go?"

"Well…" In as much detail as I could, I relayed my latest run-in with Mr. Personality. The one where he very rudely referred to Sheldon as a rat. Just thinking about it had my hackles rising until those icky scars flashed in my memory.

I had this awful feeling that those scars, or rather the horrible event that caused them, had something to do with his icy exterior. And for whatever reason, that only amplified my need to show him kindness.

"What's happening to your face right now?" Frankie transferred her well-worked dough to three separate bowls before covering them with greased clingfilm. She grabbed two orange juices from the fridge and took a seat next to me. Keeping one for herself, she handed me the other. "You've got that sad puppy dog look going." With her bottle tipped in my direction, she motioned toward my face.

"I don't know what you're talking about." My voice climbed a few octaves like it always did when I wasn't being entirely truthful.

"Is that how you're going to play it? All right." Frankie took a big gulp of her juice before setting it down on the countertop and leaning forward. "I understand that you believe there is good in everyone and that even the most lost person can be saved, but—"

"I don't—"

Her hand shot up, index finger pointing toward the ceiling. "Let me finish." When I nodded, she continued, "It's a wonderful trait to have, Maddie, it really is. You just need to realize that some people are assholes by choice and have zero plans on changing."

"Yeah, I know." I decided not to tell her that I thought there was a hell of a lot more to Mr. Personality than his grumpy mood. "So where are those sandwiches you promised me?" I asked, needing the conversation from my grumpy neighbor. I even made a show of looking around the kitchen.

Not convinced by my act, Frankie gave me a 'don't-think-I'm-fooled 'look but thankfully left the subject alone. Without saying a word, she slipped off her chair and shuffled back to the fridge.

A moment later she slid a plate in front of me. One look at it and I was salivating.

"This looks amazing." I picked up the croissant and eyed the crispy bacon, cheese, and avocado slices sandwiched between the buttery layers.

Unable to wait a nanosecond longer, I took a giant bite. The instant the different flavors hit my taste buds, my eyes widened.

"So good," I mumbled around a mouth full of food.

"Yeah?"

I could only nod since I couldn't resist going in for another taste.

"I used cottage cheese instead of butter, as well as the sweet chili jam I made the other day." I had no idea why she sounded so uncertain because if there was anything Frankie could do, it was bake... and apparently make the most delicious croissant sandwiches.

Swallowing down the food in my mouth, I resisted taking another bite long enough to tell her, "These are going to be as popular as your adult cupcakes." My gaze flicked to the deliciousness in my hands. "Maybe even more."

Frankie's face lit up and I absolutely loved it. She was doing something she loved. Following her passion and realizing her dreams. *Not like me*. But this moment wasn't about my failures, so I pushed the thought away before it had time to properly form.

"When are you putting these on the menu?" I asked.

She lifted her shoulders and let them drop. "I don't know yet. There are a few flavor combinations I still want to try out."

"I have no issues being your taste tester." I polished off the rest of my lunch and grinned just as my phone dinged from inside my pocket, reminding me that my lunch break was almost over.

Wrinkling my nose, I huffed, "I gotta get back. Am I seeing you at class tonight?"

"Of course." Frankie walked me to the door and hugged me. "Maybe we can stop by Oven and Vine afterward? Grab a pizza and a few drinks. Or a warm, willing body?"

I threw my head back and laughed. "You're impossible."

"That wasn't a no."

For whatever reason, a night out didn't sound nearly as exciting as it should have. "It's been a crazy week, Frankie. Maybe this weekend?"

My best friend eyed me carefully. "I'm holding you to it. You and me, we're going out even if I have to drag you there with my bare hands."

Grinning, I turned and started walking. "I wasn't expecting anything less."

***

I was the first to arrive for our dance/aerobics class. Lucetta had started doing these three times a week when the moms of her students begged her to do something fitness-related for the adults too. The gym in Clearwater Bay wasn't the most impressive and didn't offer a lot of variety. In fact, the only cardio training you could do there was running on a treadmill or pedaling on a stationary bike.

I shouldered the door but came to an abrupt halt when I saw Lucetta speaking on the phone. Her brows were dipped low and hands furiously waving through the air. Knowing I'd interrupted, I tried to back away slowly, but her head snapped up. "I'll call you back," she said into the phone before tossing it onto her desk. "Maddie. Hi.

Come in." With her frown still in place, she motioned for me to come closer. "I didn't even realize it was time for class already."

Feeling like I had intruded on something, which I probably had, I dragged my palms over my thighs. "I'm early, but I can come back later. Or just wait outside."

"Don't do that." She waved me off with a sigh and leaned back against her chair. Tipping her head back, she just stared at the ceiling. I wasn't exactly sure what to do. It was obvious that something was weighing on her, but I didn't want to overstep by asking.

Luckily, she put me out of my misery when she looked my way again. "My mom fell and broke her hip, and because she's as stubborn as they come, she's refusing to go to a care facility until it heals."

"She's living alone?" I guessed.

"Yeah." Lucetta blew out a breath. "And now my brother expects me to put everything on hold to drive down to Oakridge and take care of her." We hadn't had a ton of heart to hearts, but I knew that she and her mother hadn't always had the best relationship because of her dancing.

Kind of like me and my parents. Though, that particular can of worms didn't need opening at all. "I take it he can't do it?"

She looked completely defeated. "No, he's going back to London tomorrow." Leaning forward, she rested her elbows on her desk. "Don't get me wrong, it's not that I don't want to go to my mom. I actually think it'll be good for us to spend time together. I just can't leave the studio—"

The rest of her words never made it out as she lifted her head and trained her narrowed eyes at me. "You know, it would be a lot easier if there was someone who could take over the classes for me while I'm gone."

"Yeah, but you're the only dance teacher in Clearwater Bay." She cocked her brow. It took me another moment to grasp what the stare meant. "Oh, no." I shook my head vehemently. "I couldn't. Besides, I work at the hardware store during the day. I don't have the time." The words tumbled out of my mouth in a jumbled mess.

Lucetta's expression softened. Rising from her seat, she walked to where I was standing and placed her hands on my shoulders. "Maddie, don't take this the wrong way, but you can't possibly be happy there. You were born to dance."

"I already tried that," I reminded her bitterly.

Her palms were warm when she pressed them against my cheeks. "Oh, sweetie, that doesn't mean you have to stop dancing. Teaching others can be just as fulfilling."

I swallowed hard. "I don't know, Lucetta."

Her hands dropped to my shoulders again. Squeezing them, she said, "Take a day or two and think about it, okay? Whatever your dad is paying you at the store, I'll match it."

There was a very, very big part of me that wanted to scream yes at the top of my lungs. The mere thought of spending my entire day surrounded by people who understood this crazy passion was exciting.

But then there was the other part. The one that knew the taste of failure and what it felt like to have the people you love look at you with disappointment shining in their eyes.

It was that part that had me leaving the studio with a grumbled promise to think over her offer. And it was that same part that reminded me why I needed to say no.

7

ADAM

Body jerking, I shot upright and promptly landed on my ass next to the couch. It took me a full second to fully comprehend that I was sitting on the floor in my living room and not standing in the middle of a burning house.

"Shit."

Staggering to my feet, I speared my fingers through my damp hair. The nightmares that chased me from my bed every night seemed to have followed me to my couch, hellbent on reminding me that I didn't deserve the rest my soul craved.

My body creaked and groaned as I first rolled my shoulders and then my neck. Each day, I purposefully worked myself beyond the point of exhaustion, hoping for one night of peace.

Unfortunately, it seemed like the harder I worked the more determined the memories were to haunt me. I felt the walls close in, the feeling of a hand wrapping around my throat and cutting off my air supply.

Sucking air to my lungs almost impossible.

I was drenched in sweat and yet my body shuddered. Floundering my way to the kitchen, I latched onto the whiskey the instant I was able to.

The bottle was halfway to my mouth when I realized it was too early in the morning for me to attempt to numb the pain. To drown out the voices. Discarding my medicine of choice, I ventured through the glass doors in search of a reprieve.

What I found was my neighbor.

Hand splayed over my chest, I desperately tried to keep my heart from escaping its confines. I walked to the edge of the property and shamelessly observed her. She was doing the same routine she'd been doing for the past four days. And just as it had done every one of those times, watching her inexplicably calmed me.

It settled the beast inside of me. The one that threatened to undo the tiny bit of progress I'd made in the last few months.

My heart slowed its wild gallop, my breathing evened out. I couldn't explain why her dancing had this effect on me. I just knew that for the first time in years, I experienced a sense of peace I thought I'd never feel again.

I wasn't about to question it. Not when I knew it could be gone in the blink of an eye.

Disappointment rushed through my veins when she ended her routine and started heading up to her house, Fugly trotting behind her as usual. Normally this was the point where I spun on my heels and rushed inside before she saw me and attempted to strike up a conversation or something.

Today, though, I didn't want to move. I wanted to keep standing in that spot, wanted to hold on to that light feeling for as long as I possibly could. Until one of the voices slipped through the cracks and cruelly reminded me of the monster I was.

My fingers trembled when I brought them up to touch the ugly, smooth skin. I snatched them away just as fast before pivoting and storming into the safety of my house. Turning to shut the glass door, I spotted her sauntering over her lawn with that mutt hugged to her chest again.

The smile on her face rivaled the sun in not only its brightness but its beauty too.

A string of curses spilled from my lips. I didn't want to notice these things about her. I didn't want my rare sense of tranquility to come from *her*.

The loud angry thoughts inside my head were interrupted when my phone shrieked to life from somewhere. I should've stepped back. Should've gone looking for my phone. Instead, I stood rooted to the spot, trekking my upsettingly gorgeous neighbor until she slipped from my view.

I stood there staring at nothingness for a few more seconds before I finally went in search of the now-silent device.

I found it on my nightstand and immediately thumbed the screen to life. Another one of those heavy sighs I felt to the bottom of my soul blew over my lips as my sister's name stared back at me.

If it had been anyone else's name, I wouldn't even have considered returning the call. It was no secret that I didn't like dealing with people or that I had a lot of relationships to fix in my life. Even though I was pretty damn shit at it, I still wanted to rebuild the bridges I'd burned down.

It was just a little harder to do with Zoe.

I'd only recently found out that my little sister had had her own demons to fight. A lot of them actually. But because I was so busy wallowing in self-pity and pushing everyone away, she'd thought it best to take on the battle by herself.

Of course, she didn't hold it against me, but it didn't make me feel any less bad. I sucked in a few breaths and quickly hit the redial button before I could change my mind.

Zoe answered on the second ring.

"Adam. Hi. I… uhm… wasn't expecting you to call back." The surprise in her voice felt a lot like a punch to the gut.

"Sorry I missed your call." The words came out strangled; I had to clear my throat before I could continue. "I was outside."

"Oh no, you don't have to apologize," she said quickly. "Going by past experience, I figured I'd get your voicemail. In fact, I was kind of bargaining on it."

"You were?"

I heard her take a shaky breath. "Sometimes it's easier saying things to a machine." Zoe's quiet confession felt like another jab, this one hitting me right in the center of my chest. Or maybe a little to the left.

Thing was, I understood what she meant. It was my fault things were this way. I hated what I'd done to my family. How I'd turned them into such careful versions of themselves around me.

I wanted to apologize.

To make my wrongs right.

That wasn't what came out of my mouth, though. "Do you want me to hang up so you can leave a message?"

The soft laugh that filtered through the line felt like a gentle caress to my tattered soul. "That seems kind of silly since I have you on the line now."

"I guess."

The answering silence lasted so long, I pulled the phone from my ear to check if the lines were still connected. Just as I opened my mouth to speak, Zoe's voice sounded again. "Please don't feel obligated to say yes, but I... I mean we were wondering if it would be all right with you if we come down for a visit? It won't be until school's out in a few weeks, though."

She had spoken so fast, it took my brain a few seconds to decipher what she'd said. When it did, nervous tension pulled my back straight before licking its way down my spine. "Who's we?" I asked wearily.

Another shaky breath sounded at the other end. "Just me, Eli, and Molly."

They were her husband and stepdaughter. I'd only met them once. It was about eight months before I moved to Clearwater Bay. From the little I could remember, the guy seemed decent enough, and I'd tried to avoid the little girl as much as I could.

Kids asked too many questions and stared without shame.

"It's totally okay if you're not ready, Adam," my sister said, her voice soft and full of understanding I hadn't earned. "I just thought it would be nice to show Molly the ocean while she's on her break and…" She paused for a long second." I kind of miss hanging out with my brother."

Ah shit. How the hell could I say no to that? I couldn't. Not if I wanted to get back some of what I lost. But having them here in my space would mean I had nowhere to hide. I closed my eyes and dropped my chin to my chest. With a tight pinch to the bridge of my nose, I forced the words out through gritted teeth. "A visit sounds great."

The excited squeal, a few decibels too loud for my ears, should have eased some of the tension in my already tightly wound body. It did the opposite. Zoe was absolutely thrilled while I was scared shitless that I would only disappoint her.

We said our goodbyes after she promised to sort out all the details closer to the date. I was still staring at the damn phone nestled in my palm long after our conversation, an uneasy sense of foreboding slowly but surely working its way to the surface.

A feeling that still had my mind reeling hours after speaking to my sister.

Swiping the back of my hand over my forehead, I wiped the sweat from my brow. With a deep groan, I straightened my back and almost sighed with relief when my spine let out a satisfactory crunch.

I'd been hunched over my workbench, sawing and sanding the yellow pine, for the better part of the day trying like hell not to give in and beg my sister and her family not to come.

A year ago, that's exactly what I would have done. Although to be honest, a year ago I wouldn't even have answered my phone. Somewhere between choking on sawdust and sweating my balls off, I realized that building bridges wasn't meant to be easy. I was one lucky son of a bitch to still have the love and support of my family, and if keeping it meant I had to sit through uncomfortable visits and endless questions about my scars, then that's what I had to do.

Lifting my cap, I dragged my hand through my hair when a blur of gray caught my eye. Before I had time to utter the curse that lay on the tip of my tongue, Fugly was sitting beside my feet; tail furiously smacking against the ground.

"What the hell?" The dog, who clearly did not understand human, let out an ear-splitting excited yelp and shockingly thumped his tail even faster. Making a shoo motion with my hand, I groaned, "Go home."

The damn dog only seemed more determined to get on every single one of my last nerves. After another yelp, he jumped onto his hind legs and started pawing the air. Just like he had done last time. "No!" I admonished. "Go away."

To my horror, he hobbled closer and scratched my legs. I took a step back and he immediately followed. Flicking my wrist, I noted that it was still a few more hours before a normal nine to five workday would be done.

Maybe my neighbor didn't keep normal hours.

Shaking my head, I bent down scooped the mutt up, and held it to my side. Glowering at Fugly, I muttered, "Bad dog." That he seemed to understand. Flattening his ears, he let out a little whine that almost had me feeling bad for him.

Dog tucked under my arm, I hopped over the fence and marched to the glass door that looked a lot like my own. The door wasn't completely shut, so I poked my head in. "Hello?" The first thing my eyes landed on was a crate sitting in the corner of the wide space. Slowly my gaze traveled; taking in the small dinette, the slate gray L-shaped sectional and everything else in between.

There was an unmistakable home-y feeling about it all. A sliver of the feeling I felt when I watched her in the mornings made itself known. It wasn't enough to calm the madness inside me but it made me crave more. I tried to push it away as I scanned over the framed pictures lining the walls.

Every cell in my body vibrated with the need to step inside and study them.

To study her.

Annoyed, I set the dog down and spun around so fast I almost tripped over my own feet before I stomped back to the fence. Not giving two shits who heard me, I cursed a blue streak from here until Sunday.

I didn't even know why I was so damn pissed off. And that just made me even more furious. Planting one hand on the fence, I hoisted myself over in one quick motion and headed back to my workbench.

My fingers had just curled around a piece of wood when another curse fell from my lips. Sitting next to my foot was my neighbor's dog in all his ugly glory.

8

MADDIE

Deep breaths.

There were a lot of things more daunting than walking into your father's office and telling him you're not happy working for him. I knew there were. Just not for me. My heart had been making somersaults inside my chest all day. Frayed nerves barely hanging on to their last thread.

All because my dreams didn't align with what my parents thought they had to be. Lucetta and I had spoken earlier in the day. Her brother had managed to change his plans and could stay with their mother for another week. So, I had a few more days to give her my answer.

Extra time I didn't need.

I took one last steadying breath before tapping my knuckles against my dad's open office door. Head bent, thick gray brows tightly pulled together, he was scanning over a piece of paper in his hand.

I knocked again since he hadn't heard me the first time. He looked up then, the creases on his forehead forming an even deeper frown. "Maddie. Everything all right?" In my twenty-four years of being alive, I could count on one hand the times I'd dropped by my dad's office without reason.

The confusion on his leathery face completely understandable.

Inside my chest, my heart was drumming a nervous tattoo against my ribs. My mouth went dry while my hands felt like I'd dunked them in a bucket of ice water. "Yeah, everything's fine," I croaked out and immediately admonished myself. It shouldn't be like this. Needing to lay my truth bare to my dad shouldn't be this scary. "Do you have a minute?"

My dad sat back in his chair and studied me. "Sure, what's on your mind?" The way he was staring—like he was trying to figure out a complex puzzle—made my insides twist in a weird way.

Shouldn't parents know their children? Or at least know parts of them? But in that moment right there on the threshold of my dad's office he was looking at me as if I were a stranger.

It hurt. Man, did it hurt like it had never hurt before

Shoving the unwelcome feeling away as much as I could, I took a step forward then again and again until I could perch the tips of my fingers atop his desk. My dad looked painfully uncomfortable; his gaze never settling on me completely.

I cleared my throat. "I need to talk to you about something important, Dad."

He nodded tentatively. "I'm listening."

My mouth opened at the same time as Mr. White from the general store poked his head inside my dad's office. "You ready to lose some money, Fraser?"

I barely held my sigh when my dad's eyes shifted to the door. A smile that hadn't been aimed at me in a long, long time touched his lips and brought with it another pang of hurt, hitting me squarely in the chest. "Have I ever lost?"

I felt the sting of tears behind my eyes and immediately focused on the floor. I didn't want either of these men to see me cry.

"There's always a first time," I heard Mr. White say and then after a long pause. "Oh hi, Maddie. I didn't see ya there." Yup, that's me. Invisible. "You must be thrilled to be rid of that overpopulated, polluted city?"

"It wasn't so bad," I said quietly and then made the mistake of meeting my dad's glare. "Clearwater Bay is definitely better, though," I added quickly.

I heard him move before I felt his heavy arm drape over my shoulder. "Well, it's good to have you back. Ain't that right, Fraser?"

The sound that came from my dad's throat sounded like a cross between a snort and a groan. He pushed to his feet and after straightening the stack of papers, he set them aside. Those eyes of his landed on me. "We'll talk tomorrow?" It wasn't a question. Not really.

I forced a smile to my lips. "Sure, Dad. Have fun at poker night." Angling my head to the man next to me, I said, "It was nice to see you, Mr. White." Not waiting for a response out of either of them, I twisted around and fled to where my sister was sitting behind the counter.

I must've looked a fright because the instant she spotted me her eyes grew wide with concern. "What happened?"

Shaking my head, I took a moment to compose myself. "Nothing. Do you mind closing the store without me?"

"Maddie."

"Please, Jennah? It's not like I'm playing hooky." It was half an hour before closing time. But I just needed to get out of there. To get away from feeling like a disappointment.

With narrowed eyes, my sister regarded me for what felt like an eternity. A million questions were floating around in those irises and I thanked every deity I could think of when she didn't voice a single one.

Instead, she bent down and snatched my purse up before sliding it to me. "You know I'm here if you need to talk, right?" I didn't. Jennah and I weren't close. We hadn't been in years. Besides how could I explain to my sister—who couldn't set a foot wrong in my parents ' eyes—that I felt smothered. That it seemed as if I didn't fit in with the rest of them.

While they were happily trotting along living the lives they knew they were going to have, I was the one who wanted more. And it didn't necessarily mean I didn't want to live in this town. I just wanted to feel fulfilled. To make a difference. To not feel stagnant.

"Thanks. Give Tommy a hug for me, okay?" Feeling as if I might break at any moment, I rushed to my car. I had no idea how I made it home in one piece, but I'd never been as grateful to walk into my home as I was right then.

Until I saw Sheldon's crate.

His empty, dog-less crate.

My heart stopped cold right before it picked up at an alarming speed. "Sheldon?" His name came out all wobbly as I sprinted from one corner to the next. Even the smacking noises I made with my lips sounded shaky. Darting up the stairs, I kept calling him. Opening closet doors and searching under the beds.

Panic set in, my lungs and my throat seized up. Many people would look at him and see only a pet. But he was my companion. The one thing that made me feel less alone in this damn world. I'd gotten him at a shelter when friends were few during my short stay in New York.

The bond between us had been instant, and I couldn't imagine my life without Sheldon in it.

Thick, hot tears spilled down my cheeks before I even realized I was crying. Of course, this would happen. Today of all days. With my fingers laced behind my head, I stared at my bedroom ceiling. In all the time I'd had him, Sheldon had never run away. Not once. I had no clue where to even begin my search.

With a few angry swipes, I wiped away the tears and sprinted down the stairs. Maybe, just maybe, my pup was somewhere on the beach. I made it all of three steps out of the house before I skidded to a stop. It was so abrupt,

momentum threw my body forward and I almost fell flat
on my face.

Ambling toward me was my grumpy ass neighbor…
with my dog tucked under one of his thick arms. The one
covered in ink. His face a picture of determination as
those powerful legs of his took long sure strides toward
me.

I tried to swallow but my mouth felt dry. Too dry.
My gaze bounced from his legs to his broad chest, along
his tatted arm before settling on Sheldon. Who looked
happy as can be. I couldn't blame him though. The arm
holding him looked quite capable.

In the space of a breath, I had a vision of those arms
tightly wrapped around me. Holding me so close that I
could barely breathe. Making me feel comforted and safe.
I blinked and the vision, or whatever the heck that was,
was gone.

In its place, an angry-looking man glaring down at
me. A very tall and incredibly sexy man. Dark, dark eyes
peered at me down the length of a slightly crooked nose.
Those impossibly full lips curled into a snarl.

I wasn't supposed to find any of it appealing.

"Your damn rat was at my place again." How was it
even possible for a voice so low and gritty to be filled with
so much disdain?

"Sorry," was my weak reply. In my defense, having
him all up in my space like he was was a little bit
unnerving. It also gave me the perfect opportunity to
notice things I hadn't before. Like the fine lines framing
his eyes or the light dusting of freckles that spread from

one cheek to the other. And then the stubble covering his jaw that seemed to have a mixture of dark brown and golden strands.

I wanted to drag my palm over it and feel if it was as prickly as his personality. My gaze slipped to the scars on his neck. The thick welts covered his left side and disappeared into his shirt. A quick glance confirmed that they spread all the way to his left elbow.

What happened to you?

The question was there on the tip of my tongue. It was a damn miracle I didn't voice it.

"Did your momma never teach you it's rude to stare?" His voice boomed, pulling me out of my musings. I blinked once, twice, then two more times. The jaw I'd been studying seconds ago was set, the muscle ticking away like a timer of a bomb.

Then his words registered.

Squaring my shoulders, I tilted my head back and gave him a glare of my own. "No. Just like yours never taught you any manners."

A thrill danced down my spine when his eyes widened just a smidge at the tone of my voice. I was pretty sure Mr. Big and Intimidating wasn't used to people calling him on his BS.

Like he'd done the other day, he thrust Sheldon into my arms. Our hands touched for a fraction of a second, but it was enough to set my pulse on fire.

"Next time I see him on my property, he won't be so lucky," my grumpy ass neighbor growled.

I hugged my dog closer, feeling a mixture of relief and something else I couldn't quite put my finger on. "If you hurt him, I'll hurt *you*."

His lips twitched. I wasn't sure if he was holding back a smile or a snarl. "I'd like to see you try." Spinning on his heel with grace no man his size should have, he strode to the fence between our properties and hopped right over it with zero effort.

Big, loud sirens went off in my head. That man was trouble with a capital T.

I think I like trouble.

9

ADAM

I had a damn problem.

And it wasn't just my neighbor's rat who seemed to think I was his babysitter while his human was away during the day.

The little shit had showed up on my doorstep three days ago and no matter how many times I'd carted him back, he kept following me home.

Which in turn meant I had to take him back in the afternoons when my neighbor got off work, or wherever the hell she spent her days. Then of course that led to me spending a few minutes telling my gorgeous but annoying neighbor to keep her dog on her side of the fence while she stared at me with those whiskey eyes, thinking who knew what.

Her open study of me should've made me feel uncomfortable. I didn't like being under anyone's spotlight. But every time she trained her gaze on me, something shifted. I didn't understand it, nor did I attempt to make sense of it. I just knew it was there, simmering below the surface.

Unfortunately, that was only half of the problem.

The rest of it bowled down to the simple fact that instead of coming out in the morning and stumbling across my light-footed neighbor, I now waited for her. Waited like a thief in the shadows to steal a tiny bit of the joy radiating off her when she swayed and twirled like no one was watching.

My beach ballerina.

Even though the dancing she was doing was more contemporary than ballet. Yeah, I'd spent an embarrassing amount of time on the internet trying to find out what exactly it was she was doing. And I'd wanted to find out whether it was any kind of dancing that calmed me or if it was only her.

No points for guessing which one it was.

From my current perch behind my sliding door, I caught movement coming from the general direction of my neighbor's yard and I immediately shifted a little more to my left to remain out of sight.

I remained there for about a minute before gingerly opening the door and slipping outside. Long, easy strides carried me to the edge of my property, an unfamiliar zing zipping through my veins.

Until my gaze locked onto her.

In an instant, a sense of calm I had no right to wrapped itself around me like a thick blanket. My chest rose and fell with the deep drag of air I sucked to my lungs over and over again. I wanted to tip my head toward the sun and just be in that small moment of contentment.

The only thing stopping me from doing just that was the woman on the beach kicking up a cloud of sand.

How would it feel to be in the middle of that? To watch her spin and leap around me. To be close enough to learn what her hair smelled like. Or to feel her skin against mine. I wanted to know what that sweet voice of hers sounded like when she was all breathy from dancing for hours and hours.

Yeah, I had a problem all right, and it was painfully obvious who was at the center of it.

And it was because of this problem that I could tell there was something off with her routine. Her movements were sharp and choppy. Almost angry. I felt the shift inside of me, the anxious feeling of needing to know why she was upset.

I brought my hand to my chest and brushed my fingers over the scars beneath my shirt, completely transfixed on the woman slamming her fists in the sand. Her leg kicked back and, in a blink, she was on her feet again, hands reaching for an imaginary anchor in front of her.

I felt her anger, her pain, with every rough jerk of her body. She leaped through the air but instead of landing on both her feet like she usually did, she stumbled to her side before collapsing onto the sand.

Her hands shot out to her ankle, her face contorting with what I could only presume was pain. My feet were moving before my brain had time to issue the command. Sprinting down the little path that led to the beach, I reached her in mere seconds.

There was no conscious thought to my actions when I bent over and shoved my arm under her knees and hoisted her up. Not until the feeling of her body—even though it was just the side of her—was pressed up against me. Standing in a puddle with live wires touching the water from every angle wouldn't have had the same impact as her skin touching mine had.

Electricity zipped and zapped through my body without any sense of direction. I didn't know if I wanted to hold my breath or suck in a deep drag of air.

"What the hell are you doing?" the woman in my arms demanded. And because I couldn't speak, I hefted her higher and started walking toward the path. "Oh my goodness, would you freaking stop manhandling me!"

That did it. The fog clouding my brain dissipated like mist before the sun. In a move that probably wasn't very nice, I roughly deposited her back on her ass… in the sand. "Owww." She had the audacity to glare at me as if I was to blame for her pain.

Planting my hands on my hips, I narrowed my eyes. "Don't look at me like that. I was only trying to help you."

"Help me?" she cried. "You came barging down here like a freaking caveman and all but threw me over your shoulder."

Exasperated, I threw my arms in the air. "I was helping you, woman!" I jerked my chin in the direction of her leg. "How are you going to get back to your place on that?"

She pulled her shoulders back and inadvertently pushed her breasts forward. I tried not to look. I really did. But beneath the scars and pissy exterior, I was still a red-blooded man. And they were so perky yet full and would probably fit perfectly in—

"I can manage on my own." At her fierce admission, my gaze snapped back to her face. Brows pulled together; she was studying her ankle, which was a good thing considering where my attention had been a moment ago.

Those whiskey eyes flicked to mine and she held out her hand. "All right. If you could just help me up, I should be good."

Both my arms came up as I took a step back. "I thought you said you could manage *on your own*." I had to bite the inside of my cheek to keep the grin from spreading when I threw her words back at her.

Her eyes narrowed dangerously. And if she wasn't sitting on her ass with what I had a feeling was a sprained ankle, I might've felt the tiniest bit intimidated. "You're such a dick," she muttered.

And I really was. Because I stood there without so much as lifting a finger while she struggled to her feet. Straightening her spine, she pinned me with a stare so fierce my balls almost shriveled up.

And just to drive home the big FU she was throwing my way; she took a step forward and immediately winced. My feet shifted, but it was the tight shake of her head that kept me rooted to the spot.

She attempted to take another step; her entire face scrunched up in pain. Her chest was heaving, and her hands balled up into tight, white-knuckled fists at her sides.

"This is bullshit." That was the only warning I gave her before I surged forward and scooped her up once more.

If I thought holding her against me was intense before, it had nothing on the feeling that zipped through me when she willingly draped her arms around my neck. Everywhere she touched felt like it had a million nerve endings attached to it. All of them lighting up at once.

I forced my feet to move. The faster I got her home, the quicker I could retreat. Three steps into my plan and I had to stop. Eyeing her out of the corner of my eye—because I couldn't stand to look straight at her when she was so close—I asked, "Where's Fugly?"

A heavy sigh pushed past her lips. The faintest hint of strawberry tickling my nose when she shook her head. "His name is Sheldon and he's home."

Without acknowledging her words, I started moving again. A soft breeze picked up and lifted her hair, the light tresses brushing over my cheek. There was no stopping the string of curses that fell from my lips when all I wanted to do was shut my eyes and take that strawberry scent straight to my lungs.

She must've thought I was pissed off at her because she quickly gathered her hair together and mumbled an apology. I couldn't even speak past whatever the hell I was feeling so I only managed a grunt.

The woman in my arms let out another sigh, her warm breath fluttering over the side of my neck. "How did you know I was hurt?"

"What?" The word sounded rough to my own ears so I couldn't even imagine what it sounded like to her.

"You were there moments after I fell. How did you know?"

I was pretty sure my ears were turning some shade of red or pink at the very least. I couldn't tell her the truth; I knew exactly how messed up it sounded. Shrugging the shoulder she wasn't pressed to, I kept my voice steady. "Good timing, I guess."

The side of my face burned with the intensity of her stare. Still, I didn't dare look at her. I kept my attention straight ahead until we reached her sliding door.

The damn thing was cracked open a few inches again.

I aimed my glare at the door instead of her. "You really should lock your doors. It's not safe leaving it open like this."

She patted my chest, the heat of her palm searing me through the fabric of my shirt. I ground my back molars to the point of pain. "It's a small town." She huffed. "Nothing bad happens here."

"You can't really be that—"

"That what?"

I wasn't fooled by her cool tone. I knew enough to know when a woman spoke with such measured calmness, you shut your mouth and retreated to a safe distance.

Without another word, I slid the door all the way open and stepped inside her house. I couldn't explain why but it felt oddly intimate. I hated the feeling. Striding over to the couch, I set her down and before stalking to her kitchen without asking for permission.

It felt a bit intrusive to be rummaging through her freezer, but I kept reminding myself that she would have told me to get the hell out if she minded. Once I found what I was looking for, I made my way back to where she was curled up with Fugly, I mean Sheldon, nestled against her.

Covertly, I took a few fortifying breaths before I straightened her leg and slid one of her decorative pillows under her foot. Once it was elevated, I pressed the bag of frozen peas against her swollen ankle. She instantly hissed out a breath and jerked upright, which pulled a whine from her dog before he gave her cheek a meaningful lick.

"I think you sprained it," I told her.

She eyed her foot. "Yeah."

I had zero clues what to do next. Dragging a hand along the back of my neck, I took a step backward and then another and another. Just as I wanted to spin around and get the hell out of there, her soft, "Wait" stopped me in my tracks.

Not daring to move a step closer, I simply stared at her. She nibbled on her lip, it was the first sign of nervousness I'd seen on her since we met. "Thanks for the help." Her sugary sweet voice slid over my skin leaving a trail of goosebumps.

"Sure." My throat felt scratchy, I barely fought the urge to clear it.

"I'm Maddie, by the way."

I closed my eyes. I didn't want to put a name to that gorgeous face and sweet voice. She was already screwing with my equilibrium as a nameless stranger. How much worse would it be now that I knew what she felt like, smelled like? Now that I had a name to whisper in the dark.

Slowly; very, very slowly, I opened my eyes, my gaze immediately colliding with her warm one. "Adam."

"Adam," she echoed, and I had to flee.

10

MADDIE

There were moments in life that you just knew would be significant. Moments that would stay branded in your brain for the rest of eternity. Watching Adam screw his eyes shut, unable to hide the tortured look on his face, was that moment for me.

Even though he was long gone, I could still see him standing in my living room. Impossibly big and beautifully damaged. If I'd been braver, I would have asked him to stay. I wanted to; the words just wouldn't leave the safety of my mind.

My gaze flicked to the glass door that he'd shut behind him when he'd left. I grinned. I hadn't been wrong about those capable arms. At five-foot-six, I wasn't a petite little thing by any means, but he'd picked me up and carried me home as if I weighed nothing. His freaking breathing had still been even when he'd delivered me to my couch.

Closing my eyes, I inhaled deeply. He'd smelled like coffee and soap, a mix that most certainly shouldn't have set my senses on fire, and yet that's exactly what it had done. It'd been so difficult not to drop my head to his shoulder and take a deep breath of *him*. Or to lift my hand to his beard like I'd imagined doing so many times already.

And then there was the expression on his face when I'd wanted to know how he knew I was hurt. There had been the tiniest crack in those features that always seemed so aloof. Had he been watching me? And if he had, was it only that once?

Oh, I knew I should have been creeped out. But there was no way I could ignore the thrill of excitement that bubbled through my veins at the mere thought of his dark gaze on me.

I opened my eyes and sighed. I needed to stop. There was no space in my brain for Adam and his big hands, strong arms, and ruggedly sexy face. I had no right to wonder what it would feel like if he dragged his palms up my bare thighs. Would he use those hands of his to pin me down while he moved between my legs or would they explore every inch of my body?

Just thinking about both possibilities sent shivering need through my veins. And I hadn't even gotten to his mouth yet. My eyes were halfway shut, my thoughts well on their way to becoming less PG, when my phone shrieked to life from the kitchen counter where I'd left it this morning.

If it hadn't been Frankie's ringtone bouncing off the walls, I wouldn't even have entertained the idea of getting up. With a heavy sigh, I shifted to remove the now watery peas from my leg, studying it with a scrunched-up nose. The skin was a muddled mess of blue and purple, and my

ankle looked very much like Jennah's had during the last
month of her pregnancy.

The sprain wasn't bad and the pain manageable, but
only because I'd been keeping my leg still for over an
hour. From inside the kitchen, The Jonas Brothers stopped
singing for all of two seconds before the chorus of
Frankie's favorite song started up again.

Sucking in a breath, I slowly lowered my leg to the
ground before gingerly straightening to my full height.
Very much like on the beach a while ago, I took one step,
and a sharp, stabbing pain immediately shot up my leg.

"Ow," I groaned. Sheldon, bless his little k-9 heart,
whined right along with me before smothering my leg
with doggy kisses. "Thanks, buddy, but you gotta give me
room to walk." Somehow my words made sense because
he stopped licking and trotted off.

In the time it took me to cross from the living room
to the kitchen, Frankie had phoned me four times. I knew
if I didn't get back to her soon, she'd hop in her car and
drive over here without giving it a second thought.

Next to baking, worrying was her favorite thing to
do.

The instant I had my phone, I pulled up her number
and pressed the green button. She answered almost
immediately. "What the hell? I've been calling and
calling. I thought something bad had happened to you. I
was about to come over there."

"Aaand breathe." I bit my cheek to keep the smile out
of my voice.

"It's not funny." Apparently, it didn't work.

"I'm not laughing, I swear."

She might've been somewhere across town, but I felt her narrow her eyes. "Mmm- hmm, yeah. I was going to invite you over to sample the new additions to the menu, but now I'm not so sure."

This had me groaning very loudly. "As much as I would love to come over and try your delicious offerings, I can't." I sighed. "I got hurt." I explained to Frankie about the fall, choosing to leave out the part about my neighbor carrying me home.

"Say no more. I'll be there in ten." I could hear her moving about. A few cupboards opened and closed. "I'm bringing lunch."

I smiled into the phone. "I don't deserve you."

A puff of laughter filtered through the line. "Of course not, but because I'm so damn awesome, I'm letting you keep me."

"How awfully kind of you." My smile stretched even wider.

We shared another laugh and with a promise of being over soon, Frankie said goodbye. It was a good thing she knew where I kept my spare key, I thought as I hobbled back the couch, snatching up the TV remote along the way.

At least sitting back down was a little less painful than the standing up and walking to the kitchen part had been. As leaned back against the soft cushioning, Sheldon hopped on and made himself comfortable against my hip.

My hand moved to his head, fingers threading through his impossibly soft fur. "Now what to do while we wait for Frankie?" I shot him a glance. "You got any ideas?" He stared at me with his big eyes for a few seconds before burying his nose between his front paws.

Laughing softly, I poked the button on the remote and mindlessly scrolled through the channels. Nothing caught my attention, but then again, nothing would when Adam was still so firmly stuck in my head.

The scruff peppering his jaw, the way he held me, his scent. The tortured look on his beautiful face. I couldn't stop thinking about the man, and honestly, I didn't think I wanted too.

After who knew how long, Sheldon's head snapped up right before he launched off the couch and set off for the front door with a string of barks.

"Honestly," Frankie huffed out when she appeared in my living room a few moments later. "He has known me for how long? And still he yaps at me." She aimed her glare at Sheldon as he made himself comfortable next to me again.

"He's just saying hello," I told her with a grin.

She rolled her eyes before shifting her gaze to my ankle. "Ouch."

"You can say that again."

Hefting the bags in her hands, she turned headed for the kitchen. "Let me fix you lunch and then you can tell me all about it."

"You're too good to me."

"Trust me," she said, pulling out item after item. "I know."

She spent the next few minutes telling me about her plan to have a cupcake and cocktail pairing evening. Kind of like a wine tasting, she'd said, but with pretty drinks and decadent cakes.

I wasn't going to need too much convincing to attend that.

"All right, from cupcakes to sandwiches." Her smile had a nervous edge to it when she handed me a plate with another mouthwatering savory stuffed croissant.

Forgoing my manners, I lifted the treat and took a big bite. "Aaww," I moaned around a mouth full of half-chewed food. "This one is even better than the one I had the other day. My taste buds have officially died and gone to heaven."

Salty pork and sweet braised apples with just a hint of pepper danced on my tongue, reminding me how lucky I was to have a friend who loved cooking.

I went in for another bite and another, demolishing the goodness on my plate embarrassingly fast.

"So, it's good?" Frankie was sitting at the opposite end of the sectional, an untouched croissant perched on her lap.

"It's better than good. In fact." I jerked my chin toward her. "If you're not going to eat that—"

"Hands off!"

I threw my head back and laughed. "You're not eating it."

Something odd struck me then. Treats of any kind made people happy. Or most people at least. Maybe something rich and decadent would have the same effect on Mr. Grumpy Butt next door.

"I need a favor," I said.

Frankie's gaze remained on her plate, though one corner of her mouth curved upward. "I draw the line at taking you to the toilet."

"Really? You don't want to help me wipe?" My teasing earned me a sharp look and I couldn't help but laugh. "This is more a kitchen favor than a bathroom one."

"What do ya need, Maddie Cakes?"

Suddenly nervous, I shifted and set the plate down on the end table. "I want to bake your cinnamon rolls for someone as a thank you, but I… uh… don't have the recipe."

Frankie's eyes went wide, mirth making her irises even bluer. "And for whom are we baking these treats." She leaned forward, her lips lifting into a grin. "Or more specifically, what are you thankful for?"

I couldn't explain why heat shot to my cheeks so fast even my ears felt hot. "Well," I started carefully before launching into the morning's events. When I got to the being-in-Adam's-arms-part, I willed every one of my features to remain unmoving. The last thing I wanted was to explain to my friend how much time I'd spent fantasizing about the man next door.

The last word had barely left my mouth before she smacked her palm against the cushioning next to my foot. "What the hell?" I yelped. Sheldon hopped a few feet into the air, let out a loud shriek, and hopped off the couch before hurrying away.

"You could've led with that!" She looked like she wanted to shake me. "You have to tell me everything!"

I wrinkled my brow. "I just did."

"All right, play it like that, but I know there's more here." She pushed to her feet and held out her hand for me. "Come on, let's go bake."

Frankie helped me hobble to the kitchen and with my butt parked on a stool at the counter we started working on one of my favorite treats.

My body vibrated with excitement. I just wasn't sure if it was because of the impending baking or the thought of seeing Adam again.

11

ADAM

"What the hell was that?"

Sitting on the edge of my bed, I stared into the darkness. For the first time in years, my sleep hadn't been interrupted by painful memories. This time when I woke with sweat coating my skin, it had been a very different name that left my lips.

Maddie.

I'd whispered it so many times and still, the feel of her name on my tongue had the blood in my veins buzzing. I wasn't entirely sure why this woman was having this effect on me, I just knew it was a welcome reprieve from the nightmares that had haunted me for so long.

Even though it only led to a different kind of frustration.

Dropping my head, I screwed my eyes shut and heaved out a breath. The feel of Maddie in my arms was still as vivid as if it had just happened and not hours ago. As suspected, her subtle strawberry scent and kind eyes had followed me into my dreams.

Tormenting me with images of my hands fisting those honey blonde tresses while my mouth learned the taste of her skin. Those whiskey irises bored into me, and that sweet voice of hers had whispered my name breathlessly.

The cold hand of reality had ripped me from my dreams right then and I'd never been more disappointed. It wasn't rational, this sudden interest I had in her. Just as the sense of calm I could only achieve in her presence wasn't logical.

Pushing to my feet, I looked down and was reminded yet again of the very strange direction my night had taken. For the first time in I didn't even know how long, I had something that needed hands-on attention. There were absolutely zero doubts as to whose name would be on my lips when I did.

***

Unable to sit still, I'd started pacing the kitchen, only pausing every few minutes to will the slow drip, drip, drip of the coffee maker to hurry the heck up. Of course, at the very back of my mind, I knew the restlessness had nothing to do with my need for a caffeine fix.

No, the fix I was craving came in the form of a five-four, possibly five-five, packet of dynamite. Since I'd woken in the middle of the night, Maddie hadn't left my thoughts. After the obvious reason was taken care of, my mind had drifted to her and that swollen ankle.

How was she getting around?

Did she manage to eat?

Was she keeping it elevated?

Did she have someone who was taking care of her?

As much as it irritated me, I couldn't stop thinking about her. The amount of time that woman was spending running around in my mind was embarrassingly high. And I didn't know what to do about it.

Or if I *wanted* to do anything about it.

If I were honest, daydreaming about a living, breathing woman was a lot better than the alternative. The one where the past refused to retract its claws out of my battered and bruised soul.

I eyed the coffee maker again, relieved that there was enough tarry liquid in the carafe to satisfy at least one of my needs. Mug in hand, I topped it to the brim and slipped through the glass door.

As it had done for the past few days, my gaze immediately went to the beach before I realized my beach ballerina wouldn't be performing any time soon. I wasn't even close to being prepared for the deep rush of disappointment that descended over me.

The light-wood Adirondack creaked loudly as I lowered my frame into it. Sighing heavily, I took a long swallow from the steaming mug in my hand, and instead of watching the waves roll to shore, my gaze flicked to the house next door.

What are you doing right now?

An incredibly stupid idea started forming and before I had time to properly process it, I was on my feet and striding toward the fence. I'd covered half of the distance when the fog covering the logical part of my brain finally lifted and I dug my heels in.

Was I really about to hop the fence and knock on her door?

How would that conversation have gone over? If ever there'd been a time to smack myself upside the head, it was at that moment. I had no business initiating anything with anyone.

My mood changed on a dime and it wasn't particularly fair to drag anyone into that. I looked down at my hand still clutching my morning coffee. Brows drawing together, I willed the black liquid for answers.

Not just any answers. I needed to know why after all this time, I had this deep-rooting need to be different. To not be so broken that the thought of letting anyone close scared the shit out of me.

Tipping the coffee out on to the grass, I stalked back into the safety of my house, locking the door behind me for good measure. I rinsed the mug, set it on the rack, and then stared at the scenery beyond the window.

A frustrated growl tore from my lungs when the only thing I wanted to see on that beach was Maddie. My insides twisted with the confliction spreading through me. On the one hand, I was relieved at the sudden change in direction my thoughts had taken. But on the other, I knew this… infatuation or whatever the hell it was had to stop.

It wasn't healthy.

A distraction of any kind would have been welcomed with open arms but since nothing was happening, I flopped down on my couch and turned on the television. Flicking through the channels, I swore roughly when one channel was streaming a movie about a ballerina and a dance show of sorts was on the next.

Without changing it, I turned the volume down. I tossed the remote beside me, my cellphone catching my eye when the remote landed on it. Maybe it was finally time to reach out to a friend. Someone who knew me from before the accident. If anyone could give me some perspective, it would be Griffin.

He'd been as loyal as a brother even, especially, when I'd been a stupid prick and had blamed him for Angie being gone. As the memories of the unsavory words I'd spewed at him swirled around my brain, I was once again reminded how damn lucky I was.

My family, my friends, all of them could have walked away and left me to rot in the hole I'd dug for myself. No one would have blamed them one bit. But that wasn't how the people in my life did things. They stayed—even when I chased them away—and they fought like hell to drag me back.

I owed them so much.

Mindlessly staring at the muted television, I tossed the phone from one hand to the other. The last time I'd willingly sent a text to anyone had been a hell of a long time ago. So long, that I didn't even know how to initiate a damn conversation.

My gaze shifted from the wall-mounted screen to the one in my hand. I swiped the screen and opened my messaging app. After scrolling through the few numbers I had saved in my contact list; I pulled up my friend's number and stared some more.

How the hell did people do this? My thumbs fumbled over the small illuminated letters as I typed.

Me: What's up?

There. Short and straight to the point. The tiny dots on the screen started jumping almost immediately.

Griffin: Who died?

Me: What?

Griffin: You never text. Who's dead?

With a grunt, I threw my head back against the couch and stared at the ceiling. Maybe I was still upstairs, asleep in my bed because everything about the past twenty-four hours was just… weird.

I'd barely resigned myself to that idea when the phone I was still clutching buzzed in my hand, my friend's name flashing in big bold letters. Just how discombobulated I was, was evident when I poked the green button without giving it a second thought.

I didn't get a chance to utter a word before a concerned, "What's wrong?" reached my ears.

Admittedly, I felt like an idiot. I'd managed to isolate myself to the point where my family and friends figured the world was ending when they received any form of communication from me.

"Nothing," I finally breathed out. "I just wanted to check in." The familiar squeak of his truck door opening and closing sounded from his side. "Busy?" I asked.

"Nah. Just got to the station." He'd barely said the words when the background noises registered.

A sharp pang of sadness hit me in the center of my chest. I missed it. Firefighting was about so much more than putting out fires. There was a good reason why a station was called a house. You were a family bound by a mutual love for something so completely fascinating and destructive.

"You still there?" There was a muffled sound that I assumed to be his office door closing when the chattering faded.

"Yeah, still here."

"So," Griffin drawled, his Irish accent curling around the last letter. "You wanna tell me what's up with you?"

I rubbed my chest and turned my head toward the glass door and repeated, "Nothing."

A chuckle floated through the line. "Did you forget who you're talkin 'to? We might not be related by blood, but we're brothers still."

"I know."

I heard his voice, but I couldn't make out the words. Even through his closed office door, I heard the distinct sound of the fire alarm. The insistent sharp ringing calling you to action. No doubt, brave men and women were scampering around, throwing their gear on and rushing to get to the rig.

For a fraction of a second, the thrill I always got when I heard that alarm vibrated through my veins. But it was gone just as fast. Taking another part of me with it.

"Ah, shite," he groaned. "I have—"

"Go." The word felt like sandpaper clawing at the inside of my mouth and throat. The bell still ringing in the background like a sledgehammer to the heart.

"Aye," he said softly. "We'll talk later." The line went dead a second after that and it took every ounce of willpower I had not to smash the device in my hand against the nearest wall. I was living in a prison of my own making with absolutely no idea how to escape.

And just like that, the nightmare was back, only this time I was wide awake with nowhere to hide.

12

MADDIE

This is a bad idea.

With one hand clutching the rolls, I stared at the imposing door in front of me. It wasn't so much the door as the man behind it I found intimidating. Cautiously, I eyed Sheldon sitting at my feet.

"Am I being silly?"

His answering *woof* could've meant anything, but I chose to go with no. I took a deep breath through my nose and slowly released it again. After doing it one more time, I lifted my hand and tapped twice against the wood.

Behind my ribs, my heart started jackhammering as the seconds steadily ticked by. I waited and waited, but no Adam. Turning sideways, my gaze flicked between the door and the gate I'd hobbled through a few moments ago.

Then I slowly faced the door once more and quickly knocked before I could think better of it. Again, I was left staring at an unmoving panel of wood. Feeling dismayed, I looked at the rolls and then at Sheldon. "We'll just leave them here." Hopefully, Adam would find them… eventually.

The thought made me even sadder. Not just because I wouldn't get to see him—which I was inexplicably looking forward to a lot—but Frankie and I—okay, mostly Frankie—had outdone ourselves.

With a heavy sigh, I bent down to set the rolls down on the ground when the door suddenly flew open; putting me at eye-level with the homeowner's crotch. A crotch covered by a thin pair of light gray athletic shorts that did not leave an awful lot to the imagination.

There was absolutely no way the sudden rush of heat to my cheeks, and some other parts, could be helped. I straightened so fast, I almost threw my back out. And then my lungs collapsed in one fell swoop, breathing almost impossible.

Standing with one hand gripping the door and the other perched on the frame was a very, very delicious looking Adam. His skin glistened; his shirt, the same color as his shorts, a few shades darker where it clung to his sweat-soaked body like a second skin.

My gaze followed the sharp lines of his ink as it crawled along his thick, corded arm and disappeared beneath the fabric hugging his bicep. My fingers twitched with a sudden need to touch.

Adam cleared his throat and I almost jumped out of my skin; my eyes immediately flicking to his. Jaw ticking, he was studying me with dark, serious eyes that somehow had a direct line to my lady bits.

How utterly stupid.

I'd found plenty of men attractive over the years. Hell, I'd even ended up in a few of their beds. But this, this almost galvanizing feeling, was new. No man had ever set my pulse on fire with a single glance.

Until I met Adam.

I didn't know what it was about him that called out to a bone-deep part of me that I had no idea even existed. Some dormant piece of my soul that had been patiently waiting for him.

He cleared his throat again and I blushed even deeper. "Sorry, I wanted—" before I had time to finish my sentence, Sheldon jumped up and stormed into Adam's house, who immediately turned around and bent over to scoop up my naughty pup.

I really wished he hadn't done that. The tangy taste of metal filled my mouth when I bit the inside of my cheek to stop the sigh from leaving my mouth at the sight of his downright sinful butt.

He straightened and turned while I furiously tried to reign in my thoughts. One look at Sheldon tucked under his arm and all my efforts were for naught. I swear, the image in front of me was equivalent to one of those on Frankie's firefighter calendars. Adam might've been wearing more clothes, but the warning label should've read the same: *Warning! Panties in danger of spontaneously combusting.*

"I'm sorry," I spat out when my brain finally decided to work. "He isn't like that with anyone else." It was quite possible that my little fascination with this man had rubbed off on my dog. Or maybe it was Adam's fault for being so damn enticing.

"Right," he said carefully. Without making a move to hand over Sheldon, his eyes flicked to my bare feet. I wanted to curl in my purple-painted toes. "You shouldn't be walking on that."

I followed his gaze down to my ankle and shrugged. "I kept it still all day yesterday. I… uh…just wanted to give you these." Looking up, I hefted the plate in my hand higher. "It's cinnamon rolls. The best in town. Before you think I'm completely full of myself, I didn't make them, Frankie did." The word vomit just kept on coming. I wanted to bury my face in my hands but because I was still holding the stupid rolls, I couldn't.

I was also fairly certain the red covering my face had turned three shades darker.

Still focused on me, one of his eyebrows slowly quirked, "Frankie?"

"My friend. She owns Sugar Booger in town." Relief washed over me when I managed to keep it short this time.

I didn't think it was at all possible, but Adam's stare bore even deeper into mine. "Can't say that I've been."

"Oh, you're missing out. She makes the best cupcakes. People come from all over just to sample her boozy treats." I was doing it again. With a sigh, I squeezed my eyes shut. "Sorry, I'll stop."

He made a sound; it could've been a chuckle, could've been a grunt. I'd never know because when my eyes flew open his features were unmoving. Holding the plate toward him, I jerked my head in Sheldon's direction. "I'll trade you."

Those dark eyes eyed the plate. "I wasn't expecting anything."

Adam made no move to take the offering from me and I suddenly felt like a gigantic idiot. I mean, who the hell even gave baked treats as a thank you. I shouldn't have done anything. That's probably what the normal half of the population would have done.

"It's okay if you don't want them. I know Mr. Stevenson—"

"I never said that." His eyes narrowed the tiniest bit. "I want them." He said the words with so much conviction, my silly lady parts thought he was speaking about them.

My lips suddenly felt dry. I dragged my tongue over the bottom one before letting a soft, "Okay." Thrusting the plate toward him; my breath caught when his fingers dragged over mine during the transfer.

With his eyes holding mine captive, he slowly brought the plate to his nose. Nostrils flaring, he dragged the delicious cinnamon scent straight to his lungs. "Smells good." His murmur was so soft and gravelly, I wasn't certain it was meant for my ears.

"Wait until you taste me…uh…I mean it…them." Rolling my lips inward, I used every single ounce of willpower I had not to keep babbling like an idiot. I seriously needed some action because the way I was reacting to this man was beyond freaking ridiculous. Hormonal, teenage Maddie hadn't even been like this.

And to make my embarrassment even worse, Adam's face remained an emotionless mask save for his ticking jaw that picked up speed.

I reached for Sheldon and almost let out a string of curses when my palms swiped over Adam's hot skin in the process. Almost immediately, I hugged him to my chest like a security blanket. The soft whimper that came from his tiny lungs warned me I might be holding on too tight.

Loosening my embrace on my pup, I told Adam, "I just wanted to drop those off. Hope you enjoy them."

His gaze flicked to my ankle for a long moment before he lifted his eyes to mine again. "I'll help you get home."

"No!" I all but yelled. "I'm okay, thanks." With the weirdness going on in my brain and body, there was absolutely no way I could let Adam touch me. Nodding once, I turned and slowly started hobbling down the cobblestone path.

I was about halfway when he called out, "Maddie!" It was the first time I'd heard him say my name and oh how wonderful it sounded rolling off his tongue like that.

Pulling in a deep breath, I took a moment to compose myself before glancing over my shoulder. "Yeah?"

He held the plate in the air. "Thanks for these."

There was something in his eyes that touched the very bottom of my soul. The weight of his gaze burning into mine felt so intense that I had to get away. Without another word, I turned my attention forward and headed straight for his gate.

It didn't matter how fast I hobbled, that dark stare stayed on me. It followed me all the way to my house and even intruded on my dreams. Dreams that left me hot and sweaty with an insistent ache between my thighs.

***

Pressing my hand against my stomach, I willed the nervous butterflies to calm down. I'd done worse things than what I was about to do, so there was no reason for them to be all up in arms about this.

I closed my eyes and took a few calming breaths. Once I was certain I had most of my nervousness under control, I opened my eyes and walked to my dad's office. It wasn't Fraser Young I found behind the big oak desk, though, but rather my mom.

She spotted me before I had time to speak. Pulling her reading glasses off, she set them down in front of her and leveled me with a stare. "Did you come to talk about what's bothering you?"

My shoulders sagged on a sigh. "That obvious?"

"Only because a mother always knows." She beckoned me with a slight tilt of her head, and I went, collapsing onto the couch in the corner of the office with a huff. "What's going on, Madison?"

Where did I begin?

I hadn't been in the best mood all day. Adam and all his sexiness were only partly to blame. In my sleep-deprived state early in the morning, I'd made a decision. It wasn't life-altering, but it wouldn't be without repercussions.

I'd said yes to Lucetta.

Without speaking to my parents first.

And with an ankle that was still sprained.

I'd been honest about the injury, though, and Lucetta had ensured me that it wouldn't be too much of a problem. Some classes would have to be moved and others postponed until the following week. In her words, it was all doable.

"Madison?"

At the sound of my name, I blinked furiously, and Mom's worried face came into focus. "Oh, right." Swallowing past the thick lump in my throat proved to be almost impossible. "Where's Dad?" I preferred to have this particular conversation only once.

"He should be back soon. Old Dougie needed help with the kitchen sink again."

I wanted to groan. My dad would not be back soon. Whenever Dougie needed help with anything, he and my dad ended up splitting a six-pack.

My mom was still watching me intently, almost as if she was trying to pull the thoughts from my brain. I kind of wished she could.

Sitting up straighter, I ran my palms up and down my denim-clad thighs. "I don't know if you're aware," I began, "but Lucetta's mom hurt herself a while ago." Of course, my mom wasn't aware. She and my previous dance instructor didn't exactly get along. When my mom shook her head, I quickly went on, "There's no one to take care of her, so Lucetta has to go down to Oakridge for a few weeks."

I'd hoped that penny might've dropped but when my mom just stared blankly, I knew I had to explain. "She asked me to help out at the studio and I said yes."

It took a long, agonizing minute but when realization finally dawned, my mom's eyes narrowed dangerously. "Only at night, right? Because you're still working here during the day." Her voice was deceptively calm.

I knew better.

I nibbled on the inside of my cheek, trying to find the right words that wouldn't lead to an argument. "Well, I would need to be at the studio full time. Besides, it's not like I'm really needed here. You and Dad created this position for me when I came back." With my tail between my legs.

My mom shook her head ruefully and my entire being wanted to sob. That one simple action showed me just how much of me they refused to accept. "Why can't you just be normal?"

"Normal?" My voice climbed a few octaves. "And what does that look like, Mom? Losing myself little by little doing a job I hate? Or will I be considered normal when I stop thinking for myself and follow your plans for my life like an obedient lapdog?"

"Madison." Her voice had a warning edge to it but I was too far gone to heed it.

"No, Mom, I'd really like to know what it is you think I should be doing."

My mom's fingers shot to her temples, furiously rubbing tiny circles against her skin. "Anything but dance." Her sigh was loaded and heavy; it made my skin crawl and my brain buzz with questions. But then she opened her mouth and delivered her next words with so much disgust, you'd think they were poison on her tongue.

"I don't understand this obsession you have with *dancing*, Madison."

Yet again, my heart crumbled into a million little pieces. I couldn't keep doing this. I was never going to be their perfect daughter.

Lifting my chin, I looked my mom straight in the eye. "And you don't have to. It makes me happy and that *should* be enough for you."

Pushing to my feet, I held my head high and walked out of there, pretending like hell I wasn't falling apart on the inside.

13

ADAM

"I was wondering when you were going to show up."

Hands resting on my hips, I glared at the dog scratching at my closed sliding door. I hadn't had a run-in with him all day, but it was only because I had yet to go outside since I'd started working on the floor in the guest bedroom earlier in the morning.

As much as my sister and her family's impending visit had my stomach in knots, I still wanted them to sleep in a half-decent room. So, I'd abandoned my deck project for now and moved inside to sort out the guest bedroom and its adjoining bathroom.

My growling stomach was the only reason I'd come downstairs. When I did, I found the rat pawing at my door. I'd never admit this out loud to anyone, especially not his owner, but the little shit was growing on me. Just a bit.

The instant I slid the door open, the dog darted inside and parked his butt in front of my feet; his tiny paws touching the front of my work boots. "How do you always end up on my side of the fence?" Fu...erm, Sheldon tilted his head from side to side. "I think maybe your human is doing this on purpose just to annoy me."

What did irritate the shit out of me was how she kept leaving that damn door of hers unlocked. It was dangerous and not smart at all. I had half a mind to pull her over my knee and spank her ass.

Now there was an idea.

My already-wired-brain had been running in a million different directions since the last time I saw Maddie. The day she'd dropped off the delicious, completely demolished, cinnamon rolls. The absolutely last thing I'd expected to see when I peeked through the peephole was her, looking even more mouth-watering than the offering in her hands.

Black tights and a bright pink thin-strapped top had covered her curves, her hair pulled into a knot, and her feet bare. And all I wanted to do was yank her against me and find out if the real thing tasted as good as it had in my dreams.

Not doing exactly that had been a true test of willpower. By the time she limped back to her place, I was done analyzing where the sudden interest in this woman had come from. Having my thoughts and dreams filled with visions and fantasies of her was perfectly fine as long as I didn't do something about it.

Unfortunately for me, giving my deprived mind free reign on thoughts of Maddie also led to a few pressing matters that had me spending a lot more time with myself in the bathroom.

Yeah, it probably wasn't healthy, and I knew I would have to find a way to move past this *infatuation* sooner or later. Because I could never act on it. I didn't know shit about this woman, but I knew she didn't need the likes of me in her life.

Sheldon pawed at my leg, effectively pulling me from the weird place my thoughts had gone. "Go wait for your human in your own damn yard," I told the dog with absolute zero conviction.

I had a suspicion the little bastard knew I didn't mind his presence so much anymore. Groaning, I threw a thumb over my shoulder. "Come on, I think there's enough roast beef for the both of us." As if he understood, Sheldon happily trotted behind me as I headed to the kitchen.

After pulling the leftover meat from the fridge along with the makings for a loaded sandwich, I set everything down on the counter and got to work. Sheldon sat stock-still, watching me with laser precision. The only movement that came from him was when he'd lick his lips every few seconds.

When I was done, I cut my stacked sandwich in half before eyeing the bowl holding the meat I'd shredded for the dog. I was very aware that there were people who did not want their k9 companions to eat anything other than dog food.

I'd still been a probie, as green as can be, when we'd had a medical assist call. It was an elderly citizen who'd feared she was having a heart attack—turned out to be really bad indigestion. While our LT had been tending to her, Princess, her pug, had wandered up to me. At the time I'd figured the jerky in my pocket would go down a treat. Until the little old lady had spotted me feeding her dog.

Gone was the hyperventilating and moaning. She'd jumped up so fast, the LT had fallen back on his ass. And since I'd been on my haunches in front of the dog, so had I. Finger waggling, she'd come storming toward me, yelling about how her dog's tummy was going to be upset and that she was going to call me in the middle of the night to clean it up.

I'd apologized so profusely, for six months after my nickname had been *Sorry Suzie Carlisle.*

An almost ear-splitting shrill rang through the air, cutting my trip down memory lane short. I glowered at Sheldon. He was sitting on his hind legs with his front paws scratching air. As much as it hadn't amused me the first time I'd witnessed it, I was beginning to think it was kind of almost *cute.*

All I could do was shake my head at myself. Cute was a damn word that didn't belong in my vocabulary. "This is your human's fault," I told the dog, setting the bowl of meat in front of him. Maddie already looked like she wanted to hit me over the head most of the time, certainly me giving her dog human-food couldn't make matters any worse.

I was still admonishing myself when three sharp knocks sounded from the front door. That ticking thing inside my chest reacted faster than my brain, already kicking into a higher gear. My gaze flicked to the dog and I murmured, "Speak of the devil."

Without a thought, I stooped, swept up Sheldon, and headed for the front door. The insistent buzzing through my veins should have been a warning sign. A big red flashing light telling—no, screaming—at me to turn the hell around and leave this woman alone.

I just didn't want to.

It was as simple and damn complicated as that.

With a quick drag of air to my lungs, I pulled open the door and stared. It was not my enticing beach ballerina standing on my low-slung porch but rather Griffin. My friend—the only one I had—that lived over three hours away.

"What the hell are you doing here?"

Unfazed by my rather untactful greeting, he dragged a hand through his inky hair and chuckled. "Hello to you too."

I winced. "Sorry. I'm just surprised to see you. Didn't you just come off a twenty-four-hour shift?"

"Aye." He looked nervous as he shuffled from one foot to the other. "I thought I'd come see the new place."

I narrowed my eyes at him. "That right?"

"Aye." When I glared some more, he held up his hands in surrender. "I came to make sure you're all right. I didn't like the sound of ya over the phone." Reaching behind him, he pulled out an envelope and handed it to me. "And I wanted to deliver this in person."

I studied the piece of stationary in my hands. Black with golden script and decorative swirls in each corner. A wedding invitation. My thumb swiped over the letters. Behind my ribs, an annoying fluttering made itself known.

My throat felt thick when I finally spoke. "Congrats, man." I moved to the side and motioned for Griffin to come in.

He stepped inside, gave me one look, and barked out a laugh I did not appreciate. His gaze shot to my arm; eyebrow arched high, he asked, "New friend?"

I gave Sheldon a downward glance and shook my head. "He belongs to my neighbor."

"Your neighbor?" he echoed as we headed down the hall toward the living room. "And you're what... dog sitting?" The way he'd asked it made my skin prickle with uneasiness.

"Not exactly, no."

Just as we turned into the living room, Griffin shook his head. "I'm more interested in the view you kept going on about when you moved here."

Nodding, I changed directions toward the sliding door instead. A minute later, we were standing outside; facing the ocean, and taking fresh salty air to our lungs.

Hands tucked inside his pockets; my friend sucked in a deep breath. "This is bloody gorgeous. Rae would love it here," he mused.

The wistful sound in his voice when he spoke his girlfriend's name—his fiancée now, I guess—had my heart doing that funny thing again. That thing where I was reminded of the dead empty space inside of me.

The one I wasn't aware of until—

"She wanted to come today," Griffin said. "But her brother is moving this weekend." I glanced at him out of the corner of my eye but said nothing, which is probably why he added, "They're very close and since he's moving over four hours away, they're having a sibling day."

I nodded as if I understood. I really didn't. It shamed me that Zoe and I didn't have the kind of relationship that required a *sibling day*—whatever the hell that was—when one of us moved away. A small voice at the back of my head, the one I usually told to screw off, whispered that it wasn't too late to fix things.

Sheldon wiggled under my arm, reminding me that I was still holding the damn dog. I leaned down. But before his paws had time to touch the grass, her achingly sweet voice filled my ears.

"I really don't know why he keeps coming over to you."

Beside me, Griffin's amused whisper came through clenched teeth, "That's your neighbor?"

With a heavy sigh, I straightened and headed to where Maddie was standing on her side of the fence. The moment I laid eyes on her I could tell something was off. Her beautiful eyes were red rimmed, like she'd been crying for too long. Her blond locks weren't neatly tucked into the knot on top of her head, and that lush bottom lip of hers looked like she'd been chewing on it. Hard.

A pain so sharp shot through my chest, I had to stop myself from pressing my hand to the spot. I had this inexplicable need to jump over to her side and just hold her.

Until my nosy friend sidled up beside me. The pain I'd felt mere seconds ago was instantly replaced with something else entirely. A big blotch of angry that only seemed to spread further through my veins when Maddie's eyes shot to my left and her gorgeous mouth curved upward.

I'd never wanted to smack Griffin more in my life.

For reasons I didn't even care to dissect, I wanted that damn smile to be aimed at me. And when she shoved her hand over the fence and introduced herself, I had this intense urge to press *my* palm against hers if it meant I could keep my friend from touching her.

Yeah, no doubt there was something very wrong with me.

"Oh, I love your accent," she cooed when Griffin spoke to her. My gaze flicked between the two of them, molars grinding together. I didn't like this. Any of it. This woman was messing with my equilibrium. She'd waltzed up to this fence with her honey-sweet voice and whiskey eyes and made me batshit crazy.

That was the only explanation I had for doing what I did next.

With a grunt or maybe it was a growl, I thrust her dog into her arms. "He keeps coming here because you keep leaving—" angrily, I stabbed my index finger in the direction of her door "—that thing open. It's not safe. Not for you and not for that damn rat of yours. And it annoys me!" By the time I was done with my little tirade, I was breathing hard.

Then the look on her face registered and a punch to the balls would've hurt less. She looked confused and so damn devastated. Licking her lips, she shut her eyes and swallowed hard. The action drawing my gaze to the slender column of her throat.

I wanted slide my fingers along her skin, curl my hand around the back of her neck and—

"Really?" she whispered. "We're back to that?" Her hand came up to pinch the bridge of her nose. I knew I had to apologize; the words just wouldn't come. Like an idiot, I stared as she slowly opened her eyes and shook her head. "You know what? Whatever. I don't have the energy to deal with you." Without another word from either me or her, she pivoted and fled to the safety of her house.

"What in the seven hells did I just watch?" Griffin's voice sounded so suddenly; my entire body jerked.

I scrubbed a palm over my face and breathed out a deep, heavy sigh. "Hell if I know." My gaze flicked to Maddie's house once more before I turned my back to it. "I need a drink. How 'bout you?"

He stared at me for a moment before saying, "If your couch is available, I won't say no." Pulling his phone from his pocket, he swiped the screen to life. "I'll call Rae to let her know I'll be home tomorrow."

Leaving him outside, I stalked to the kitchen and grabbed the bottle of Jack and two tumblers. When I returned, he'd made himself comfortable in one of the Adirondacks facing the ocean.

I slumped into the one beside him and after pouring two fingers 'worth of whiskey into both glasses, I handed him one and set the bottle on the ground. Leaning back in my seat, I savored the feeling of the alcohol burning its way down my throat.

"So what's the deal with the pair of you?" my friend asked after a long stretch of silence.

"Nothing," I muttered into the glass.

He sat up and studied me to the point where I felt uncomfortable. "You like her." There was no question in his voice; he was stating a fact. A very accurate one.

Scoffing, I looked him in the eye. "Have you already forgotten the exchange you witnessed moments ago? There's no like between me and her."

"Yeah, I'm not buying it." His all-knowing gaze pinned me with a hard look. "You know Angie would want—"

"Don't talk to me about what my dead wife would want," I growled.

Griffin, ever unfazed by my antics, shook his head. "As much as it hurts me to say this, you need to hear it. Angie might not be amongst the living anymore, but you are. Don't waste what is left of your life by shutting down any chance at happiness you might have." He picked up his drink and settled back against the Adirondack as if he hadn't just given me a shit ton to think about.

14

MADDIE

Eyes squeezed shut, I pressed two fingers against my temples and massaged.

"You're supposed to be the cool one," the reason behind my sudden headache whined.

Cracking my eyes open, I stared at the seven-year-old looking at me like I'd just taken away his ice cream. Which coincidentally I had. But it was eight in the morning, and his mother would kill me if I let him have it for breakfast.

Or at the very least, she'd never let me watch him when she ran errands again. As much as this little boy drove me batty, he made me happy in equal amounts. He was by far the brightest light in the Young family.

My hands came to rest on my hips, my uninjured foot slowly tap-tapping against the wooden floor. "Three scoops of ice cream and half of the bottle of chocolate sauce is most definitely not healthy. Your mom will have both our butts if you eat that."

My nephew, Tommy, narrowed his hazel eyes—the same shade as my sister and mine." But if you don't tell her and I don't either, then how will she know?"

I bent over, putting us at eye-level. Lifting two fingers in the space between us, I motioned for him to come closer. He leaned in eagerly, more than ready to hear whatever secret I was about to divulge.

The sharp edges of my teeth dug into my cheeks as I tried to stop myself from smiling. "Moms know everything!" I said very loudly.

Tommy's little face contorted; I would've given anything to snap a picture of his sullen expression. "Not cool, Auntie Maddie." He crossed his arms in front of him and gave me the biggest pout he could. "Not cool."

I threw my head back and laughed. By the time I was done wiping the tears from my eyes, he was still glaring at me. I ruffled his curly light brown hair as I moved past him to get breakfast ingredients from the fridge. "Why don't you take Sheldon outside? I'll be out with some French toast in a minute."

His eyes flicked to the confiscated frozen treat. "You know, if I grabbed that and ran, you wouldn't be able to catch me."

He was taking a dig at my limping. Exactly a week had passed since I'd sprained it, and it was definitely getting better. So much so, that I'd already let everyone know Tuesday's exercise class was going forward as planned.

Grabbing an orange from the fruit bowl in front of me, I tossed it in the air a few times. "Yeah, but I can still throw like a champ."

Tommy sighed and rolled his eyes way too dramatically. "You're no fun anymore." Shoulders sagging, he muttered at Sheldon to follow him.

The entire time while I prepared our toast and added sliced strawberries to the plate, my smile stayed firmly in place. It was still there when I made my way outside, arms loaded with food.

Until I saw what the hell Tommy was up to.

Head nodding, arms going every which way, he was happily chatting away with my neighbor. The one I'd been actively avoiding since the day he'd reverted back to being a dick. All because he didn't like my dog or the fact that I kept my door open.

Asshole.

I set the tray on the patio table and took slow strides to where they were standing. I'd almost reached them when Adam's eyes flicked my way. Those dark irises looked like they were drinking in the sight of me and my heart just about turned over on itself. I hated it. Hated that he was the only man my body was reacting to so fiercely.

He gave me a quick once over followed by a slight tilt of his head before his attention shifted back to Tommy. I was vaguely aware of my nephew's excited babbling about some sort of aircraft—he had a fascination with anything that could fly—but it was the way Adam was giving the boy in front of him his undivided attention that held me captive.

With his feet spread and those thick arms crossed in front of his even thicker chest, he could've easily looked intimidating if it weren't for his missing scowl and softened gaze.

He listened patiently while Tommy excitedly tried to figure out how many words he could spew out in a minute. My heart squeezed. There was no doubt that my sister was giving her son the best possible life she could. But the way he was talking to Adam—a practical stranger—showed me how hungry he was for a father figure in his life.

Jennah's boyfriend of four years had gotten her pregnant on their graduation. When he found out he was going to be a father, he'd upped and left Clearwater Bay, never to be seen or heard from again.

" Isn't that so, Auntie Maddie?" Tommy suddenly asked.

I blinked and two sets of eyes were trained on me. It was only one of them that had electricity zipping up and down my spine. "What?" The word came out all pitchy.

Every cell in my body called for me to look at Adam. But if the heat of his stare was already setting me on fire, there was no way I could face it head-on. That was why my gaze stayed trained on my nephew. He did not look impressed with me at all.

"I said, I am going to be a pilot when I grow up."

My mouth lifted into an easy smile. "Yeah, you're gonna do everything your little heart desires."

Obviously, that was not what he wanted to hear. Nose scrunched up, he shook his head. "You're being weird."

Something that sounded a lot like a chuckle came from the other side of the fence but when I looked up, Adam's face was impassive. But his eyes, though, they were studying me. I wanted to hide from it. Afraid he'd see through the cracks and learn my deepest darkest secrets. Afraid he'd see—

"What happened there?" Tommy's curious little voice sounded. I looked his way and was mortified to find him pointing at Adam's neck.

My gaze quickly snapped back to Adam again, my blood turning to ice when those ten-foot walls were back up. I hadn't forgotten how he'd reacted when he'd caught me staring and I wasn't going to stand for it if he spoke to my nephew the way he had to me.

I squeezed Tommy's shoulder. "Hey, we should let Mr.—" I paused, realizing I didn't know his last name "—Adam get back to work. Besides our breakfast is getting cold." I could tell he wasn't happy about it, but he grumbled a goodbye to Adam and lumbered over to the patio table.

Because I didn't know what to say, I pivoted and started making my way back to a sulking Tommy. Three steps. That's how far I managed before Adam's deep, gritty voice washed over me.

"Maddie."

One word. One freaking word and tiny bumps chased their way up and down my arms. I stopped walking and stared at my feet. I really wished he wouldn't say my name like that. Like it was a prayer or maybe a plea.

I took a much-needed breath and then another before I glanced at him over my shoulder. He'd shoved his hands into his shorts 'pockets. And even though I wasn't standing right in front of him, I could still see his jaw muscle steadily tick-tick-ticking.

He wet his lips and if I didn't know any better, I would have sworn he looked the tiniest bit nervous. But this was grumpy ass Adam, so it couldn't have been that. Sheldon barked somewhere behind me, Adam's gaze flicking to where I presumed my dog was.

Still, neither one of us said a damn word. It was beginning to feel a little awkward. He was the one who'd called out to me and if he wasn't going to say anything then I wasn't going to keep standing there like an idiot.

With a sigh, I tore my eyes away from him and continued walking.

"I'm sorry."

This time when I came to a halt, I spun around and faced him.

His uneasiness was clear as day when he shuffled from one foot to the other. One of his hands scrubbed over the back of his neck, the action making his tatted bicep pop deliciously. "I shouldn't have been so rude."

I crossed my arms in front of me and popped my hip. "When are you referring to exactly? You know, since rude has pretty much been your default setting."

He winced. Only slightly but I didn't miss it. "Right." The word slowly rolled off his tongue. "How 'bout I start with Monday?" I narrowed my eyes but didn't say anything. "It wasn't my intention to snap. I just got so damn frustrated with you and that open door."

I parked my hands on my hips and glared at him. "You kinda have the wrong definition of an apology."

He brought both his hands up and dragged his fingers through his hair and over his neck. "Sorry." His sexy as sin voice was laced with so much defeat, it made my heart ache. "I haven't done this in a long time."

Taking pity on him, I half-smiled. "Apology accepted. This time." It was quite a sight to see his massive shoulders sag with relief. "I'll see you around, Adam." For the third time, I turned and walked away from him. Only this time the slightest smile touched my lips.

15

MADDIE

"Ooooh, that one looks promising."

I glared at Frankie over the salted rim of my margarita glass. We'd barely arrived at Oven and Vine for a girls 'night out when she started looking for potential hookups...*for me*. Licking my lips, I set my glass down on the coaster and glared some more.

"What? You're not even going to look?" She leaned sideways and cast an appraising look to someone or something over my shoulder. "You're missing out," she mused. "He's got that tall, dark, and handsome thing down pat."

I dragged my finger up and down the smooth service of the stem of my glass. "You know," I said dryly, "I came out to have a few drinks with my friend." I stabbed my index finger in her direction. "That would be you, by the way."

"Yeah, but you need some action too, and what kind of friend would I be if I didn't try and make that happen." Frankie curled her tongue around the straw sticking out of her fruity drink and waggled her perfectly shaped brows. Once the straw was nestled between her puckered lips, she sucked up a good amount of alcohol.

I shifted my focus, choosing to aim my frown at the countertop instead of my friend. When she'd texted me earlier in the day, I'd thought a night out was the kind of distraction I needed to help me forget about a certain six-foot-something man who seemed to have the ability to look straight into my soul.

But now that I was out, all I wanted to do was go back home and sort through the mess inside my head. Because really, Adam should not be taking up so much of my thoughts. I shouldn't care about how he got those scars. Or what had happened to make him so angry at the world. And I most definitely should not have been thinking about his mouth or how badly I wanted it on mine.

"Evening, ladies."

At the sound of the smooth voice to my right, I shot a death stare at the woman to my left. It did not discourage her one bit. She raised her hand and wiggled her fingers at the man next to me.

"Can I get you something to drink?" My eyeroll could not be stopped. "Maybe a glass of wine, or perhaps you'd like a refill of what you're having?" My eyes narrowed at Frankie's twitching lips. She knew how much I hated wine.

"I'm good, thanks," I answered as I turned to face him. He was incredibly handsome. Like he could be on the cover of *GQ* handsome. A big, friendly smile showed off perfect teeth. There was no scruff covering his chiseled jaw, and even though I couldn't make out the color of his eyes in the dimly lit bar, I could still see them sparkle.

Yeah, this guy certainly did not want for female attention. And yet I didn't feel the tiniest bit of interest.

He stuck out his hand, the smile on his face spreading wider. "Jack."

I eyed his hand before gingerly slipping mine into his. "Maddie." Jack's fingers curled around mine and I waited. Waited for a zip of electricity. A fluttering low in my belly. Anything really.

It never came.

As irrational as it may have seemed, I blamed Adam for this. Before he came along, a guy like Jack would have piqued my interest. Hell, I might've been tempted to see where the rest of the night might lead.

But because some deeper part of my being was so unfathomably drawn to Adam, the prospect of a guy like Jack didn't entice me whatsoever.

"Maddie." Instead of getting those pesky little goosebumps at the sounds of my name, I wanted to scrunch up my nose. "Forgive me for being forward." He smoothed down his tie with his free hand; the other one was still firmly wrapped around mine. "But have you had dinner yet? I'd be so honored if you'd join me."

I was going to kill Frankie. The moment Mr. Polite over here released my hand, I was going to jab my friend in the boob. Slowly retrieving my captive hand, I pasted a polite smile on my face. "I've actually already eaten, but thanks anyway." It was on the tip of my tongue to tell him that my dear, dear friend was famished, but I let the words roll away.

He rubbed at his chest. "Ouch." That big smile was back. "Maybe next time?"

My head bobbed up and down. "Mhm, maybe."

Jack flashed his teeth once more before he wandered away. Arms folded in front of me, I angled my head Frankie's way. "You called him over, didn't you?"

She stuck her tongue out and tried to pull her straw closer, giving up when she kept missing. "I don't know what you're talking about." Something over my shoulder caught her attention. She straightened her back and her eyes grew wide. "Wow! Isn't that your neighbor?"

I spun around on the little stool so fast, I almost fell on my ass. My gaze zeroed in on the door, but none of the laughing crowd loitering at the entrance resembled Adam.

It took my brain a minute to catch up.

There was no way my vague descriptions of the man could have painted an accurate picture of him. No way my sneaky friend could've known what he looked like.

"I knew it!" Frankie exclaimed smugly when I faced her again. "First the rolls and now this…What exactly is going on between you two?"

A heavy sigh blew over my lips. "His name is Adam, and there's nothing going on."

With her elbow perched on the countertop, she rested her chin against her palm. Big, curious eyes roamed over my face. "But you want there to be?"

Yes. No. I pulled my shoulders to my ears and let them fall again. "I don't know, Frankie. I'm curious about him and I definitely find him attractive." Even though she was the person I trusted most in this world, I didn't tell her about the inexplicable pull I felt to Adam. If I couldn't make sense of it, I could only imagine what it would sound like to her ears.

"There's nothing wrong with being curious." She nibbled her lip. "Whatever you do, just be sure to keep both eyes open."

I reached forward and wrapped my fingers around the hand resting on her legs. Her caution was understandable, especially since her ex had done such a number on her. "I promise." I squeezed her fingers and tilted my head toward our half-empty glasses on the bar. "Are we having drinks or what?"

16

MADDIE

I took a fortifying breath before releasing my white-knuckled grip on the steering wheel and stepping out of my car. When I'd arrived home after drinks with Frankie last night, there'd been a message from my mom asking me to join them for Sunday lunch. It didn't take a genius to know what it was about.

I'd worked my last shift at the hardware store on Friday, and I would put money on the fact that my parents were planning on getting me to change my mind. Honest to goodness, I didn't understand their strong aversions to dance or why they couldn't accept how much it meant to me.

Knots twisted and folded in my stomach as I walked up the steps that led to my childhood home. I had so many happy memories there, and the ones that weren't so happy were directly tied to one thing.

It saddened me to my core and not for the first time, I found myself wishing I was more like Jennah. The only time my parents ever went off on her was when they learned about her pregnancy. And even that hadn't lasted long before the excitement of having a baby in the house took over.

I smoothed my hands over my hair, checking that every strand of my ponytail was in place. My palms swept over the flower print of my summer dress before I quickly tapped my knuckles against the door.

A tiny bit of relief washed over me when it flew open to reveal my sister. Maybe if she was there, this was just a family lunch and not the intervention I thought. A sweet smile touched Jennah's lips when she said, "I was wondering when you'd get here."

Flicking my wrist, I checked the time and frowned. "I'm not late. Mom said to be here by one." My eyes met hers. "It's not even twelve-thirty yet."

My sister grabbed me by the wrist and pulled me inside. The delicious smell of rosemary and lemon permeated the air. I closed my eyes and inhaled deeply. "Mmm, Mom's roast chicken."

"Hey." At the sound of my sister's snapping fingers, I opened my eyes. Jennah looked a bit odd when she checked over her shoulder a few times. Leaning closer, she whisper-shouted, "I need all the details on this neighbor of yours my son can't seem to shut up about."

A groan rumbled its way through my chest. "There's nothing to tell." Didn't I just have this conversation with Frankie less than twenty-four-hours ago? I dropped my chin to my chest and pinched the bridge of my nose. "What's Tommy on about?"

"Well," my sister drawled. When I looked at her, she was grinning. "Oh, just that he has *super cool scars* and that Auntie Maddie had a big smile on her face after she spoke with him."

I narrowed my eyes. "You're making that last part up."

"You're not denying it," Jennah accurately pointed out. "So, spill. I didn't even know someone had bought the old Nichols house."

Jennah and I might've been related by blood, but Frankie knew more about the goings on in my life than my sister did. And it was solely my fault. When my parents had started saying things like *'Why can't you be more like your sister?',* I had distanced myself from her.

Of course, it wasn't fair to Jennah; she'd never said or done anything to make me feel like I was less than her. Unfortunately for us both, my bruised ego had needed someone to act out on.

"Uh, yeah." I pulled my ponytail over my shoulder and wrapped it around my finger. "He's been living there for a little over a month now. He generally keeps to himself; I think Tommy caught him on an odd day."

My sister's blonde head—a few shades lighter than mine—slowly moved up and down. "And the scars? Are they bad? Is that why you were looking at those horrible pictures the other day?"

"Jennah, I don't—"

"Madison!" My mom came rushing in, wrapping me up in a hug the moment she reached me. For all our disagreements, it was moments like these that I cherished. They might've had their faults, but they were still my parents. And I loved them dearly. Winding my arms around my mom, I hugged her right back.

Jennah closed the door and together the three of us headed outside to where Mom had set the table on the patio. Tommy and my dad were throwing a baseball back and forth, and I had the slightest bit of regret that I didn't bring Sheldon. Much like Adam, my dad also referred to him as a rat. So I often left him home when I came to my parents.

And thanks to Adam, he didn't even have fresh air blowing through the house since I'd kept the sliding door closed all week.

Before my mind had too much time to latch onto a certain broody man, I took the lemonade my mom held out and settled in one of the chairs. Choosing to focus on their current conversation on how to get Tommy to eat vegetables instead.

Unfortunately, all I could do was listen since I didn't have anything to offer on the topic. And hell, if watching them laugh and chatter didn't have me feeling even more like an outsider.

The odd thing was, I didn't exactly want to be different. I liked who I was, and I was okay with my dreams not fitting theirs. I just wanted their acceptance.

Just as the sadness settled in my bones, my dad and nephew joined us at the table. Tommy's smile was big and beautiful when he launched his little body at me and gave me the biggest hug.

"Auntie Maddie! Have you asked Mr. Adam about the marks on his neck yet?" Excitement burned bright in his eyes when he pulled out of the hug and perched his hands on my shoulders.

Next to me, Jennah stopped talking, and I felt her stare bore into the side of my head. "No, buddy, I haven't. Some people don't like talking about stuff like that so it's better to wait until they decide to tell you themselves."

Tommy scrunched up his face and pushed his lips out in a pout. "I know, but they look so cool. I bet the story of how he got them would be even cooler."

I didn't think the story would be cool at all. Deep down, I had a feeling it would be absolutely heartbreaking. Obviously, I couldn't say that to the little boy in front of me. Smiling, I simply said, "I bet."

In typical kid fashion he let it go and the conversation quickly moved to the *awesome* airplane model he'd seen at the toy store and how desperately he *needed* it. The more he spoke about it, the more dramatic he became. Which, in turn, had all of us laughing.

It felt so incredible to be able to share a laugh with my family. Our differences momentarily forgotten.

But I should have known better. Should've known that the peace wouldn't last.

We'd just devoured Mom's roast chicken and delicious sides when my dad leaned back in his seat and spoke to my sister. "We might have to open an hour later tomorrow. I want you and Madison to get the new stock that arrived on Friday on the shelves first."

A bucket of ice over the head wouldn't have the same bone-chilling effect his words had. Bowing my head, I took a deep breath through my nose. Held it. And then slowly released it. Lifting my gaze to my dad, I kept my voice steady. "Dad, did you forget? I start at the studio tomorrow."

He waved a dismissive hand through the air. "You were serious about that?'

Even though I wanted to shrink back and look away, I held his stare. "You know I was."

His face morphed; anger making the veins in his neck pop out. "Dammit, Madison. When are you going to get over this? I would think that year in New York showed you how stupid this dancing business is." His voice boomed with each hurtful word he spat at me.

Out of the corner of my eye, I spotted Jennah jumping to her feet and grabbing Tommy. "Really, Dad?" Wrapping a protective arm around him, she gave me an apologetic look before ushering her boy inside.

My gaze flicked to my mom; she looked upset but weirdly it wasn't aimed at me. No, her what-the-hell-do-you-think-you're-doing glare was directed at her husband. Insides shaking, I pushed to my feet and turned my attention back to my dad. "And *I* had hoped by now you would have seen dancing makes me happy."

My dad jumped to his feet too, pointing an angry finger at me. "You are wasting your life on something that has no future. You're—"

"Fraser," my mom said, her voice low and stern. "That's enough."

Dad's eyes looked almost wild as he turned them to my mom. Nostrils flaring, he ground out, "You, more than anyone, should know better, Carolynn." When my mom didn't say anything else, my dad threw his hands in the air and stomped off.

The back of my eyes began to sting, and I cursed my stupid heart for getting bruised so easily. Without looking at my mom, I let out a shaky breath. "I think I'm going to go."

"Madison—"

"Thanks for lunch, Mom. It was delicious, as always." Not sparing her another glance, I headed back to my car, choosing to go around the house in case I ran into my dad or sister inside.

Those tears that'd threatened earlier finally fell when my parents 'house disappeared from the rearview mirror. Thick and hot, they rolled down my cheeks, showing no sign of stopping. Not even when I pulled into the safety of my own driveway.

Angrily, I swiped at them as I got out—slamming the door for good measure—and shuffled around the side of my house to get to the backyard. If anything could bring peace to my jumbled-up insides, it was the ocean.

That was until I saw Adam standing at the edge of his property. There was no way I wanted to face him in the state I was. Stopping in my tracks, I quickly spun around and attempted to retrace my steps.

I didn't get very far before his gravelly voice sounded. "Maddie."

Why did he have to say my name like that? Why did my entire being yell at me to turn around and go to him?

It was because of those questions and the intensity of what I was feeling that I muttered, "I can't deal with you right now."

17

ADAM

My eyes followed Maddie as she rushed around to the front of her house. Digging my heels in, I forced myself to stay put when every fiber of my being wanted to go after her. This sudden marrow-deep need to find out why she looked so sad was as abrupt as it was unwelcome.

I'd barely had time to fully process the despondence in her sweet voice before this desperate need to comfort her had taken over. There was a part of me that knew fighting the urge to go to her would be futile. But I had to resist; I was in no shape to offer her any form of comfort.

Maddie disappeared around the corner, and I released a slow breath through my nose. Whatever was the matter with her wasn't my business. I kept repeating those words like a whispered prayer as I strolled back into my house.

The thing was, I didn't want to listen to myself. I'd gone out there intending to make small talk. I wanted to attempt to be her friend or at the very least just be in her presence for a little bit. Because whenever Maddie was around, there was a certain calmness inside of my soul I couldn't get anywhere else.

I used to think it was her dancing that had that effect on me, but I quickly realized it was the woman herself.

Whatever energy radiated from her wrapped around me like a blanket and settled in the deep, dark corners of my being.

However, my plan had gone to shit the moment I was faced with her tear-stained face and slumped shoulders. Whatever words I'd wanted to say had dissolved on my tongue, never to be voiced.

With my mind still firmly fixed on the woman next door, I headed upstairs to continue working on the guest bedroom. The plastic that covered the floor I'd finished a few days ago crinkled under my boots as I walked to where I'd dropped the scraper earlier when I heard Maddie arrive home.

Hands perched on my hips, I glared at the tool as if it had offended me. How the hell was I going to be able to work when all I saw was her…looking so damn disheartened. Tilting my head back, my gaze shifted to the ceiling.

Nice people checked on their neighbors all the time, right? Look at Maddie, she was the epitome of nice and she brought me baked goods to say thank you. So it wouldn't be all that weird if I knocked on her door just to make sure she was all right.

With a new plan taking root, I bolted back down the stairs and skidded to a stop in front of my glass door. Would it be rude if I showed up empty-handed? I had never done anything like this, I seriously had no clue what the right etiquette was.

"Shit," I muttered under my breath.

Scratching the side of my face, I mentally scanned the kitchen cupboards. They weren't stocked with the kind of things you gave to someone to make them feel better. And I was fairly certain, giving her half a bottle of Jack would be frowned upon.

I was about to say screw it and just go over there when I remembered the gift basket Zoe'd had delivered to my place when I'd just moved in. Although I'd eaten my way through most of it, a bottle of red wine and a small box of dark chocolates remained.

I shuddered when I thought about it because I couldn't stand the taste of either, but women liked wine and chocolates, right? When Zoe and I were younger and she'd been upset, chocolate had always been her go-to. Albeit in liquid form. She always said chocolate was the cure for anything.

Finding the items was as quick as opening a few cupboards. After I tucked the sweets under my arm and grabbed the wine, I hurried next door before I had the good sense to change my mind.

My steps slowed somewhat the closer I got to her door. If I hadn't been so busy pacing myself, I would have laughed at how nervous I suddenly felt. My palms were clammy, and my heart was slamming against my ribs in very much the same way as a teenager going out on his first date.

It was ridiculous.

I sucked in a breath but before I could hold it for a few seconds, the air went whooshing out of my lungs.

That damn sliding door was open again. Why the hell was she so damn determined to be unsafe?

Gritting my teeth, I brought my hand up and tapped it against the glass with a lot more force than was needed. From somewhere inside, I heard the little rat let out a string of barks. They grew louder and louder until the curtain moved and he came trotting out. It was kind of laughable how he immediately stopped yapping the instant he saw me. Tail wagging, he parked his butt in front of me, those big eyes completely focused on me.

"Where's your human?"

Jumping on his hind legs, Sheldon let out a shrill sound that had me thinking this dog actually understood me.

Stranger things had happened.

Bending down, I scooped him with my free hand then without thinking it through, I moved the curtain with the bottle. "Maddie? It's Adam," I called out as I stepped inside. Again, the home-y feeling of her place hit me in the chest. I couldn't even remember the last time I'd felt like this walking into someone's home.

Hell, this feeling even eluded me in my own space.

Still tucked under my arm, the dog wiggled. I bent down and set him on the floor with the words, "Go find her, boy."

His tiny paws spun in place on the polished wooden floor before he darted off. Since I had a moment alone, I walked up to the frames lining the wall and studied them in the way I'd wanted to when I'd first stepped foot in her house almost two weeks ago.

Every single one of the snapshots told a story of a woman who loved life. There wasn't a shot in which her smile wasn't big and carefree. I was still staring at the picture of her sticking her tongue out at the camera with both her arms wrapped around a woman with inky black hair when footsteps caught my attention.

It sounded like they were coming from the stairs, so naturally, that's where I went. Big. Mistake. Maddie was halfway down, her arms up in the air tangled in a shirt that only covered her face.

My gaze flicked to her breasts hidden beneath a bright orange sports bra then slowly trailed down her midsection before finally settling on the sparkly stone winking at me from her belly button. My swallow— amongst other things—was hard. Really, really hard.

I tightened my grip around the bottle to stop my itching fingers from reaching out and brushing over her toned middle. From digging into her soft skin just so I could hear what sound she'd make.

While my brain was conjuring up a million different things I wanted to do to this woman, Maddie wiggled and mumbled a frustrated, "Oh for shit's sake" before wiggling some more.

I bit back a curse of my own and squeezed my eyes shut in prayer to every deity I knew; begging for the strength to get through what I had to do next.

Once my eyes were open and the woman in front of me still struggling to get her shirt on, I set the wine and chocolates on the nearest table and approached her as if she was a bomb that could go off at any second.

With each step carrying me closer to her, my heart thumped louder and faster.

When I was finally close enough, I reached out and grabbed her shirt, but instead of allowing me to help, Maddie let out a blood-curdling scream. She thrashed and kicked like a wild animal. Her bare foot connected with my shin, pulling a muttered curse from my lungs.

"Hold still," I growled. "I'm trying to help you."

She froze instantly. "Adam?"

"No, it's the damn tooth fairy." The words came out strained, and my throat felt as if I'd been swallowing down sandpaper. "Can I help you now? Or would you like to kick me some more?"

She remained stock-still, her head doing something under the fabric. I sighed. "Words, Maddie."

"Yes," she breathed out.

I nodded even though she couldn't see me. Curling my fingers tightly around the hem of her black t-shirt, I slowly dragged it down her body. She shivered when my knuckles brushed over her satiny soft skin. My own body did something similar.

It was very tempting to let my hands drop to her hips once the shirt was righted. To feel her. Touch her. But with strength I had no idea I possessed, I let them fall to my sides as I moved two steps down.

"I knocked," I explained, hooking my thumb over my shoulder. "I wanted to give you…" Swallowing the rest of my sentence, I darted back to where I'd left the wine and chocolates.

I almost fell backward when I spun around and Maddie was already standing there. Her hair was a mess, her cheeks still blotchy. The tip of her little button nose a deep shade of red. And still, I found her beautiful.

So damn beautiful.

Shoving the items toward her, I grumbled, "For you."

Sheldon chose that moment to make his presence known again. Parking his butt in front of me, he pawed at my leg. Maddie eyed him and shook her head. "He really likes you." The words were so softly spoken, I wasn't entirely sure they were meant for my ears.

I bent down and gave the mutt a scratch behind the ear, my gaze never leaving Maddie. Face scrunched up, she studied the bottle of wine and chocolates for a long, agonizing moment before her eyes met mine. "W-what's this for?"

Licking my lips, I rose to my feet. I'd never felt so uncomfortable. My skin was too tight, my heart ten times too big, and a thousand beats too fast. "I...uh..." I dragged my fingers over the spot where my scars hid under my shirt. "You looked upset earlier. I wanted to cheer you up."

"You did?" She sounded so amazed. Had no one ever done something nice for her? Or was she shocked that *I* was attempting to do something nice? I knew where I'd put my money. "That's so...unexpected," she went on. Her attention shifted back to me. "I knew there was a sweet spot somewhere beneath all that grumpiness."

I let out a snort-chuckle. "Don't sing my praises just yet. That—" I jerked my chin toward the treats in her hands, "—was left over from a housewarming gift my sister sent me." Maddie's brow wrinkled. Nibbling on her lip, she studied me with those big eyes. "What?"

"You have a sister?" she asked, her tone careful.

"Yeah."

"Mhm," she murmured. "Interesting."

It was my turn to frown. "Why exactly is that interesting?"

Maddie's shoulders rose and fell in a small shrug. "I just figured with your level of tact, you had to be an only child." The most wonderful thing happened then. Her lips twitched before curving into the most brilliant smile that made my heart hiccup. "I'm sorry." She maneuvered around me, bumping her shoulder against my arm as she did. "I couldn't resist."

"Funny."

The sweetest sound filled the room when a small laugh escaped her. "I try." Looking over her shoulder, she winked before continuing on into the kitchen. Because the space was open-plan, I had a clear view of her from my spot in the living room.

I also took the opportunity to shamelessly study her. Along with the black t-shirt, she was wearing orange camouflage tights that stopped just below her knee. The skintight material did nothing to hide her finely toned legs. For a quick second, I imagined what it might feel like to have them wrapped around my waist as I mercilessly—

Biting the inside of my cheek, I stopped that thought dead in its tracks and placed my folded hands in front of the bulge inside my pants before I embarrassed myself. "How's the ankle?"

Maddie faced me and held on to the counter where she'd set down the wine and chocolates. Bending her knee, she lifted her leg and flexed her foot. Gifting me with another grin, she said, "Much better." She dropped her leg. "I'll be back to dancing soon."

Even from where I was standing, I could see her face light up. I understood that kind of passion that bubbled out of your pores because it was so big, you couldn't contain it. An image of her tear-stained face flashed before me. My brows dipped low. "Why were you so sad earlier?" The question was out before I could stop it. Regret shortly on its heels.

Her face fell. "It's nothing." Shuffling away, she opened the fridge and stared at the contents for a long while. "Can I get you anything to drink?"

My first instinct was to say yes. I wanted nothing more than to share a drink with her—even it was just a glass of water. This woman intrigued me. I wanted to get to know her and oddly I wanted to let her in.

Which was why I said, "No, thank you." Maddie's gaze snapped to mine. The expression on her face one I couldn't decipher. But something about it tightened the knots in my stomach. "I have to get back."

"Right. Of course."

Why did I feel like I'd just kicked a puppy? And why in the name of all things holy did I want to stomp to where she was standing and taste her mouth? I took two steps backward. "Take care, Maddie."

Making a one-eighty, I prepared to flee to the safety of my house. To a place where she wasn't. I'd made it all the way to her door when her voice halted my steps.

"Hey, Adam." Our eyes met over my shoulder. "Thanks for checking up on me."

Because I didn't trust myself to speak, I gave her a quick nod and got the hell out of there. I should have known better than to think that Maddie's beautiful face wouldn't follow me.

18

MADDIE

I couldn't recall another time in my life where going to work had a smile spreading across my face. Even when I'd been in New York, furiously chasing my dreams, I hadn't experienced the zing of excitement that coursed through my veins as I pushed through the doors of Soulbeat.

Taking in the mirrored walls and wide-open space felt a hell of a lot like coming home. Something behind my breastbone shifted, clicked into place and a lightness touched my soul.

"Maddie. Hi." Lucetta came rushing forward and threw her arms around my shoulders when she reached me. "Thank you so much for doing this," she breathed.

I hugged her back with everything I had in me. In her mind, I might've been doing her a favor, but it was the other way around. Dancing was such a core part of my DNA, and she'd given me an opportunity to surround myself with people like me.

"It's me who should be thanking you," I told her honestly.

She pulled back and gave me the biggest encouraging smile before leading me over to her office. My eyes went

SLOW BURN

a little wide at the scattered papers covering the table. I wasn't OCD at all, but this was a mess, even for me.

As if reading my mind, Lucetta gently patted me on the shoulder. "I'll show you where all these go in a minute, but I need you to look at this first." Handing over one of the pages, she continued, "It's a list of all the classes; their days and times as well as the students in each."

"Okay." My eyes furiously tracked over the page. I had no idea Lucetta's little studio was so busy. There were easily between five to six hours 'worth of classes every other day during the week along with the two exercise classes on Tuesday and Thursday nights.

My stomach twisted violently, nerves suddenly pushing bile into my throat. Lucetta had been doing this for years. There was no way I could come even close to reaching her standards. The absolute last thing I wanted was to cause her dancers to move backward.

"Hey." I blinked and her hands were on my shoulders, gently guiding me to face her. "You've got this, Maddie. I believe in you." I swallowed down the big fat lump in my throat because besides her and Frankie no one else had said them to me. "You have a gift. It's not something anyone can teach. It's an intricate part of who you are."

Closing my eyes, I blew out a slow breath before opening them again. "I've got this," I whispered Lucetta's words.

She squeezed my shoulders and smiled. "Come on, let me take you through everything. I have about two hours before I need to leave."

I used up every minute of the time she had left. Asking question upon question until I felt at least somewhat comfortable. By the time the first class gathered at noon, I was still nervous but excited too.

It helped that our town wasn't the biggest and since I'd lived here almost all my life, people knew me. A few of the moms even told me how thrilled they were I was helping out.

And with that kind of encouragement, it wasn't hard to dive into the first class and then the second and the third. Before I knew it, time had literally flown by and the day was done.

Slumping into the chair behind Lucetta's desk—which was probably my desk now—I released a satisfied breath. It'd been way too long since I'd spent so many hours on my feet. I'd forgotten how draining it was. No doubt, I was tired to the bone, but I was also so incredibly happy.

I threw my head and grinned at the ceiling like an idiot. Lucetta was right, this was who I was. It was woven into the very essence of my being. Without dancing, I was an incomplete version of myself.

"That big smile can only mean your first day was good."

At the sudden sound of Jennah's voice, my entire body jerked, and I almost fell off my chair. "Holy shit! You can't do that!" I wheezed out, clutching my chest.

One side of her mouth tipped up. "Sorry." Leaning against the doorframe of the office, she scanned the studio over her shoulder before returning her gaze to me. "You were always different when you were here," she mused. "Almost weightless. Free."

I cocked my head and studied her long and hard. We never spoke about these kinds of things. The closest we'd ever come to talking about what this world meant to me was when she begged me to stop doing it for my own sake.

After the day I'd had, the last thing I wanted to do was get into it with my sister. I bit my tongue and chose my words carefully. "I guess I am." I toyed with the messy bun on top of my head. Aiming my gaze at a spot on her shoulder, I gave her a piece of my truth, "Expressing myself this way has always been easier. I dance whether I'm happy, angry, or sad. Sometimes it's safer than saying things we can never take back." My eyes met hers and I laughed. "It's also a lot cheaper than therapy."

She laughed too, but it wasn't a happy sound. "Maybe you could teach me a few moves."

My brows pulled together along with the band tightening around my heart. "Jennah, are you okay?"

The smile tugging on her lips was laced with so much sadness, I wanted to go wrap my arms around her. But that wasn't how things were between us. I realized then how much I hated it. She was my sister. I shouldn't have been hesitant to go to her.

I pushed off my chair at the same time as she spoke. "Do you have plans tonight?"

Not sure entirely what I was expecting but it wasn't that. "None that I am aware of." My eyes narrowed. "Why?"

Jennah's fingers curled tighter around the strap of her purse hanging over her shoulder. "Tommy's with Mom and Dad so I thought we could go for dinner at Oven and Vine. Get a head start on Mom's birthday plans?" Our mother was turning fifty in a few weeks, and my sister and I had been talking about throwing her a big party to celebrate.

"Sure. I'll meet you there in a bit. I just need to take a quick shower and get changed."

***

Thirty minutes later, we were seated in one of the booths next to the large windows that overlooked Main street. Jennah had a glass of white wine in front of her while I'd opted for a soda. The silence that'd been stretching between us wasn't comfortable at all, and I had zero clues on how to fix it.

Across from me, my sister picked up her wine and took two huge gulps. Since she wasn't a big drinker, my eyes widened with confusion. "Thirsty?"

She swiped the inside of her hand over her mouth. The intensity burning behind her eyes when she leveled me with a stare had uneasiness prickling over my skin. "Why aren't we close, Maddie?"

Good thing I didn't have anything in my mouth because it would've come right back out again. Sure, I'd been wondering the same thing, but never had I even imagined that she had too.

Leaning forward, I poised my folded arms on the table and pulled my shoulders up. "I don't know, Jennah. It's probably my fault. I always kind of envied you for being the golden child."

Her brows furrowed, deep lines marring her forehead. "Golden child?"

I sighed heavily and turned my attention to the cars driving by. I'd had these thoughts for years. Finding the right words shouldn't have been so difficult. I was just so terrified of accidentally hurting her.

"Will you talk to me, please?" Jennah begged.

My gaze found hers again. One look into the eyes that looked so much like my own and I knew she deserved the absolute truth. "Do you still remember when Mom and Dad found out that I'd been going to dance classes instead of soccer practice?"

She winced. "Yes."

I closed my eyes and swallowed hard at the memory. Drawing in a deep breath, I opened them again. "Well, later when Dad demanded I never set foot in Soulbeat again, he asked why I couldn't be more like you."

Something that looked a hell of a lot like understanding fell over Jennah's face. It gave me strength to go on. "All I ever wanted was for us to be best friends but that stupid incredibly hurt part inside of me envied you. Jennah, I was so jealous of your ability to be the perfect child. The one who wasn't a disappointment."

My sister reached across the table so fast, I startled. Her fingers curled around my wrist and squeezed tight. "Oh, Maddie." She searched my eyes. "I'm not making excuses for anyone, but somewhere over the years, I've come to think that our parents really didn't know any better. Hell, they still don't."

She stared at her hand wrapped around my arm. "When I fell pregnant with Tommy, Dad took me to Mathilda's Diner for burgers and milkshakes." Slowly, her focus shifted back to me. "I'd stupidly thought it was to assure me that everything would be all right. That we'd get through it together."

A mirthless laugh escaped her lips. "Yeah, I was so wrong. Dad laid into me about how irresponsible I was to throw my future away like that. He did some comparing too, and even though I am two years older than you, I'd never felt more inferior than I had that day."

She leaned forward; eyes boring into mine. "You know what else?" Biting my lip, I shook my head. "The only reason why it's so easy for me to fall in line with their plans is because I'm not half as brave as you are."

"That's not true," I insisted fiercely. "You're raising a kid all by yourself. That's pretty freaking brave, if you ask me."

At the mention of my nephew, a genuine smile touched her lips. "That was forced bravery. I really didn't have any other choice."

The waitress appeared. A tender look on her face as her gaze flicked between Jennah and me. She pulled her notepad out. "Are we ready to order?"

Meeting my sister's gaze, I grinned. "We sure are."

***

Funny how one dinner with my sister could change so much. We weren't suddenly best friends, but I understood her better and vice versa. I was already smiling when I walked around to the back of the house; it only grew wider when I spotted Adam standing at the edge of his yard.

In the dim light of the moon, I could only see enough to know he was facing the ocean. Keeping on my side of the fence, I wandered to where he was standing. Although most of the big blue was hidden under the darkness of night, the sound of the waves gently lapping against the shore filtered through the air.

"That has to be my favorite sound," I confessed quietly.

A deep, "Mhm," rumbled through his chest and had me shivering on the spot. Adam was quiet for so long after that, I couldn't help but feel like I'd intruded on his moment of peace. I was about to go inside and leave him alone with his thoughts when he spoke.

"You feeling better today?"

Turning to face him, I was surprised to find him already looking at me. Soft light spilled from his house and cast shadows over his face. He looked dark and mysterious and painfully beautiful.

"Yes, thank you."

That rich, gritty voice was soft and low when he spoke again. "That's good." The little butterflies in my stomach fluttered about furiously and when he stepped closer my heart joined in too.

He casually draped those thick arms over the fence, his gaze zeroing in on me. In the darkness, I couldn't see the look in his eyes, but I felt the heat of his stare all the same. "I'm curious," he murmured.

"About what?" Goodness, I sounded all kinds of breathy.

"It's been a while since your dog has flown the coop."

Somehow, I'd imagined him saying something else entirely. But that could've been a byproduct of my endless fantasies about the man. Laughing quietly, I shook my head. "Well, yeah. A certain someone—I'm not naming names or anything—complained profusely about my dog and the door I used to leave open for him. So now I close it and poor Sheldon has no fresh air," I said very dramatically.

A deep chuckle rumbled through Adam's chest and rolled over my skin, instantly presenting me with my new favorite sound. I had the urge to close my eyes and beg him to let me hear it on a loop.

"Whoever said such a thing must be the biggest asshole in the world." I could still hear the smile in his voice and as much as I wanted to tease him, something inside of me wouldn't let me.

"Or maybe he's just misunderstood."

Adam didn't utter a word for such a long time; I was certain I'd overstepped. I opened my mouth to apologize but he spoke first. "You know you could always leave Sheldon with me during the day."

It was my turn to be silent. From the moment I'd met this man, he made no secret of the fact that my dog was the bane of his existence. Now he was offering to dogsit? Also, did he not have a normal job like the rest of us? "You don't have somewhere to be during the day?"

It might've been my imagination, but he looked slightly uncomfortable. "I...uh...no, I don't. Watching him won't be a problem."

That was a vague answer if I ever heard one. Unfortunately for my curious little self, he didn't need to explain his comings and goings. "Careful," I told him. "I might think you're actually nice."

His comeback was swift. "Maybe I just wanna be nice to *you*?" The way he said it made my skin tighten in the best way possible. Goosebumps chased up my arms and down my spine. My nerve endings felt like live wires feeding electricity into my veins.

This was dangerous.

He was dangerous.

Like a thunderstorm slowly rolling in, ready to cause havoc wherever it touched.

But instead of running and shielding myself, I wanted to step straight into the middle of it. Wanted to feel the full force of it wrapped around me.

"Think about it," he said. "The offer stands." With that, he pushed off the fence. I bit my lip as I watched that big body amble toward the house.

I was in so much trouble.

19

ADAM

I hardly recognized the man staring back at me from the mirror above my sink.

The dark patches that'd been beneath my eyes for the better part of three years were steadily fading away. Life had been breathed into the hollow stare I had come to expect to see every morning.

And those were just the changes on the outside. Inside of me, things had shifted. The deep-rooted hate that'd consumed me for so long was finally making room for something else. Or possibly someone else.

It wasn't lost on me that since Maddie had come into my life, the nightmares had stopped. No more razor-sharp claws slowly digging away at my sanity. No more sleepless nights filled with nothing but bad dreams of the woman I couldn't save.

The dreams were still there. They just verged on the edge of fantasies and featured an entirely different woman. One with whiskey eyes that I wanted to get lost in.

Still regarding my reflection, I pulled my brows together. Hand brushing over my chest, I realized that for the first time since the accident Angie could enter my thoughts without a bout of self-loathing following on her heels.

Over the past few days, I'd done a lot of thinking. Mostly about what Griffin had said and specifically what he thought Angie would want. And he was right. Wallowing in what was, was no way to live.

I didn't know where I was going to go from here. And certain wounds ran so deep, I wasn't sure they'd ever heal. But I wanted to try. Small steps. And I was going to start with Maddie.

I hadn't lied the previous night; I wanted to be nice to her. I wanted to be her friend. And, yeah, maybe I wanted to taste her lips and find out what sounds she made when her buttons were pushed just right.

But more than that, I just wanted some of the good in her to rub off on me.

Bending over, I splashed my face with cold water and felt my mouth stretch into a grin. When I'd decided to move to Clearwater Bay, my dad had taken me aside and told me that he believed I would find the peace I was craving here.

If he only knew how right he'd been.

The generic ringtone of my phone sounded from my bedside table. I chuckled when I saw an incoming video call from my mother. Flopping down on the bed, I swiped the green button. Mom's confused face immediately filled the screen.

"Adam…I wasn't expecting you to answer so quickly." Her brows pulled together, eyes blinking rapidly.

"I was close to the phone."

She leaned closer to the little camera, searching for who knew what before she pulled it away from her softly lined face. "You look different." From her tone, I couldn't tell whether she thought it was a good thing or not.

Nodding, I admitted, "I've been sleeping better."

She smiled then. It was big, bright, and beautiful. "That's good. Your father will be so happy to hear that." A little sigh escaped her lips. "He worries about you. We all do."

"I know, Mom. And I appreciate it."

My mother fell silent, eyes shining with unshed tears. My heart did that funny thing again. And for all the changes that'd taken place, seeing my mom cry still was something I didn't have the strength for. Because if I saw those thick tears roll down her cheeks, I'd wonder how many of them she'd shed over me.

I cleared my throat. "You doing good?"

"Oh, yes." Her lips curved upward again. "Your dad and I have been going to Bingo nights at the community center." Laughing, she shook her head. "A sure sign that we are getting old now."

"Nah, not old, just wise." I winked and my mom howled with laughter. The sound, so joyous, bubbled straight from the happiest depths of her, and it was impossible not to grin.

With a few swipes of her fingers, she wiped away her happy tears. A second later, she looked about as serious as a heart attack. "I've missed you."

I knew exactly what she meant because I'd missed me too. There was a time, not too long ago, where I thought I'd never be able to be like this with anyone again. Swallowing down the emotion lodged in my throat, I stared at my mom's face. "I…I'm not…" For whatever reason, the right words wouldn't come. "There's a long way to go still," I finally admitted.

My mother's smile never wavered. "Of course there is. You've been to hell, and finding your way back was never going to be quick or easy."

Deep inside me, something else shifted. The sure click of it finding its place, lifting another small rock off my shoulders. I opened my mouth to tell my mom how right my dad had been, but before I could utter a word, two sharp knocks sounded from the front door.

My heart jumped inside my chest.

There was only one person who would be standing outside my door this early in the morning. "Someone just knocked. Can I call you back later?"

She blinked rapidly. "You have company?"

"Yeah."

I bit the inside of my cheek to keep my grin from spreading when her mouth opened and closed a few times. Two more knocks sounded. I pushed off the bed. "I gotta go now." And then before I could stop it and possibly because she needed to hear it, I reminded her, "Love you."

Her eyes were shining once more when she repeated the words back to me with a wobbly goodbye at the end. Phone still clutched in my hand, I bolted down the stairs.

Fingers curled around the handle, I took a few steadying breaths before I pulled it open.

As I suspected, Maddie was standing on my porch with her dog tucked under her arm. When he saw me, his tail furiously swished back and forth. My gaze flicked to the woman holding him. Was she just as happy to see me?

"Morning," she greeted sweetly. "I brought Sheldon." My eyes zeroed in on her mouth when she rolled her bottom lip over her teeth. I wanted to suck on it until the taste of her was burned onto my tongue.

Gripping the door tighter, I shifted from one foot to the other and forced my gaze to hers. The way she was staring at me, like she was seeing me and not the scars I wore, had the hair on my arms and neck standing up.

"It's still okay, right?" she asked, her voice quiet and unsure.

Clearly, whenever she was around, I was incapable of logical thinking. I blinked and then blinked again. "What?"

She licked her lips and I almost offered to do it for her. "Sheldon."

"Right, of course," I stammered, feeling like a bigger fool than I looked. I jerked my head in the excited dog's direction. "He come with special instructions?"

Her long blonde ponytail swayed side to side with the shake of her head. "Nope, just a warning." Maddie's mouth lifted into a mischievous smile. "If you love your shoes, keep him far, far away from them."

"Got it."

I lifted my hands to take the dog from her, but she pulled him just out of my reach. "You sure you want to do this? It's okay if you changed your mind."

"Maddie." I leveled her with a stare. "I offered, didn't I?"

It was my own fault she was second-guessing me. The little bastard and I hadn't started on the best foot, but if it weren't for him, I would never have needed to talk to Maddie.

Her gaze flicked between me and Sheldon before she reluctantly handed him over. There was no avoiding touching her during the transfer and as it always did, the parts of my skin that touched hers felt alive.

"My cell is on there as well as the studio's number." She thrust a small piece of paper toward me. "Please call me if anything goes wrong."

With the dog secured under one arm, I stepped forward and placed my hand on her shoulder. "Relax. Everything is going to be fine."

Those big eyes of hers flicked to where I was touching her before ever so slowly trekking up along my arm, over my shoulder, and finally settling on mine. They roamed over my face for a few breath-stealing seconds. "Okay." The word might've left her lips in a whisper, but it didn't hold an ounce of hesitancy.

Lifting my hand from her shoulder, I took the card with her contact details from her. I was still studying her neat scrawl when she spoke again. "I appreciate you doing this. If there's anything I can do to return the favor, just ask."

Oh, I could think of a few things, but I doubted they were the kind of favor she was referring to. "I wouldn't say no to cinnamon rolls."

The way her beautiful face lit up right then nearly did me in. "You liked them?"

"A little more than like," I confessed. "They were gone before sunset."

She nibbled on her lip again. "Getting you rolls is the least I can do. So consider it done." With a soft smile, she said goodbye and turned on her heel. She didn't make it very far before she stopped, and a curse fell from her lips.

She shook her head as she slowly turned to face me again. With a sigh that almost sounded defeated, she put one foot in front of the other until she was standing before me again.

The look of dread on her face was enough to give me pause. "You okay?"

Her lip disappeared between her teeth; eyes focused on me. "I forgot what day it is," she almost whispered. I was about to remind her it was Tuesday when she spoke. "Every Tuesday and Thursday we have dance aerobics."

Since my brain function was severely slowed whenever Maddie was around, it took me a few seconds to catch up. "You're going to be late."

Worry pulled her brows together. "Yeah. Are you still okay with watching him?"

"No."

Her eyes went big. "Oh...okay then?"

Flattening my lips into a thin line, I tried to keep myself from grinning. "Maddie, I'm kidding. It's fine. What difference is a few hours going to make?"

"I don't want you to think I'm taking advantage."

She could take whatever the hell she wanted if it meant I got to spend a couple of minutes with her. "You're not," I assured.

Closing the distance between us, she bent over and nuzzled Sheldon, who was still happily tucked away under my arm. The subtle scent of strawberries tickled my nose, and not closing my eyes and breathing it in was almost impossible.

When she peered up at me, my heart stuttered. "Thank you, Adam."

I couldn't speak. I was too damn afraid if I opened my mouth, I'd beg her to say my name like that again. Like it was something wonderful. Instead, I nodded and stared after her like a fool until she disappeared from view.

I wasn't sure what this woman was doing to me and oddly enough, I didn't entirely hate it.

20

MADDIE

"There's something wrong with your…" Frankie pointed a finger in my direction and circled my face. Wrinkling her nose, she looked at me as if I'd just thrown up all over the floor.

I threw my hands in the air, palms facing the ceiling. "What?"

"You're grinning like someone who's had an orgasm, or maybe a few of them." Moving around me in a slow circle, her gaze flicked up and down the length of me. "It's disgusting."

A snort-laugh sounded from my throat. "I wish." Pinning her with a stare, I added, "Maybe I'm just excited for class."

Frankie cocked her head and pursed her lips. "Yeah…No. I bet it has something to do with these." Lifting her hand, she dangled a paper bag in front of me.

The sweet smell of cinnamon wafted around me and I could actually feel my smile grow. "Ah! You brought them. Thank you." I moved to take the bag, but she snatched her hand away. "Hey!"

Her index finger furiously wiggled from side to side in front of my face. "Nah uh. Before I hand them over, I want to know what, or—" her eyes narrowed suspiciously— "who they're for."

"Who says they're not for me?"

"You ordered a dozen cinnamon rolls, Maddie." Pausing, she gave me a *'come on'* look. "They're for the grumpy idiot next door, aren't they?"

"Maybe." I quickly turned my back to her and pretended to study something on the wall.

Frankie wasn't having it. She simply pushed at my shoulder over and over until I looked at her. "So," she drawled, eyes twinkling with mirth. "You've been seeing more of him then?"

It was ridiculous how my smile couldn't be stopped when I filled my friend in on everything that'd happened since I saw her last. By the time I was done, she was grinning with me. "You like him?"

"He intrigues me," I rectified.

She regarded me for a few agonizing seconds. "But you wouldn't pull away if he tried to kiss you, now would you?"

Luckily for me, the studio door flew open and a group of laughing women filed in, saving me from admitting to my friend how right she was or how desperately I actually wanted that very thing to happen.

Next to me, Frankie sighed heavily when the newcomers came bouncing toward us. There was no way we could continue our conversation and by the time class was done, we'd probably be too exhausted.

While we waited for the rest of the group to arrive, nervousness settled in the pit of my stomach. As agitated as I had been to walk the little ones through their routines, it has been easy to find my footing with them.

But these were grown women who came into the studio expecting something specific. Something that they got from Lucetta. What if I couldn't deliver? What if, just as in New York, I wasn't good enough.

Sensing that something was off, Frankie touched her hand to my elbow. After excusing us from the group, she led me to the back of the room. "Whatever is going on up there," she motioned toward my head, "cut it out."

Gaze flicking to the last four women pushing through the door, I wet my lips. I didn't like the feeling eating at my gut or the little voice in my head reminding me of my failures. But I didn't know how to stop it either.

"Hey. Look at me." Frankie's hands were warm when she cupped my shoulders and stepped in front of me. "You've got this, Maddie Cakes."

That right there was why she was my person. We didn't need big speeches or endless words of wisdom. One look and I knew she had my back just as I had hers.

"Thank you. I needed that," I told her.

"I know. Now let's go shake our booties."

Which is exactly what we did after I lined up our playlist. For an hour we shimmied, gyrated, and grapevined until sweat covered our bodies and a simple breath set our lungs on fire.

And as much of a high as that gave me, it didn't come close to the feeling I got when class was over, and everyone thanked me. Some of them even going as far as to say it was the most fun they'd had in a while.

For as long as I could remember, people always used the saying those who can't do, teach. It was one of the reasons why I never looked into it. To me, teaching was admitting that I'd failed. But after only two days at Soulbeat, I realized it didn't even come close to being that.

Because failing didn't leave you feeling on top of the world when the day ended, and it definitely didn't fill your veins with excitement for the following day.

"Don't forget your rolls." Frankie's voice pulled my attention to her. We were standing on the sidewalk outside Soulbeat. She'd insisted on staying with me while I locked up.

"Thanks," I said, taking the offered bag. "And thank you for always being here when I need you."

"Aah shucks, Maddie Cakes." Slicing a hand through the air, she waved me off. When she quickly averted her eyes, I knew I wasn't the only one feeling emotional. "Don't go getting all mushy on me."

"Wouldn't dream of it."

"Good." Frankie jerked her head toward my car. "Now get out of here."

After we said our goodbyes, I slipped behind the wheel of my Prius and started the short journey home. The closer I got, the more the butterflies living inside my stomach fluttered.

Just knowing I was about to see Adam had my wires crissing and crossing in the best way possible. And when I finally knocked on his door, my heart had joined in. Furious in its effort to push past my ribs. It didn't surprise me when the door flew open to reveal a ruggedly sexy man dressed in a skintight black tee and faded jeans with my dog almost lovingly tucked under his arm.

What did have me double-taking was the delicious smell permeating the air. The sweet smell of cinnamon, pungent turmeric, and smoky cumin assaulted my senses. I was salivating.

It genuinely wasn't fair. He looked like *that* and apparently, he could cook too. Or maybe there was a person of the female variety in there preparing a yummy smelling meal for them.

I didn't like how that particular thought made me feel.

"I hope he didn't give you too much trouble." I took Sheldon from Adam. The sneaky little guy almost seemed reluctant to go. I couldn't blame him, though. If I had those arms wrapped around me, I wouldn't want to be tugged out of them either.

"No trouble."

" Thanks again for helping out today." Lifting the bag in my hand, I held it out to him. "Your rolls, as promised."

He made a noise and took the bag from me, immediately opening it up and taking a whiff. "Smells good."

"Almost as good as the smell coming from your kitchen."

Adam eyed me over the rim of the brown paper bag. "You're more than welcome to join me." His voice was steady, I had no clue if he was asking to be polite or if it was a legitimate invitation.

"I wouldn't want to impose."

Lowering the bag, he scratched the back of his neck with his free hand. "You're not. I was going to ask anyway."

My eyes roamed over his face. "That so?"

"Yeah." Nodding once, he shuffled from one foot to the other. "I figured you might not be in the mood to cook after such a long day."

My smile was wide. "You better watch out," I told him. "Your niceness is showing."

His lips twitched as he opened the door wider. "You coming in or not?"

"Well, since you asked so *nicely*." I stepped inside but stopped when I was next to him. Our gazes met and the air rushed out of my lungs in one fell swoop. "I guess I'm coming in."

21

· ADAM

I closed the door and took a few seconds to try and calm my thumping heart. This—having her here in my space—felt big. When I turned around, Maddie was making her way down the small hallway.

I stayed a few paces behind her and tried to imagine what the place must look like to her. I didn't have happy snaps or intricate art pieces lining my walls. In fact, the off-white paint was stained and had started to peel in a few spots.

It was cracked and broken, just like me.

We rounded into the living room, Maddie's hand shot out, her fingers trailing along the wall. They were small and delicate. Feminine. Was her touch like that too?

"I'm curious." She eyed me over her shoulder. "Why did you buy this house? From what I've heard, it's not even a fixer-upper. More like a lost cause."

Sheldon, who was still tucked against her chest, must've wiggled because she dropped to her haunches and set him down before straightening again. The instant the dog's paws touched the wood, he scampered to where I was standing and pawed my leg. Lowering myself to his level, I gave him a quick scratch behind the ears.

The intensity of Maddie's eyes on me slammed into me from across the room. My gaze lifted to hers and what little air I had in my lungs got knocked the hell out. My blood felt hot, too hot for my body. My skin too damn tight.

"What?" I finally croaked out.

Our gazes were still locked as I slowly pushed to my feet. The connection only severed when her eyes flicked to the dog at my feet. Maddie's brows pulled together and when I followed her gaze I almost choked on a laugh. Not at all bothered by what was happening around him, Sheldon had one leg stretched out while he happily licked at his privates.

"He's never been like this with anyone else but me. Not even Frankie." When I didn't say anything, she blinked rapidly. "I don't mean *that*." Her hand motioned toward the dog. "He's usually just so skittish, but with you—"

"He has no boundaries," I finished dryly.

She grinned. "Yeah."

I pulled my shoulder up. "Maybe he gets a kick out of annoying me." With a quick jerk of my head, I motioned for her to follow me. "What can I get you to drink?" Once inside the kitchen, I opened the fridge. One look at the empty shelves and it was painfully clear how I had not thought any of this through.

With the door gripped in one hand, I faced Maddie and winced. "I have water and whiskey."

The smile never left her lips. "Water is fine, thanks."

"Sorry." I grabbed a glass from the cupboard and after filling it with ice I set it along with a bottled water on the counter where Maddie was standing. "I usually put in my grocery order on Wednesdays."

"It's really okay." Unscrewing the cap, she filled the glass and then brought it to her mouth. My eyes were glued to the slender column of her throat as she greedily swallowed down almost half of her drink.

I had visions of brushing my knuckles along her skin and lowering my mouth to the spot where her pulse was ticking. Quickly averting my gaze, I moved to the stove. Lifting the lid on the curry, I carefully stirred the concoction.

I'd wanted this. Wanted her here in my space where I could just be in her presence. But I didn't take a moment to think about how it would affect me. How I'd want more. And I wasn't talking about something physical. I wanted to sit with her and beg her to tell me about who she was, what her wants and dreams were.

I wanted to know everything.

My eyes fell shut when I heard her move behind me. In those few seconds before I felt her presence to my left, I willed my frantic thoughts to calm the hell down.

"Mmmm."

I opened my eyes; Maddie was leaning over the pot, using her hand to wave the aroma toward her nose. She took one last whiff before straightening and turning her body toward me.

Her gaze flicked to my scars and for the first time since I'd had them, I didn't immediately want to turn away. Maybe it was because her face never contorted with disgust or possibly because her eyes didn't shine with pity.

She looked at me with curiosity. Like I was some sort of intricate puzzle that she needed to solve. Still studying me, the pink tip of her tongue darted out and slid along her bottom lip. "Can I ask you something?"

Those knots in my stomach twisted and turned. I swallowed roughly as I pushed away from the stove and began pulling plates out. "Sure," I rasped over my shoulder. "But I can't promise to answer."

Especially not if she was about to ask about the fire.

"You intrigue me, Adam. First, you move in here in the middle of the night. Then you nearly chewed my head off when I just wanted to introduce myself." She was moving again; I heard her soft footfalls steadily approach. "And as far as I can tell, you don't leave the house." Maddie came to a standstill next to me as the last words fell from her lips.

Taking a breath, I stared at my hands planted on the counter. "How would you know if I left the house or not?"

She made an incredulous sound. "Have you seen yourself?" My entire body froze, my stomach sinking to the floor like a rock. She must've noticed. Within a breath, her hand was curled around my bicep. "I don't mean…" Out of the corner of my eye, I saw her shake her head. "You're a big guy, Adam, and you're not exactly terrible to look at. It's a small town, and tongues would have been wagging if you'd been spotted."

Head still bowed, I looked at her. "Not terrible to look at?"

Her cheeks went from pale to bright red within a second flat. I swear, it was the prettiest sight. She tucked a few strands that'd escaped her ponytail behind her ear. "You know what I mean."

Straightening, I leaned my hip against the counter and folded my arms in front of me. "I really don't."

Maddie mimicked my stance and I couldn't help but steal a quick glance at her chest. "Actually, you don't get to ask a question. I still haven't asked mine."

I cocked a brow. "You sure about that?"

"Oh yeah." She nodded once. "I made a few observations but didn't ask a single thing."

It scared the shit out of me to say, "Well, what do you want to know?"

With one arm still tucked beneath her breasts, she tapped her chin with her index finger. While she was pondering over her question, I came up with an idea of my own. Right when her pretty lips parted, my finger shot up.

"Just a sec." I waited until I had her undivided attention before I continued, "I think it's only fair that I get to ask you something too."

Maddie rolled her lip between her teeth, eyes roaming over my face for the longest time. "Okay," she answered carefully. "But can we eat while we partake in this game of twenty questions." With a small smile, she patted her stomach. "I'm starving, and the aromas coming from that pot aren't helping matters much." Pinning me with a stare, her tone turned serious. "I might bite when I'm hangry."

You can bite me anytime you want. I had to press my tongue against my cheek to keep the words from spilling out. "All right."

Dishing up, we silently moved around each other. Each brush of our arms or stolen glance charging the air between us. By the time we were seated opposite each other at the small dinette, every cell in my body felt alive and on fire.

When Maddie picked up her fork and eagerly tucked into her food, I found myself holding my breath. Slowly lifting the fork to her mouth, she trained her eyes on me. My heart ground to an abrupt halt before it fiercely started hammering against my ribs.

Her mouth closed around the bite of food, her lids fluttering closed a second later. I was about to take a much-needed pull of air when the most sinful, most sensual sound came from the back of her throat.

"Mmm," she moaned. "This is sooo good."

The air lodged in my throat wasn't the only thing that needed to go the hell down. Shifting in my seat, I snatched up my water and poured it down my throat when I really wanted to tip the contents over my head.

If I was going to make it through this dinner—that I had wanted—I needed to get a handle on my damn hormones. Surely, at the age of thirty-four, it shouldn't be that difficult a task?

One... two... three... four...

"You're not eating." Maddie's remark interrupted my slow count to ten. "Not hungry?"

Oh, I was hungry all right. Just not for the food in front of me. "Just waiting for the inquisition to begin." I kept my tone light, hoping she wouldn't take my phrasing the wrong way.

One corner of her mouth lifted. "Hmm, or could it be that you're patiently waiting to ask whatever it is you want to ask?"

Loading my fork with chicken, my gaze flicked to hers. "Maybe."

Instead of speaking, Maddie went in for a few more bites. "This is really good," she said with a little sigh. "If I weren't such a terrible cook, I'd ask for the recipe." She reached for her water and lifted the glass to her mouth, awarding me with the most brilliant smile before taking a small sip.

After returning the glass to the coaster, she pushed her almost empty plate aside, then leaned forward slightly, those eyes of hers sparkling. "You ready?"

No, I most certainly wasn't. But I couldn't say that. Leaning back in my seat, I swiped my palms down my thighs. "Ask away."

Maddie's eyes flitted to my neck. My stomach turned over on itself. I'd talk to her about whatever the hell she wanted, just not the fire. Never that. Under the table, my leg started bouncing on the spot. The need to jump up and hide so effing strong.

But then her gentle stare met mine and within the space of a breath, my frayed nerves started to settle

"Why Clearwater Bay?" Her voice was quiet and curious.

Giving her an evasive answer would've been so damn easy, but I found that wasn't the first thing I wanted to do. I pushed my plate to the side and rested my elbows on the table.

"I needed solitude. A place to heal without everyone—as well-meaning as they were—looking over my shoulder." The urge to stop talking was so strong but I shoved it away. "I shut down and I needed to find myself again."

My heart was beating too fast and too loud. It felt as if a million insects ran over my skin, I barely suppressed the shiver. I hadn't told her anything and yet it was the most I'd told anyone.

She leaned in as close as the table would allow. "And? Have you?" Her words were soft, the expression in her eyes gentle as they roamed over my face.

"I'm getting there." I heard the conviction in my voice. Felt the truth of it in the marrow of my bones. "My turn?"

She swallowed. "If you must."

I didn't need to think about it, I've had the question bouncing around in my head for the better part for two days. "Why were you upset the other day?"

Shifting her focus to a spot on the table, she pressed her lips into a thin line. It hadn't been my intention to put her on the spot like that, there simply was this burning need inside of me to know what or who had made her cry.

But I didn't want that information at any cost to her. "You don't have to answer if you don't want to," I reassured.

She was quiet and unmoving for so long; I wasn't entirely sure whether she heard me. Just as I opened my mouth to repeat what I'd said, she spoke, "For as long as I can remember, I wanted to dance. It's a part of me as much as the organs that keep me alive." Her tone sounded as heartbroken as the expression on her face had been when she'd come home in tears.

Slowly, ever so slowly, she lifted her golden gaze to mine. What I saw made my heart hurt. "I was sad because someone told me following my dreams, doing what I love, is nothing more than a silly notion."

By the way her cheeks turned pink, I got the impression that she shared more than she'd intended. It still wasn't enough. As angry as I had been at the world, violence had never entered my mind.

But seeing the look in Maddie's eyes, remembering her tear-stained face; I wanted to find this asshole and force him or her to take back those hurtful words. My body vibrated with an intense need to protect her from people like that. People who thought nothing of stepping on someone else's dream. Idiots who tried to snuff out the lights of people who shone brighter than them.

I had a feeling it was this need that pushed the words from my tongue before I had time to check myself. "That's the biggest load of bullshit I've ever heard. If it's what you want to do, you should do it. With the way you dance, you should be up on a stage somewhere."

Maddie's eyes narrowed dangerously. "How would you know?"

I shifted uncomfortably. Scrubbing a hand over the back of my neck, I searched for the right words to say. The ones that didn't make me sound like a complete creeper, even if it was true. "I've seen you on the beach in the mornings."

"You've been watching me?" It wasn't an accusation. I saw it in the soft way her eyes danced over my face.

Refusing to look away, I confessed, "I have. It happened by pure accident when I came outside one morning. The way you moved—" I shook my head, still remembering the feeling. "—touched something right here." My fingers came up and tapped against my chest.

Those eyes of her roamed over my face like they couldn't settle on one spot. Without thinking, I reached across the table and covered her hand with mine. When she sucked in a sharp breath, I quickly released her again. "Maddie, I'm sorry if knowing that makes you uncomfortable. The thing is…"

Pinching the bridge of my nose, I drew in a steadying breath. "Your dancing is quite possibly the most beautiful thing I've ever seen."

Eyes taking up half of her face, Maddie's head slowly moved side to side. "I need a minute." And then she jumped up and rushed out of the kitchen.

22

MADDIE

I was certifiable.

I had to be. It was the only explanation I had for what was going on inside of me. Adam had just confessed that he had been watching me in the mornings. Not that it was a surprise since I already had my suspicions.

No, the real shocker came when the butterflies in my stomach decided to take flight at his words. I understood that any normal person's reaction would've been to feel uneasy or at least some level of discomfort.

My brain knew that logic. But my heart...that little traitor didn't. It had bounced around excitedly at the mere thought of moving him with my dancing. Because dance was art and art was supposed to evoke strong feelings in whoever witnessed it.

"Maddie, I'm sorry."

His voice sounded from across the room. I spun around slowly. Adam was standing inside the arched entryway that separated the kitchen and the living room where I currently found myself in.

"Watching you was a rude invasion of your privacy." That deep gritty voice sounded as tortured as the look on his face.

All I wanted to do was go to him, wrap my arms around his neck and tell him that I didn't flee the table because of what he said but rather because of the strong emotions swirling inside of me. This all-consuming hunger to learn more about him and to find out what his kiss tasted like.

Which just proved I was completely batshit crazy.

"Please say something?" It was his broken plea that finally pulled me from my stupor.

I dug my heels in to keep myself from rushing over to him. Sucking in a deep breath, I fidgeted with the hem of my shirt; searching for the right words to say. "It's not a private beach. I've always known someone was bound to see me."

Those eyes of his studied me so intensely, it made my toes curl. He took one step, then another and another until he was close enough to touch. Balling my hands into tight fists at my side, I stopped myself from doing just that.

"You knew?"

I dragged my tongue over my suddenly dry lips. "Not for sure, but I had a feeling. You were there awfully fast after I fell."

Adam cocked his head and arched an eyebrow. "And still you showed up every morning without fail?" The seriousness in his stare had warmth spreading through my veins with the speed of a wildfire. "You wanted me to see?"

It was more of an observation than a question. He wasn't wrong. Maybe I hadn't put a conscious thought to it, but somewhere in the very back of my mind I knew he'd see me, and I might have wanted to perform...*for him.*

In front of me, Adam had gone completely still save for his gaze rapidly bouncing between my eyes. He reminded me of a wild animal finally crawling out of his hiding spot. One wrong move and he'd retreat.

"Maybe..." the word came out scratchy. Clearing my throat, I tried again. "Maybe I like having your eyes on me."

He squeezed his lids together like my words had pained him somehow. I itched to reach for him. To drag my fingers over his short beard and up to smooth out the deep lines marring his forehead.

"Adam."

When he parted his lids and captured my gaze with his, I almost gasped at the sheer determination burning in his eyes. There was no mistaking that he'd made a decision and was about to act on it.

My breath caught in my throat when he lifted his hand and slowly, oh so slowly, trailed his fingers along my jaw. Dark, dark eyes carefully trekking the movement of his thumb scraping over my mouth.

Delicious shivers worked their way down my spine while tiny bumps popped up all over my skin. My lips parted on their own, a tiny puff of air escaping almost immediately. The urge to close my eyes and just feel was so strong, so intense, giving into it would have been so easy. But if I did that, I would've missed the way Adam's tongue darted out and swept across his lip.

Almost like he couldn't wait to taste.

I wanted that. Wanted his mouth on mine. His hands in my hair and my body pressed tightly to his. I wanted it so badly, I felt the tug of that need low in my belly. And then as if he could read my thoughts that big frame of his steadily leaned forward or maybe it was me moving closer.

I didn't care which was which. Not when I was so close to finally finding out what it would feel like to kiss this man. This man that'd plagued my every thought and dirtiest dreams for over three weeks.

His hand, rough and calloused, cradled my cheek. My lids instantly fluttered closed at the contact. A soft moan sounded from somewhere at the back of my throat when Adam's hot breath blew over my lips.

I was so ready for this.

Until the shrill sound of a phone coming to life rudely interrupted what could have been a wonderful moment. I wanted to curse. Adam did. One profanity after the other rolled off his tongue. He dropped his hand and with a few backward steps, he put unwanted distance between us.

Somewhere in the living room, the phone was still ringing. I wanted to grab it and smash it to the floor and possibly stomp on it too. Not that we could go back. The moment was gone, and judging by the look on Adam's face, it was going to stay gone.

When the generic ringtone finally died down, silence filled the room. And for the first time since I'd arrived, I felt awkward. A quick glance at Adam confirmed he felt it too. His hands were shoved into his pockets while he tried to stare a hole in the floor.

A complete and utter miserable feeling descended over me. This sudden uneasiness that hung thickly in the air was the last thing I wanted. Honestly, if I could backtrack, I would.

I turned my attention to the couch where Sheldon was curled up into a little ball, happily snoring away. He wasn't going to be happy with me for disrupting his sleep, but he would just have to suck it up because there was no way I could stay.

Smoothing my hands over my hips, I opened my mouth to tell Adam I was leaving when our discarded dinner caught my eye. He'd worked hard on that meal; the least I could do was clean up.

Avoiding Adam, I slipped into the kitchen and started gathering the plates all the while cursing the stupid manners my mom had instilled in me.

"What are you doing?"

He might've spoken softly, but I still jumped at the suddenness of his voice. For such a big man, he sure had light feet. Or maybe I was too busy sulking to hear him approach.

My eyes locked onto his. There was so much emotion swirling in those dark irises; pity I couldn't decipher even one. "I'm clearing the table."

His brows pulled together. "Why?"

I couldn't stand the way he was looking at me. It made me feel hot all over, but it also held so much warning. Focusing on the plates in my hands, I spat out the words as quickly as I could. "I think I should go, but leaving you with all these dishes feels wrong."

He startled me once again when without warning he pulled the plates from my hand and shoved them onto the table. "Maddie, I—" The damn phone started up again. I shut my eyes and dropped my chin to my chest.

I didn't believe in fate and the universe giving us signs but damn if this one didn't have bright neon lights flashing around it.

"Shit," Adam muttered. "Let me just turn the ringer off."

He started to move, I quickly opened my eyes and gripped his forearm. His skin was warm and the muscles beneath my fingers jumped. "It's okay. I really should get going."

Adam parted his lips but seemed to think better of what he wanted to say and snapped them shut again. Nodding stiffly, he said, "All right, if that's what you want."

Talk about being all over the place. *I* was the one who wanted to go and yet when he didn't ask me to stay, my heart filled with disappointment. No wonder women were always being accused of not knowing what we wanted.

Because clearly, we didn't.

"Thank you for dinner." I removed my hand from his arm, and his gaze immediately shot to the spot I'd been holding on to. Deep lines marred his forehead as he studied it with the intensity of someone solving a difficult math problem.

Turning my back to him, I gathered the dishes once more. I didn't get very far before his raspy, "Leave it," rolled over my skin. Everything about this night, this man, rattled my bones. Perching my fingers atop the table, I kept my gaze in front of me.

"Are you sure?" I asked. "I don't mind—"

"I'll do it." He didn't sound angry, but he definitely wasn't happy either.

With a quick jerk of my head, I spun around. "Okay." Taking a wide step around him, I snatched Sheldon from the couch and headed to the front door. My heart sank a little when our goodbye was almost as awkward as our first meeting.

My mind spun in a million different directions and by the time I was safely tucked into my bed, there was only one thing I was certain of.

Adam whatever-the-heck-his-last-name-was was messing with my head and I didn't like it.

23

ADAM

Like the idiot I was, I didn't stop Maddie from leaving when every cell in my body begged me to. Instead, I stared at her retreating back like a damn idiot. Thing was, I was scared shitless.

Everything about Maddie terrified me. Without even trying, she'd touched the darkest corners of my soul and breathed life into parts of me that I thought would forever stay dead. The more time I spent with her, the more I wanted to be around her. To touch her. To kiss her.

I'd been so close to doing just that and for all my cussing, I now realized the phone ringing when it did was probably a good thing. Because I didn't need to do it to know that one taste of Maddie would never be enough.

Sure, she'd wanted me to kiss her, but what then? What happened afterward? Would it even be possible to maintain a friendship—not that we were even there yet— after a hot and heavy make-out session?

I didn't think so.

And that right there was the reason I let her walk out.

When she was out of sight, I closed the door and rested my forehead against it. For her own sake, I'd give her space. Keep my distance until I had a handle on this all-consuming need I had for her.

I didn't have anything more than friendship to offer, plus I came with baggage that was even too heavy for me. Pushing off the frame, I busied myself with tidying up before I dragged my ass upstairs.

Since I knew sleep would be impossible with Maddie running laps through my mind, I headed for the guestroom and started painting. How utterly monochromatic my life was was painfully obvious with each stroke of white I applied to the walls.

I'd put money on the fact that Maddie would've chosen a color that was soft, feminine, and inviting. Just like her. The roller paused halfway; a string of curses fell from my lips. I couldn't even perform a simple task without thinking about her.

That was pretty much how the following two days went. I'd walk into the living room and the look on Maddie's face right before I almost kissed her would flash in front of me. The image would trigger a myriad of sensations in my body that either had me cursing a blue streak or going back upstairs.

Other times, I'd prepare the wood for the deck and instead of focusing on the task in front of me, I'd stare at her house like a freaking creeper. It was ridiculous to miss someone you hardly spent time with, but I did.

I wanted to see her. To ask her about her day, and much to my own surprise, I wanted to give the little rat a scratch behind the ears. Which was why I found myself hopping over the fence on Friday night.

I would just have to deal with whatever the heck I felt because not seeing her at all was a hell of a lot worse than fighting the constant need to get my hands on her.

My brows pulled together in a deep frown when I approached the sliding door. It was halfway open with the curtains slowly blowing in and out of the house. Before I had time to knock, Sheldon started barking and came trotting out a few seconds later.

Dropping to my haunches, I gave him a scratch behind the ears which quickly turned into a belly rub when he flopped onto his back.

Out of the corner of my eye, I caught movement by the curtains. "Holy shit," I muttered under my breath the instant I looked up. Maddie was leaning against the frame with one hand holding onto the door.

My gaze greedily, hungrily, raked over her body. I started at her bare feet and slowly made my way up her toned legs and over the tiniest sleep shorts I'd seen. On top, she was covered with a loose-fitting shirt that slipped over her shoulder. It didn't escape me that there was no visible bra strap.

I ventured higher still. It was the first time she had her hair loose and my fingers itched to feel the strands against my skin. When I reached her eyes, those whiskey irises were guarded. Watching me thoughtfully.

"Hi," I croaked out. Giving Sheldon one last rub, I straightened, my gaze never leaving hers.

"You have something against the front door?" When my brows furrowed, Maddie clarified, "I always find you this side, never in front."

"Uh." I scratched the scruff on my chin. "It's closer…but I can use the front door if you'd like."

Her face was so serious, I got the impression she was about to tell me to get lost. That was until her lips twitched before stretching into a bright, beautiful smile. "I'm just messing with you. Wanna come in? I don't have a fancy curry to offer you, but I did pick up a pizza after work."

I gave her a grin of my own. "Sounds good."

Maddie pushed off the frame and opened the door further. I started moving but instead of going in, I stopped in front of her and got a whiff of her subtle strawberry scent. Peering down the length of my nose at her, I pointed my index finger skyward. "Are there mushrooms on this pizza? If there is, I'm gonna have to decline."

Her eyes narrowed. "Your ass can stay outside then."

Splaying my hand over my chest, I pretended to be hurt. "You're mean."

"Nope, just hangry."

"Ah! Is this the part where you bite me then?"

Maddie's eyes leisurely traveled up and down the length of me. The way she was nibbling on her lip as she did, had me shifting from one foot to the other. When she pinned me with a stare that looked more like a heated promise, I knew I was beyond screwed.

"Maybe." How was it even possible for a voice so sugary sweet to sound downright sinful? I wanted to know what it would sound like when my name fell from her lips in a breathless whisper.

Shit. Wasn't this exactly why I'd stayed away for the past couple of days? To reel in these rampant thoughts. Get a grip on my hormones that were embarrassingly unstable.

"Relax." Maddie drew my attention back to her. "I won't bite. Not yet, anyway. And there are no mushrooms on the pizza. Just a lot of meat." Without waiting for a response, she spun on her heel and sauntered deeper into the house.

And because I liked the torture, my eyes stayed glued to her perfectly rounded ass until Sheldon's sharp yap interrupted me. With a lot of effort, I shifted my focus from Maddie to the little shit sitting at my feet. "What?"

Another shrill sound left his mouth before he trotted after his human, bushy tail in the air. I threw my head back and begged for the strength I needed to get through this night without so much as laying a finger on Maddie.

A task that was surely going to require superhuman strength since said fingers itched to explore every single inch of her body. After a few steadying breaths, I stepped inside and immediately smiled when some dance show was playing on her wall-mounted TV.

"What can I get you to drink?" Maddie called from the kitchen. "I have OJ, water, and the wine you brought over."

Frowning, I joined her. The bottle of wine still stood on the countertop. "I don't drink wine," she admitted softly.

My gaze immediately shot to hers. "You don't?"

Maddie shook her head, her cheeks turning the prettiest shade of pink. "Don't like the taste."

"Why didn't you tell me?"

In the space of a breath, she was standing in front of me with her fingers curled around my arm. As it did that night at my house, my skin felt alive under her touch. Jolts of electricity rushed through my veins and zapped at my heart.

Tilting her head back, she met my stare head-on. "What you did was so thoughtful, I didn't want to ruin the moment." Her lips curved into a shy half-smile. "I devoured the chocolates, though."

A chuckle rumbled through my chest. "I don't drink wine either."

The half-smile turned into a full-blown grin. "Well, look at that…We actually have something in common."

"I guess we do."

Maddie moved back to the fridge, and I immediately missed the warmth of her touch. After I told her I was good with just water, she pulled two bottles from the fridge and tossed me one.

I followed her back to the living room, where a pizza box was sitting on the coffee table. She flipped the lid and grabbed a slice for herself before plonking down on the couch and motioning for me to do the same.

It was only after both of us demolished two slices each that I broke the comfortable silence that'd fallen between us.

"So?" I eyed the TV for a beat before settling my gaze on her again. "This is what you get up to on a Friday night?"

She made a face. "I know. I'm the most boring twenty-four-year-old on the planet."

I'd known she was young; just didn't think I had a decade on her. Not that knowing her age suddenly changed things. I felt what I felt, it couldn't be helped.

"What's happening to your face?" Maddie leaned closer and made a show of inspecting me. "You look like you're doing math." Pulling her foot up, she tucked it under the leg dangling off the edge of the couch.

With a chuckle, I shook my head. "I was trying to think of an adequate word to describe you because boring isn't it." I, too, made myself comfortable. Turning sideways, I leaned back against the couch and spread my arm across the top of it. The way her eyes softened and roamed over me, made me feel funny. I couldn't remember when last someone looked at me like that. "What?" I croaked.

"You're sweet."

I scoffed. "I most definitely am not."

Leaning forward, way forward, she invaded my space. I balled my fingers into tight fists to keep from reaching for her. "That's what you want people to believe," she said seriously. "But I see you, Adam."

It was on the tip of my tongue to tell her the man she saw was the one she brought out in me. I'd hurt enough people over the past three years to know there hadn't been too much good in me.

Because I couldn't handle the weight of her stare, I averted my gaze. What would she say or think if she knew about that part of me? If I admitted how horribly I'd failed the person I was supposed to love the most?

Her tastefully-decorated, memory-lined walls started to close in on me. The invisible band around my chest pulled taut, and the air refused to leave my lungs. I jumped up and surged through the open door where I could drag fresh, salty air to my lungs.

"Adam?" Maddie's warm, soft hand landed on my back and I swore under my breath. "I'm sorry if I overstepped."

Pinching my eyes shut, I bowed my head. The last thing she deserved was me freaking out on her. I took another deep breath through my nose and opened my eyes again. Pivoting slowly, I felt her hand drop from my back. Without thinking, I reached forward and grabbed her wrist.

Her pulse was racing against the tips of my fingers. It matched my own heart's wild thundering. "You didn't overstep," I assured her. "I'm not a good person, Maddie. I've done things I am not proud of." I gave her a long, hard stare. "And you really shouldn't look at me through rose-colored glasses."

Maddie pressed her free hand against my chest, splaying her fingers across the general vicinity of my heart. "No one's perfect. And when I look at you, glasses or not, I like what I see."

"You shouldn't."

She shrugged her bare shoulder. I wanted to lean down and sink my teeth into her skin just so I could lave it with my tongue. "There are a lot of things people tell me I shouldn't do, and yet I still do them."

"Like dancing?"

"Yeah." Gaze never leaving mine, her hand moved from my chest to my arm, the tips of her fingers brushing over the sharp lines of the ink crawling up my skin. "Tell me, Adam, are you passionate about something?"

It wasn't just the curiosity in her eyes that pushed me to speak; I actually wanted to tell her about this part of me. This part that I hadn't spoken to anyone about in years. "I used to be. Since I was a little boy, I'd wanted to fight fires. It always fascinated me how firefighters ran into burning buildings when everyone else ran out. The day I put out my first fire, I knew why. There's this rush I can't explain. You know you might die doing it, but at the same time, you can't fight the pull it has."

At the mention of firefighting, her eyes trekked over the scars visible to her, but she remained silent.

"How come you never ask me what happened?"

Maddie's stare never wavered. "It's not that I don't wonder about it because I do. It's just...I don't know." She shook her head slightly." It's your truth to tell, and you should be able to do it when you're ready not whenever people ask."

I was done for.

This woman. This gorgeous, incredibly smart woman was burrowing so deep beneath my skin, I didn't think I'd ever get her out.

Or that I wanted to.

24

MADDIE

I was in too deep.

Way too deep with the very real possibility of drowning. In all things Adam, of course. We'd had a moment the previous night. Right there under the stars in my backyard, we shared something. It wasn't deep or overly personal, but somehow it only cemented this indescribable connection I had to him.

And although there was no kissing, everything about it had felt intimate. Almost as if, piece by piece, our souls were bared to each other.

Or it was possible that I was so ridiculously sexually frustrated I'd started sprouting some weird-ass poetry. With the lack of stimulation I was getting, I definitely wouldn't count it out.

Leaning back, I dug my fingers in the sand. The sun had only just made its appearance; shades of pinks and oranges streaked through the sky while the waves gently lapped at the shore.

I took a deep breath through my nose and shook my head at Sheldon, who was scavenging for crabs.

"Mind if I join you?"

The butterflies in my stomach immediately took flight at the sound of Adam's gritty voice. Cupping a hand over my eyes, I turned and tilted my head back. In the crisp morning light, he was so damn hot, it made my heart stutter.

A light gray t-shirt hung loosely from his torso. The arms were ripped off, giving me just a peek of the stacked muscles hiding underneath the cotton. If he was standing at the other side of me, I probably would've gotten a glimpse of the scars there.

My gaze traveled lower and I bit down on my teeth. Hard. He was wearing those can't-really-hide-anything gym shorts again. The ones that left no doubt about the fact that he went commando.

The kind that promised whatever the fabric was covering would most likely be a welcome stretch that would feel oh-so-good.

Because my legs were stretched out in front of me and crossed at my ankles, it was easy to squeeze my thighs together without him noticing. I cleared my throat and tried very hard not to think about his shorts or rather what was under them or the things I could and seriously wanted to do.

"Not at all." I sounded all kinds of pitchy but if Adam noticed, he didn't say a thing.

Keeping his eyes on me, he lowered that massive frame of his onto the sand with zero amount of effort. He pulled his legs up and casually draped his forearms over the tops of his knees. His focus shifted to Sheldon still furiously digging. "No dancing today?"

I grinned at him. "You sound disappointed. Were you hoping to catch the show?"

Serious eyes bore into mine. "I was, yeah."

It was so tempting to tell him that I'd be more than happy to give him a private show—the frustration was very real. Luckily, I caught the words and quickly swallowed them back down.

"I get a lot of dancing in now that I am at the studio every day." My mouth curved upward on its own. Soulbeat—dancing—was undoubtedly my happy place. Somewhere I could be who I was without judgment.

"You didn't always have your studio?"

I shook my head. "I still don't. My old dance instructor needed someone to fill in for her." Not sure why, but I couldn't bear to look at him when I said the next part. "I…uh…used to work at my parents 'hardware store."

"Hmh."

I gave him a curious look but before I could ask what the hell *Hmh* meant, Sheldon came darting across the sand, tail happily wagging at the sight of the man sitting next to me. He skidded to a stop between Adam's legs, kicking up sand in every which direction, and let out an excited bark.

"Hey, buddy," Adam cooed, giving my dog a scratch behind the ears that had his eyes rolling back in his little head. Not proud of it, but I was kind of jealous of my dog just then. I wanted this man's hands on me. Had a few itches he could scratch too.

"Your parents were the ones who told you that you couldn't dance?" His remark had the effect of a bucket of ice over the head—and lady bits. No one could have their parents and sex in their brains at the same time.

I eyed Sheldon, who seemed to be in a state of bliss, before following the lines of Adam's tattoo along his corded arm and over his broad shoulder. When my gaze finally landed on his, he was already watching me.

What did he see when he looked at me like that?

"They wanted me to study accounting and for a while I did." My insides twisted when I recalled how miserable I was. How spending every day looking at numbers sucked the life out of me little by little.

"What happened?" Adam asked quietly.

My tongue slipped over my lips. "I woke up one morning and decided I was done."

"Good for you."

"Oh no, it really wasn't. I went to New York, determined to be the next best thing, and fell flat on my face." This was the part that stung like nobody's business. "I came back home with my tail between my legs a year later and started working for my parents the next day." I laughed dryly. "If it hadn't been for my grandma leaving me this house in her will, I probably would've still been in my childhood bedroom."

Saying the words out loud made me feel so inadequate. And it sounded a hell of a lot like I was a quitter.

I didn't like accounting, so I quit.

I couldn't get a decent job as a professional dancer, so I packed up and came home.

My throat burned with the sudden bout of tears I tried to keep inside. I didn't want Adam to see, so I focused on the waves gently rolling over the sand.

A calloused palm landed on my knee, drawing my attention back to the man beside me. He regarded me for the longest time; those dark eyes roaming over my face. "Success isn't always measured in what we accomplish," he finally rasped. "Sometimes we find it in the things we learn along the way."

I couldn't speak past the thick lump in my throat. Hell, I could hardly breathe. The way he made me feel, I wished I could find the right words. Something to describe the crazy but wonderful feeling he evoked inside of me.

Unaware of what he was doing to my insides, Adam lifted his hand and toyed with the strands hanging over my shoulder. "I like your hair like this." His murmur was so soft, so sensual, it had delicious shivers dancing down my spine.

"I like *you*." The words slipped from my tongue before I had a second to check them. But once they were out, I didn't regret saying it.

Adam's eyes turned darker. "You shouldn't." The fingers tangled in my hair moved, his grip getting tighter the closer he got to my scalp.

"You keep saying that," I breathed out.

"Mhm." His gaze bounced between my eyes and mouth. By the tortured look on his face, I knew he was trying to decide what to do. And as desperately as I wanted to beg him to just kiss me already, I needed him to get there on his own.

To crave this as badly as I did.

I knew the exact moment the war within himself was over. Impossible as it might've seemed, those dark irises turned even darker. The fist in my hair gripped tighter as he leaned forward and pulled my face to his at the same time.

Every single cell in my body felt alive. My nerve endings buzzing with anticipation. Behind my ribs, my heart was beating so fast, almost too fast. The wild thundering in my ears so loud, I was certain Adam could hear. He wet his lips. I felt the warmth of his breath feather over my mouth. There was barely half an inch between us.

I parted my lips when I felt the slightest touch of his against mine. *Finally, finally*, I thought.

"Madison. That you?"

"Are you freaking kidding me," I groaned. Adam pulled back and immediately angled his body sideways; hiding his left side from the man slowly ambling toward us.

I raised my hand and waved. "Hi, Mr. Stevenson."

Sheldon, who at some point must've scurried away, came trotting back and parked his butt next to Adam. I shook my head.

"Lovely morning, isn't it?" Mr. Stevenson said with a wide smile when he finally reached us.

Pushing to my feet, I returned his smile. "It sure is."

The older man's head bobbed up and down while he gave a now standing Adam a curious look. "You fixin 'up old Ronnie Nichols's place?'

"I am, sir."

At Adam's tight tone, my gaze shot to him. His jaw was ticking as he held a stiff arm out to Mr. Stevenson and introduced himself. He looked uncomfortable. So terribly uncomfortable. My heart squeezed a little.

"I was hoping I'd run into you today," Mr. Stevenson told me. "You know my son, Billy?" It wasn't really a question, but I nodded anyway. "He and his lovely wife, Angela, just had a little boy. They named him after me, you know?" He puffed out his chest, the smile on his face stretching wider.

"How wonderful! Congratulations."

He was beaming; it was impossible not to smile right along with him. Unless your name was Adam and your grumpiness was showing.

"They invited me to go visit for a while. You know, meet the little man and all," Mr. Stevenson babbled on. "I was hoping you'd keep an eye on the place for me. Agnus from the library will stop by once or twice a week to water the plants, so you don't have to worry about that."

"Of course."

After he thanked me profusely, Mr. Stevenson slowly strolled along the beach. I watched him for a while before I turned my attention to Adam. He had his serious frown aimed at the ocean.

I poked him with my elbow. "You're being a grumpy butt."

He half-glared at me out of the corner of his eye. "I'm being quiet," he said matter-of-factly. "There's a difference."

"Oh, yeah?" I moved to stand in front of him. Hands perched on my hips. "Enlighten me. What goes on up there," I pointed at his head, "when you are being *quiet*?"

Was he thinking about how we should pick up where we left off before Mr. Stevenson interrupted us? Gosh, I really hoped so.

"I just realized I have never seen a single dance movie."

Huh. Not where I thought the conversation was going but I played along anyway. Grabbing my chest in mock horror, I squeaked, "What? Tell me it isn't so."

His lips lifted into a grin that didn't quite reach his eyes. "Nope. Not one."

"We have to fix this, Adam. It's a serious problem."

"It is?"

I nodded furiously. "Yes! We can't be friends unless you've watched at least one of the classics."

One dark eyebrow slowly arched. "That so?"

"Yup."

"Well, then I guess you better school me." He bent forward a bit. "Because I really want to be your friend, Maddie."

I knew he didn't want to be just friends. The heat simmering in his eyes proof of that. But for reasons that probably had a lot to do with the scars coating his skin, he needed to slow down.

And I was perfectly happy with going as slow as he needed to.

25

MADDIE

I was in the middle of going over the merchandise list for Soulbeat when the sound of footsteps reached my ears. From his perch on the doggy bed next to the patio table where I was working, Sheldon lifted his head and angled his ears.

That's how I knew it wasn't Adam coming over for an impromptu visit. It was stupid how I was a little sad at that since I had seen him just this morning. But I was quickly realizing that however much time I was spending with him, wouldn't be enough.

There were still so many things about him that I didn't know. Things I wanted to ask about.

"Auntie Maddie!" Tommy squealed. I had about a second to brace myself before his little body slammed into mine.

I squeezed him tight. "This is a nice surprise." Over his shoulder, I noticed my sister approaching with caution in her steps. We'd never really done the spontaneous drop-ins. My heart contracted a little when I thought about all the things we'd missed out on because I had purposely closed myself off to them.

Jennah wiggled her fingers in a small wave. "I hope it's okay?" she asked jerking her head toward Tommy hopping onto my lap. "He's been begging to come since yesterday."

"Geez, kid, what have you been eating?" I poked him in the ribs earning me happy peals of laughter. "You're heavy." Shifting my attention to my sister, I gave her a genuine smile. "It's more than okay. I'm happy you're here."

The relief that washed over her face at my words quickly turned to curiosity as she scanned my backyard— spending a few seconds extra on the house next door.

"I thought we could discuss Mom's birthday since we didn't get to it the other night." Jennah slipped onto one of the chairs and eyed my computer. "Unless you're busy?"

With a shake of my head, I closed my laptop. "Not busy at all." I tried to shift in my seat, but my nephew's butt-bones dug into my legs. I jabbed his ribs again. "You need to stop growing because you're getting way too big to sit on me."

Tommy tilted his curly head backward and beamed. "Mom says I'm getting big and strong now because I'm eating my vegetables."

I widened my eyes. "Say what now? You're actually gobbling up your veggies?"

He nodded his little head vehemently and Jennah laughed softly. "Well," I drawled. "Because you are so *big and strong*, you might break my legs." I made a show of that being the worst news; clutching my chest and looking toward the sky. "What am I going to do without my legs?"

If I thought my little performance was going to amuse the seven-year-old sitting on me, I was dead wrong. Tommy rolled his hazel eyes. "Girls are so dramatic." As quickly as he got on, he slid off my lap. "I'm going to go play with Sheldon." Smacking his lips and patting his leg, he lured my dog to the grass where a game of chase immediately ensued.

"I swear." Jennah shook her head. "He is not even a teenager, but he sure is acting like one."

My gaze flicked to hers. "At least he's not bringing girls home yet."

My sister let out a tortured groan. "Oh please, no. I can't even."

"Do you remember when Casey wanted to take you out for a milkshake, and you told him he had to pick you up at home?"

Jennah covered her face with her hands, shoulders shaking with silent laughter. "That was so bad," she mumbled from behind her palms. "Dad cleaned his freaking shotgun right there on the porch." Eyes that reminded me so much of my own peeked at me through her fingers. "Casey asked Tabatha Collins out the next day."

Laughter burst out of both us, and I couldn't remember a time where Jennah and I had ever been like this. Which made me all the more thankful for this moment and the opportunity to rebuild the relationship we should've had.

When the happy sounds that were long overdue finally ebbed, I wiped my mouth with the back of my hand. "I have wine if you'd like some."

My sister's eyebrow slowly climbed toward her hairline. "You drink wine now?"

"Nope." I shuddered. "I still think it's nothing more than rotten grapes."

"Ohhhkay. Then why do you have it?"

"Funny story." I stood from my chair and motioned for her to follow me into the house. Once in the kitchen, I handed my sister the bottle and filled her in on how it ended up in my possession.

I tried to keep my voice and face even as I spoke about Adam, but judging by the huge grin on Jennah's face, I knew I was failing miserably. That in itself was somewhat troublesome. If I was having a hard time keeping emotion off my face, I was in way deeper than I thought.

"And when are we meeting the mysterious man?" my sister inquired after her wine was poured and we were back on the patio.

A visual of how uncomfortable Adam had been in front of Mr. Stevenson flashed before me. "I don't know," I told her honestly. He might not have opened up to me, but from the things he wasn't saying, I knew that Adam's scars ran a lot deeper than the ones I could see.

Tommy's laughter drew our attention to him where he was lying flat on his back on the grass with Sheldon furiously licking at his face.

"Maybe you can invite him to Mom's birthday bash?" Jennah quietly said from beside me.

My gaze flicked to the house next door. Perhaps there was the slightest chance that he'd go with me. The thought alone made me feel giddy. Shifting in my seat, I eyed my sister. "Speaking of…there won't be a party to invite him to if we're not planning it."

With a quick tilt of her head, she brought her glass to her lips and took a delicate sip. "So, I was thinking." She set the glass down and ran her thumb and index finger up and down the stem." We could do it at the community center. Maybe have fifty balloons drop on her when she walks through the door."

My sister kept coming up with new ideas. Every one better than the previous one. The little details she thought of and how she could envision the layout and which colors would go where. All of it amazed me. *She* amazed me.

"What?" she asked when I simply stared. Her hand shot to her chin, furiously wiping over her skin. "Do I have wine dripping from my chin?"

I shook my head. "You missed your calling, Jen. You should totally be doing this for a living."

Her cheeks flushed, and I knew it had nothing to do with the wine she was drinking. "I don't know. It seems irresponsible to chase after this now. I have Tommy to think about. Securing his future is the most important thing for me."

Reaching for her hand, I covered it with mine and squeezed. "You're a good mom and I know you're giving him the best you can. But you deserve to be happy too. You could always do this on the side. See how it goes."

I could practically see her wheels turn, and it filled me with warmth to think she was really considering this.

We spent the next three hours planning our mother's party and chatting about anything and everything. By the time I walked her to her car, I was genuinely sad to see her go.

When Tommy was secured in the backseat, Jennah surprised me by spinning around instead of sliding behind the wheel. She launched herself at me, wrapping me up in her arms. The crushing hug she was giving me had a gigantic lump forming in my throat.

"I'm so happy we got to do this today," she breathed into my hair. The slight trip in her voice betraying her emotions.

My arms around her tightened. "Me too, Jennah." I swallowed and swallowed, but the lump refused to go down. The backs of my eyes stung, and my nose burned with the tears I was holding in.

After way too many years, I finally had my sister back.

26

ADAM

Yet again I found myself watching Maddie, only this time it was more than me wanting to stay in the shadows. I didn't want to intrude on what looked like an intimate moment between her and her sister.

You didn't have to be a genius to know the two women were related. They shared the same blonde hair and the same facial features. And right now, they were locked in an embrace that had my heart doing strange things and my brain drifting to my own sibling.

I missed the days where I'd been comfortable enough to simply pick up the phone because I wanted to hear my little sister's laugh. Or when she used to show up out of the blue to torment me with her *boy troubles*.

I missed Zoe. Missed my family.

The sputter of an engine coming alive drew my attention to the driveway next door in time to see the Honda pull out and roll down the street. Maddie stood stock-still until the early evening swallowed the retreating taillights.

Emerging from where I was standing, I made my way to the fence just as she pivoted. When she spotted me, the smile playing on her gorgeous lips stretched even wider. My heart stuttered in response.

There weren't words—there probably were, I just didn't have them—to adequately explain how it made me feel when she looked at me like that. All I knew was, I wanted to see a hell of a lot more of it.

I opened my mouth to greet her but before a single sound could come out, Sheldon darted around the corner. His shrill barking reaching a new octave the closer he came.

"Looks like someone is happy to see you." Maddie laughed.

I planted my hands on top of the fence and pinned her with a stare. "He the only one?"

"No." Her answer came without hesitation, loosening the band around my chest a little more. My gaze flicked to Sheldon sitting against the fence; head tilted back, tongue lolling, he was watching me expectantly. "I've been thinking about those movies you were on about," I told Maddie when our eyes locked again.

"Oh yeah?"

"Yeah." Nodding, I dragged my palm over the back of my neck. "If you're not busy, I thought maybe you could *enlighten* me."

That beautiful smile that always touched some deep, dark part of me grew bigger and brighter. "You wanna have a movie night?"

Holding my gaze, she sucked her bottom lip into her mouth, rolling it over her teeth.

My entire body went up in flames because, shit, I wanted to nibble too.

"Something like that." The words came out hoarse, scraping against my throat like sandpaper.

The way her features lit up with excitement was so damn beautiful and infectious; I felt my own lips curve upward in return. Smile still in place she said, "You better get over here quick. School's about to start."

I wasted no time hopping over the fence and quickly stooping to pick up Sheldon. Almost immediately, he attacked my face with his tongue, even managing to lick the inside of my nose.

Maddie laughed when I pulled my head back and groaned. "All right, buddy, I'm happy to see you too." With a chuckle, I scratched behind his ear.

"You know." Maddie nudged my arm with her shoulder. "If you'd shown up five minutes earlier, I could've introduced you to my sister."

The band that'd loosened earlier pulled taut again. Uneasiness crawled down my spine and made my skin feel tight. There were things I couldn't dance around anymore. Things about me Maddie needed to know.

I just didn't have the balls to come right out and tell her.

Choosing to remain silent, I followed her through her front door, down the long hallway, and into the living room. Sucking in a breath, I held it and dropped to my haunches to set Sheldon down. Slowly released it as I pushed to my feet.

Hands perched on my hips, I faced Maddie. But she was already watching me, those eyes of hers filled with curiosity as they roamed over my face.

"You don't like being around people, do you?" There was no judgment in her voice when she asked the question.

"It's not that I don't like it. People, in general, make me uncomfortable." Rocking back on my heels, I slipped my hands inside my pockets. "They're always staring." Her face softened and I hated it. "Don't do it, Maddie," I begged. "Don't pity me." I didn't think I would be able to handle it.

She shook her head, her pony vehemently swinging back and forth. "It's not pity you're seeing." I closed my eyes and almost immediately snapped them open when I felt her palm land on my chest. "I was staring too, but not—"

"I don't mind *your* eyes on me," I confessed roughly.

The moment the words left my lips, her gaze tracked up the tattoo on my right arm, over my shoulder and settled on my mouth for a long, hot second. "Good," she finally said when her eyes met mine, "because I don't think I can stop looking."

Good thing my hands were in my pockets, so I could somewhat hide how her words were affecting me. My lack of control over my body was becoming damn annoying. I swear, all she had to do was lick her lips and I was straining against my jeans like a fucking teenager.

So her words coupled with that heated stare had my body going from zero to one-hundred in the space of a breath. "Stop looking at me like that."

Feigning innocence, Maddie's lips lifted into the sweetest smile that had the dirtiest things running through my mind. "Like what?"

"Nothing." I took a step back and her hand fell from my chest. "Are we doing this movie thing, or what?"

Her right shoulder steadily lifted to her ear before falling back down. "If you insist."

Yeah, I insisted all right. Because if we didn't, I might've ended up with my mouth on hers. Or possibly buried deep inside her. A groan threatened to vibrate through my chest at the thought alone.

How would it feel when her body moved with mine? What sounds would she make?

" Are you even listening?"

I blinked a few times until Maddie's snapping fingers came into focus. "Huh?"

Laughter spilled from her lips while she rubbed at her temple with two fingers. "Where the heck did you just go?" Not giving me time to answer, she shook her head. "Never mind. Before you spaced out, I asked you if you'd mind if I took a quick shower before we started the movie?"

I gritted my teeth to keep a curse from rumbling free. I was already having a hard time with my rampant thoughts. How much worse was it going to get now that I could add the idea of her lathering up her naked body?

"Not a problem."

If she noticed the strain in my voice, she didn't show it. Bouncing on the balls of her feet, she smacked her hands together. "Great! I won't be long." Turning she sprinted for the stairs. I couldn't tear my eyes off her ass even if I tried.

My fingers itched to squeeze, and my mouth tightened with the need to bite.

"Oh!" she skidded to a stop so abruptly there was no way she missed the way I was checking her out when she spun around. "If you could make yourself useful and get the popcorn going, that would be awesome."

"Geez, you're bossy." I was smiling even as I said it.

Grinning, Maddie pivoted before meeting my gaze over her shoulder. "Don't pretend you don't like it." And then she was off again, darting up the stairs and disappearing from view.

My fingers trembled slightly when I dragged them through my hair and released a slow breath. Shaking my head, I ambled to the kitchen. I had to open and close a few cupboards before I found a bag of microwave popcorn.

When it was done, I grabbed two drinks of water from her fridge and settled on the chaise part of her sectional. Because her television wasn't on, I could hear the sound of running water coming from upstairs.

She was up there.

Naked.

Dragging a lathered-up sponge all over her body.

I threw my head back against the soft cushioning and pulled a breath through my nose. I held it for a few seconds before slowly blowing it out through my mouth. Yeah, it didn't help. My entire body still vibrated with the need to stomp up the stairs and replace the sponge with my hands.

Or my mouth.

Probably both.

I was well on my way deeper into fantasyland when Sheldon hopped onto the couch, his sudden presence giving me a small reprieve from the movie playing inside my head. He turned around and around before flopping down and snuggling up against me.

I smiled.

Who the hell knew a little creature that resembled an overgrown rat could paw his way into my heart? With a sharp shake of my head, I dug my fingers into the soft fur on Sheldon's head and scratched behind his ear.

Something that could only be described as a happy sound came from him before he tried to snuggle even closer to me.

"I think you bewitched my dog."

Hearing her voice, my head snapped up and my mouth went dry. Maddie was sashaying toward me looking like she'd just stepped out of one of my dreams. The small sleep shorts and loose-fitting tee she seemed to favor at night gave my fingers inches upon inches of skin to itch over.

The way her damp hair spilled over her shoulders had my mind running in a million different directions. All of them ending with the strands tightly wound my around my fist and my mouth crashed to hers.

But I couldn't do any of that, it wouldn't be fair to Maddie to bring my kind of fucked into her life.

Pushing thoughts of Maddie and her sinful mouth to back of my mind for the time being, I shrugged my shoulders and dryly stated, "Maybe he just likes my roast beef."

She made a noise but said nothing, sauntering to her TV unit instead. I couldn't keep my gaze from following her even if I tried. Something I very much regretted when she bent over to pull a stack of DVDs from the cabinet below the TV.

I bit the inside of my cheek so hard; the irony taste of blood filled my mouth. My hands curled into tight fists at my sides while I scanned the couch for a throw pillow. Anything to keep her from seeing my tented jeans.

"Okay." Blissfully unaware of me turning ten different shades of blue, Maddie flipped through the cases in her hand. "Oooh, we should start with this one." She murmured the words more to herself than me which was a damn good thing. I didn't believe I'd be able to string two words together let alone a coherent sentence.

After she popped the DVD into the player, she snatched the remotes from the coffee table and plonked down next to Sheldon. She was so close to me, if I stretched out my arm across the top of the couch, I'd be able to brush my fingers over the back of her neck.

I wanted to do just that.

Instead, I focused on the opening credits rolling over the screen while the band begged someone to be their baby. My eyebrow arched high. Whatever bumping and grinding the people on screen were doing, it sure as shit wasn't dancing.

"Uh, what exactly are we watching?"

Maddie grabbed the bag of popcorn and opened it. After popping a few into her mouth, she turned to me and grinned. "Only the best movie ever."

My brow climbed even higher. "Which is?"

"Are you kidding?" Her eyes grew wide. "You've seriously never watched this?"

My gaze flicked to the TV where big, bright pink letters scribbled across the screen informed me the film was titled *Dirty Dancing*. Fitting, considering the first three minutes resembled some kind of foreplay.

"Nope, can honestly say I have not."

My face must've given away my reservations because Maddie burst out laughing. She reached over Sheldon and patted my thigh. "It's not that bad, I promise."

I focused on her delicate fingers splayed across my leg. "If you say so."

"All right." She patted my leg once more before removing her hand. "Tell you what, if by the end you still hate it, I'll watch whatever you want me to watch."

My gaze sought hers out. "Anything?"

"Yup, anything."

I narrowed my eyes and thought of the one movie my sister hated. Not because it was bad, but the ending was so unexpected. I, of course, thought it was genius. "Even *Braveheart*?"

Maddie wrinkled her nose and I had the urge to kiss the tip of it. "Of all the movies in the world *that's* the one you pick."

I tapped my chin and pretended to think. "How about *300* or *Gladiator*?" Her groan told me she'd seen both and most likely didn't want to again.

She threw another piece of popcorn into her mouth and after chewing and swallowing it down, she said, "Luckily I don't have to decide until this one is done."

"Only if I like it," I quipped.

She shot me a self-assured grin. "Oh, you'll *love* it."

"That so?"

"Yes! Now shh and watch the movie."

"So damn bossy," I muttered, giving my attention to the screen. For all of ten minutes. I'd wanted to concentrate on what was happening on the television, but as if it had a mind of its own, my gaze kept flicking to Maddie. Not only did she know the movie word for word but the smile playing on her lips never wavered.

"This is such a good part," she said quietly, forcing me to pay attention to what was happening.

The girl made some comment about carrying a watermelon that Maddie found absolutely hilarious. I had to wonder, as the heroine stared at the hero of the story, if I looked like that whenever my gaze followed Maddie.

Could she see the amazement, the wonder, the want on my face?

When the pair finally made it to the dancefloor together, it was my turn to chuckle because that girl's stiffness in her hips had nothing on mine. "I'd probably break something if I tried that," I muttered, pointing at the screen.

I barely had time to blink before Maddie was up on her feet, pulling me right along with her. Her hands landed on my hips and I sucked in a sharp breath.

She was manhandling me; trying to rotate my hips first left then right while I thought of ice creams and cold showers.

"You're stiff as a board," Maddie exclaimed. *Yeah, no kidding.* "You have to loosen up. Like this…"

Every rational thought left my body the instant she took my hands and set them on her hips. Beneath my palms, I could feel the warmth of her skin seep through the soft layers of her clothing.

I wanted to grip her tighter and pull her body flush against mine. I needed it almost as much as I needed my next breath.

"Shit. Maddie…wait." I took a big step backward; almost falling over the chaise when the back of my legs hit the couch.

"What's the matter?" She moved forward, but I stopped her with a jerky shake of my head. The confused look on her beautiful face nearly killing me.

"Gimme a sec." My voice was so rough, I doubted she heard me.

"Did I do something wrong?"

I swiped my palm over my mouth, barely hiding my uncomfortable chuckle. "You didn't do anything, Maddie. It's me."

Despite the warning look I gave her, she advanced on me. Touching her hand to my chest the instant she was able to do so. Electricity zipped through my veins. The heat of her touch searing me even through the fabric of my shirt.

Every nerve ending in my body felt alive and on fire.

"Could you not touch me for a minute?" I snapped.

But this woman, this gorgeous creature in front of me, knew exactly where my frustration was coming from. Taking another step closer, her palm swept up and curled over my shoulder.

Her breasts grazed my chest when she pushed onto the tips of her toes. I had to grit my teeth and use all my strength not to bow my head. If I did, not even a breath would separate our mouths and there was no way I'd be able to resist tasting her.

Of course, Maddie was unaware of the war raging inside of me.

"Oh." She dropped back onto her heels. "I'm sorry, you said…" She shook her head and muttered, "I thought you wanted me too." The words were so soft, but she might as well have yelled them from the rooftops.

She made a move to turn around, but my hand shot out first, fingers curling around her wrist. One tug was all it took for our bodies to mash together. My other hand possessively wrapped around the back of her neck, pressing our foreheads together.

We were so close, my lips brushed against hers with every word I spoke, "I want you so bad, it fucking hurts."

Tilting my head slightly, I finally, *finally*, sealed my mouth over hers. My eyes fell shut. Maddie sighed. Soft pliable lips met mine, and it took every bit of strength I had not to swallow her whole.

Another sigh blew into my mouth when she opened up, giving my wondering tongue permission to slip inside. We matched each other stroke for hungry stroke. The kiss wet and dirty as we both tried to give as good as we were getting.

Maddie's arms banded around my waist, the action bringing our bodies even closer together. A groan filled with pure need rumbled through my chest when she hummed at what she felt pressed against her.

I wanted to hear more of it.

Wanted to taste more of her.

My hand slipped into her hair, winding her silky tresses tightly around my fist while the other slid down and over the curve of her ass. Curling my fingers, I squeezed hard and pressed her soft body even deeper into my hard one. Her moan was loud and needy and so damn sexy. As was the way her mouth was moving over mine in the same insatiable way I wanted her.

Like she too couldn't get enough.

Maddie lifted her leg, dragging her knee along my outer thigh. My hand dropped and gripped her tighter, fingers digging into her hot skin. Hard. I wouldn't be surprised if bruises matching my fingertips showed up the next morning.

Another animalistic sound rumbled through my chest when she rocked her hips against mine. It felt so damn good, the bulge straining against my zipper jumped in excitement.

If a kiss could feel this big, this consuming, how much more magnified would it be when I lost myself in the warmth of her body?

I wanted it.

Wanted to own every inch of her and give her all of me. Wanted, no needed, to hear my name on her lips when pleasure ripped through her body. It was the only thing I could think of until I felt her hand slip beneath my shirt and reality slapped me in the face.

Up until now, she hadn't given me a single reason to believe she'd look at me with repulsion, but she also hadn't seen what was hidden beneath the cotton of my tee.

Even more, I wasn't ready for her to see.

Gripping her wrist, I dragged her hand up and pressed a kiss to the center of her palm. My eyes locked onto hers. One look at the want shining in those whiskey irises and I figured I was likely the world's biggest idiot. "Nothing's rushing us."

She stared at me for a long second before her gaze dropped to my mouth and stayed there even longer. "We're going slow." Her eyes flicked back to mine. "Got it."

Is she…? Oh yeah, this gorgeous woman was full-on pouting. Barking out a laugh, I cradled her cheeks between my palms and pressed my mouth to hers in a quick smacking kiss. Before either of us had the opportunity to deepen it, I pulled back and took her hand in mine.

"Come on, Let's finish this movie so you can decide whether we're watching *Braveheart*, *Gladiator*, or *300* next."

27

MADDIE

I popped one eye open and immediately grinned. It hadn't been a dream at all. The hard body I was snuggled up against was very real. My hand swept over Adam's broad chest, loving the feel of his warmth seeping into my skin even through the barrier of his shirt.

He was still asleep, so I took the opportunity to shamelessly study him. I hadn't seen his face look as relaxed as it was at that moment. There was no clenching jaw or brows tightly pulled together. Or a delicious looking mouth pressed into a thin line.

Naturally, my brain zeroed in on the amazing kiss we'd shared the previous night. One touch of his tongue and my little world had flipped on its axis. As far as I could remember a single kiss had never felt so intense.

So monumental.

I wanted to close my eyes and relive the moment over and over again, but instead of doing exactly that, I took in the rest of his gorgeous features. All the while wondering about the man he was before he moved in next door. The things he'd witnessed and endured. And who he'd been before all of it had happened. I had a hard time envisioning him as anything else than the grumpy butt next door.

Mostly, because I didn't want him any other way.

"I can feel your eyes on me." His voice was groggy from just waking up, even sexier than his normal raspy tone.

Tilting my head back, I found him studying me through thin slits. I smiled and said, "You love it."

His answering grin had my heart bouncing like a rubber ball, and when he opened his eyes and I experienced the full weight of his stare, the breath whooshed straight out of my lungs. How was it even possible that the man could look so sinfully sexy first thing in the morning?

Also, if he kept looking at me like that, I was definitely going to climb all over him. Because I wasn't opposed to another taste. Maybe even more. Almost like he knew exactly what I was thinking, Adam's big hand curled around my hip and he pulled me on top of him. He was half-lying, half-sitting with his shoulders leaned back against the back of the chaise part of the couch with me straddling his massive thighs.

"Hi." Rough, calloused palms dragged up my bare legs until his fingers could toy with the bottom of my shorts. I wanted them higher. A lot higher.

"We fell asleep on the couch," I said in lieu of greeting, trying my best not to roll my hips to get some much-needed friction.

"Mhm, I guess we did." His hands were on the move again, brushing over my shorts and dipping under my shirt. Up and up they went, until he splayed his fingers over my ribcage. I shivered when the pads of his thumbs brushed the underside of my breasts.

Live wires wouldn't have had the same effect as his big hands on my skin. Skin that felt alive with electricity zipping over the surface. Low, low in my belly there was an insistent tug warning me if he didn't do something soon, I might spontaneously combust.

"Touch me, Adam."

I barely had time to feel embarrassed over being so forward when he shifted his hands and filled them with my breasts. His thumbs moved in slow circles before his fingers squeezed and pulled a moan from the back of my throat.

Tiny bumps peppered my skin while my blood turned to molten lava. My entire body hummed with pleasure. But I needed more. So. Much. More. Digging my knees into the soft cushioning of the couch, I rolled my hips over his hard body and almost whimpered at how good it felt.

"Shit," he groaned. Abandoning my chest, he smoothed his hands over my hips before shoving them down the back of my shorts. Curling his fingers into my bare skin, he helped me move over him. "So good."

Adam tipped his head back, his jaw muscles tight as he continued to push and pull. Over and over again. Without warning, he surged up, covering the back of my head with his palm and pulling my face to his.

He kissed me as if I was his last meal and he wanted to remember every single detail. Our tongues coiled and twisted while our hips rocked to a crazy rhythm. I was about two seconds away from bliss when he flipped us so fast, it made my head spin. As did the image of him hovering over me with those dark, dark eyes boring into mine.

But it was the expression on his face that did me in.

He looked at me like he worshipped me and wanted to do the dirtiest things to me at the same time. I wanted that. Oh, how I wanted that.

His sinful mouth twitched before his head slowly dipped. I wet my lips in anticipation. My body was already buzzing and ready for another taste of Adam. Only he didn't kiss me. He ran the tip of his nose along my jaw before nudging my head back. His mouth closed over the skin below my ear from where he nipped and sucked his way down my neck.

The sensations he was creating with his teeth, tongue, and the stubble covering his jaw had goosebumps chasing up and down my skin. I weaved my fingers through his short hair and scraped my nails down the back of his head.

Adam growled before giving me a little more than a nip. It wasn't gentle but I definitely didn't mind it. The needy whimper bouncing off the walls a testament to that.

"You like that?" he rasped. When I nodded, his hooded gaze locked onto mine and he bared his teeth in a wolfish grin. *Bye-bye panties*." Then you'll love this."

Needy state or not, I raised my eyebrow. "You sound extremely sure of yourself."

He aimed another one of those panty-melting smirks my way before grabbing my shirt and pulling it over my head. After tossing it aside, he stared at my bared breasts and slicked his tongue over his lips.

That was the only warning I got before he descended and covered one with his hand, closing his mouth over the other. Within the space of a few heavy breaths, I'd turned into a moaning writhing mess of bones while this man did wicked, wicked things to my body.

His hands were freaking everywhere. *Everywhere.* Touching me. Teasing me until there wasn't a single coherent thought left in my brain. Then he was on the move; kissing and nipping a hot path down my body, settling those massive shoulders between my thighs.

I was vaguely aware of Sheldon barking at something, but I couldn't be too bothered not when Adam had his fingers hooked in the waistband of my shorts and he was looking at me like he was about to rock my world.

There wasn't a part of me that didn't ache or throb with the desperate need for this man to give me a release. To push me so far over the edge that catching my breath would be impossible.

I was so ready for it when he pulled at my shorts and dragged his teeth over my hipbone, my entire body surged to life. Back arching, hips bucking. His tongue was hot and wet as he slowly licked his way to the other side.

"I'm gonna devour you until the only name leaving your lips is mine."

Yes! Yes, yes, yes.

" Yoo-Hoo, Maddie-Cakes."

Adam's head whipped up, eyes frantically searching mine. "The fuck?"

Groaning, I rolled my head back and cursed myself for ever telling Frankie where the damn spare key was or that she could use it whenever she wanted to. I was so damn close to getting a release from all this pent-up tension that'd been building and building over the weeks.

She couldn't have waited another hour or so before showing up? The couch dipped, effectively pulling me from my little pity party. When I lifted my head, I found Adam standing with one hand gripping his neck while his gaze flicked between the hallway and the glass door. It took my lust-fogged brain a minute to catch up, and I swear the pure panic on his face had my heart twisting.

I pushed to my feet and after covering my breasts with one arm, I touched my palm to his chest to gain his attention. When his eyes collided with mine, the look in them reminded me of a wild animal. One that felt cornered and scared.

"Go," I said softly, jerking my head toward the door.

He didn't argue. Simply took the out I gave him and even though it hurt just a little that I wouldn't be able to introduce him to my best friend, I understood where he was coming from.

Pushing the sadness away, I scanned the floor for my shirt. I'd just pulled it over my head when Frankie waltzed into the living room, cradling a grocery bag in each arm. "I was out there knocking for ages," she complained. "So, I decided to use the spare key."

Eyes narrowing, her assessing blue gaze scanned the length of me. I stood as still as a statue when all I wanted to do was fidget. "Why didn't you answer the door?" She was staring at a spot on my neck as she asked the question.

"Didn't hear you knock."

"Mmm-hmm." Frankie's head slowly bobbed up and down. "And why is that?"

I licked my lips nervously. If I confessed to her why the sound of her knocking never registered, she'd want to know where the heck Adam was hiding. And then I'd have to tell her about his difficulty being around people.

I didn't want to do that. It was Adam's truth to tell, not mine.

"You're covered in beard burns!" Her screech sounded extremely close all of a sudden. I blinked and blinked again, only to find her standing in front of me, studying the marks on my neck as they were some new discovery.

"Uhm," was about as far as I got before my phone chimed to life. I'd never felt more relieved in my life. Shooting her an apologetic look, I snatched it off the coffee table and pressed it against my ear without checking the caller ID.

"This is Maddie," I said into the phone as I turned my back to avoid Frankie's death-glare.

"Hi Maddie, It's Lucetta."

"Oh! Hi." We'd been keeping in touch via text messages so the fact that she was calling was a bit strange. "How is your mom?"

"She's in a lot of pain, but we knew the healing process would be slow." She paused for a beat. "Especially for someone her age."

"And you?" I asked tentatively. "Are you doing okay?"

I heard her deep intake of breath. "I am. I've had a lot of time to reflect on my life and the choices I've made while I've been down here."

"That's great." *I guess*. There was something in her tone that gave me pause. A little niggle of foreboding trickled down my spine.

"Look, Maddie, I know this is out of the blue, but I don't think I'm coming back to Clearwater Bay."

I couldn't hide my surprise. "You're not?"

A sigh filtered through the line. "No. My mom needs me here, and we're finally breaking down the walls that'd been between us for so long."

I was happy for Lucetta. From the little I knew, I understood that her mother didn't approve of her dancing career. But I couldn't help but wonder, "What's going to happen to Soulbeat?"

In the silence that followed, I wandered to the glass door. Instead of looking out over the ocean, my gaze drifted to Adam's house. "That's actually why I'm calling," Lucetta finally said.

Another beat of silence followed while I waited with bated breath. "I'll be selling the studio, Maddie."

My head was spinning. All I could manage was a muttered, "Okay." Once Soulbeat was sold, I'd have to go back to the hardware store. It was the last thing I wanted. Working in that store would crush my spirit. It sounded harsh, but it was the truth.

I wanted to teach. I'd known from the first moment I stood in for Lucetta. I wasn't destined for a big stage and bright lights and that was completely fine. But not having dance in my life anymore wasn't.

"Are you still there?"

I squeezed my eyes shut and cleared my throat. "Yeah, I'm here."

"Soulbeat has been my life for more years than I care to count," Lucetta began. "I started that studio with nothing more than a degree and a dream." She drew in a deep breath and I opened my eyes; Adam's house still in my line of sight. "I don't want just anyone taking over."

"Of course not," I agreed solemnly.

"This is short notice, I know, and rest assured I won't pressure you into making a decision right away."

A fluttering of hope bloomed in my chest. "Lucetta, what are you talking about?"

"I want you to take over the studio, Maddie. There's no one else I trust more."

My head started to spin again. So much so that I had to smack my hand against the glass door to steady me. Lucetta was still talking, mentioning figures and ways for us to make it work.

"You've given this a lot of thought," I stated when I finally found my voice.

Her response came without hesitation. "I have."

On a shaky breath, I promised her I'd give the decision some real thought and let her know what I wanted to do. By the time we said goodbye and I stabbed the red button, my entire body was shaking.

Frankie appeared by my side a second later. Eyeing her out of the corner of my eye, I let out a nervous laugh. "You're never going to believe what just happened."

The words spilled from my lips without pause. Frankie curled her fingers around my arm and led me to the couch, never once interrupting my frantic ramblings. I loved her all the more for it.

Once I was done talking, I fell back against the couch with a heavy sigh. Tilting my head toward the ceiling, I covered my face with my hands and groaned. "I don't know what to do."

"Well, what do you want to do?"

Dropping my hands, my head rolled to the side. "Of course I want to buy the place. Not only does it have immense sentimental value to me, but teaching…" I shook my head." It's given me new love for this art."

Frankie's smile spread wide. "There's your answer."

"It's not that simple." I sighed again just thinking about it. "I have savings, but not nearly enough to cover the costs."

Ever the optimistic, my friend patted my leg. The grin on her lips never left as she pushed to her feet. "There's always a way. Now, come on, you can fill me in on those beard burns while you test the new sandwich combinations I want to try out."

My gaze stayed glued to her back as she headed into my kitchen. She made it sound so easy, and maybe it was. The real question though was exactly how far was I prepared to go to chase after my dreams.

28

MADDIE

Adam: *I'm sorry I left like that.*

I read over the text for what felt like the hundredth time. It had come through almost three hours ago when Frankie had still been here. She'd done such a great job at distracting me with food, I hadn't even heard my phone.

After I'd walked her out and came back inside the blinking light on my phone caught my attention. And then I saw Adam's message.

Yes, I somewhat understood why he felt the need to flee. But if I were being honest, it'd hurt me a little too. And that just made me feel guilty. I didn't know what it felt like to walk around with scars on my body.

Just because I didn't see him any differently didn't mean others would too. Somewhere at the very back of my mind, a little nagging voice tried to make itself known. What if this thing with Adam grew into something more? Would he always stay in the shadows? Was I going to go to the movies or Oven and Vine alone?

I shook my head and forced that silly little voice to shut the hell up. She was getting way ahead of herself.

Thumbs hovering over the keyboard, I waited a few seconds before I typed my reply.

Me: *It's okay. What's not okay, though, is the frustrated state you left me in.*

It took a while for the little dots to start jumping.

Adam: *I can take care of that.*

I laughed; it sounded a little irritated and nervous. There was nothing I wanted more than for Adam to come and freaking finish what we started but I had to go see my parents. While I still had the nerve.

Me: *I'm going to hold you to that as soon as I get back from my parents.*

When his response popped up, I laughed even more. It was so Adam to just send a thumbs-up emoji. Nibbling on my lip, I slipped my phone into my back pocket and tried very hard to ignore the insistent fluttering in my heart when I thought about the man next door.

The man who had six-foot walls around his heart and still managed to break through every single one of mine. The man who made my knees weak and my heart skip a beat. He was also the one burrowing so deep into every part of me, it was almost impossible to imagine a day without him.

Those thoughts were scary as hell.

No doubt I was falling. Hard. I just wasn't sure whether he'd be there to catch me before I hit the ground.

With a deep breath, I shelved that particular line of thought. I had more pressing matters to attend to.

***

The knots in my stomach twisted tighter and tighter the closer I got to my family home. By the time I walked up the steps and knocked on the door, I was so nervous I thought I might throw up.

I actually almost did when my mom opened the door and greeted me with a wide smile. One I hadn't seen much of lately. The nausea rising in my throat made way for something else entirely when she pulled me to her chest and whispered against my hair, "I'm so happy you're here."

Pulling back, I smiled at her. I wanted the band so tightly wound around my chest to expand, but I knew it wouldn't. Not until I'd spoken to my parents. "Is Dad home? I want to talk to you both."

A mask of worry veiled her features. Her hands shot to my shoulder and gripped them firmly. "Are you all right? Did something happen?"

Swallowing hard, I chose to only answer her first question. "I'm not sick if that's what you're worried about, Mom. I just really need to talk to you and Dad."

Slowly her head bobbed up and down, I could tell she wasn't buying it. Thankfully, she remained quiet as she led me through the house.

My gaze bounced from picture to picture lining the walls. It hadn't been all bad, my childhood. It was only when I started dancing that this wall was erected. One, in all fairness, I hadn't even attempted to climb over. Hopefully, after today we could remove a few of the bricks.

"He's out here," my mom said as we walked through the kitchen and out the back door. My dad was sitting on the patio nose deep in a book. On the chair next to his was my mom's knitting basket.

It must've been nice to simply be in each other's presence while you were still doing something for you. Unexpectedly—or maybe not so unexpectedly—my mind drifted to Adam. He'd happily sit on the beach or anywhere else—where there were no people—and watch me dance. I wasn't sure how I knew; I just did.

And that thought had something else entirely blooming inside my chest.

"Look who stopped by." My mom sounded so thrilled, I felt bad for not coming over more often.

Dad lowered his book and lifted his eyes to mine. I wanted to press my hand against my stomach to keep the knots from twisting and churning. "Madison." He jerked his head in greeting. "What brings you over?"

Deep breaths, Maddie. This was it. The moment that probably could make or break my already fragile relationship with my parents. I took a few more steadying breaths as I dragged a patio chair closer and steadily lowered myself onto it.

My gaze bounced between both my parents before it settled on my dad. "You know how I've been filling in for Lucetta while she's away?" Dad rolled his eyes, and I forced the rest of the words out of my mouth when they wanted to shrink back down my throat.

"She's not coming back and she wants me to take over. Not only will I be able to do something I love but I'll have the opportunity to finally earn a living off of this. The thing is, I only have about seventy-five percent of the amount she's asking, and I was hoping I could—"

"No!" My dad bellowed. "There's no way in hell, I'm going to support this craziness. You can just for—"

"Fraser." Mom reached over and placed her hand on Dad's.

He wasn't having it. Shaking her off, he jumped to his feet and towered over me. "I shouldn't have entertained the idea of this silly hobby. I know how it can destroy."

"Destroy?" I pushed to my feet so fast, my dad had to take a step back. "What on earth is dancing going to destroy? It makes me happy, Dad. And the only one destroying anything is you!"

"Madison," he warned.

"No! All I have ever asked of you was to support my dreams. I'm not you, Dad. That hardware store doesn't bring me joy. I hate it. Because you love it more than your own daughter."

My dad's face turned bright red, the veins on his forehead and neck bulging with fury. He looked to my mom then glared at me before stomping off like an enraged beast. I never knew what real heartbreak felt like until I watched my dad walk away from me like that.

I wanted to cry. I wanted to yell. But mostly I wanted to run away. To be somewhere safe where it was okay to be me.

"Maddie." My mom clasped my hands in hers and pulled me back into my seat. "We should have been honest with you a long time ago. I don't even know why we never said a thing."

I'd never, not once, seen my mom look so forlorn. A part of me wanted to throw my arms around her and just hold her close. I might've done that had it not been for the hurt little girl inside of me demanding to be heard and understood.

"What are you talking about?" I flinched at the ice in my tone.

My mom let go of my hands and smoothed hers down the front of her floral skirt. Her gaze drifted to a spot on the fence, and when she spoke, her voice sounded almost hollow. "There's a reason your father and I don't like dancing."

"That's putting it mildly." I snorted. "You hate it, Mom. Probably because it makes me happy."

Her eyes snapped back to mine lightning fast. Brows pulled together she searched my face. "Is that what you believe?"

I felt the sting of emotion at the back of my eyes and I willed it to stay put until we were done. "It's kind of hard to think anything else when you haven't even given it a shot."

Not once in my life had I spoken to my mom the way I was speaking to her right now. The fact that she wasn't admonishing me about it should've been a warning for what was to come.

"Did you know your father had a sister?" my mom asked softly. I gaped at her because no I hadn't known.

My dad barely spoke about his childhood other than he'd lost both his parents in a bus accident at the age of twenty.

When I said nothing, my mom gave me a wistful look. "You were named after her." She shook her head. "To this day, your father believes we cursed you when we gave you your name."

"What? Why?"

Smiling ruefully, my mom reached for my hand and I let her take it. "Your father's younger sister—your aunt—loved dancing. She lived and breathed it. And, oh Maddie, she was good too. Just like you."

There was a huge ball of emotion lodged in my throat. I could barely breathe around it, let alone swallow. I had no idea my mom had ever seen me dance. And I wanted to know all about the hows and whens right after I learned more about my namesake.

Mom gave my hand a gentle squeeze. "She was two years your dad's junior, and she had more drive and determination in her little finger than most people had in their entire lives."

After sucking in a rough breath, my mom's gaze shifted back to the fence. By the deep lines on her forehead and the sharp angles of her brows, I knew she was lost in some memory.

"What happened to her?" I asked in a whisper, afraid my interruption might startle her to her senses. Then Madison of the past would be lost to me forever.

"She had big dreams of joining the ballet and performing on the world's biggest stages." My mom didn't look at me as she spoke. "And your dad encouraged her to follow those dreams." Her eyes finally met mine. "He was her biggest cheerleader."

Oh, how I wished she hadn't said that. The knife stuck in my chest twisted and sliced away another piece of my heart. Why? Why couldn't he have been *my* cheerleader then too? Gritting my teeth, I willed the stupid tears to stay away.

Maybe it was written all over my face, or it might've been a mother's intuition, but she knew. She was out of her chair and crouched in front of me faster than I could blink. Unlike me, she allowed the emotion to wet her cheeks.

"It's not your fault your father has not forgiven himself over what happened to his sister." Mom wiped a rough hand over her cheek before splaying her fingers over my leg again. "When he thinks of you dancing, all he sees is the way he found his baby sister in some dingy motel that charges by the hour."

"What are you talking about?" I wasn't entirely sure if I wanted to hear the rest of this history lesson. But wanting something and needing it were two different things. And I needed this. Desperately.

Before she straightened, my mom gave my thighs a reassuring squeeze. Using her index fingers, she wiped beneath her eyes as she settled back in her seat. "When it was time for your dad to leave the house, Madison begged him to take her with. She had no interest in finishing school. She just wanted to dance."

Bowing her head, she watched her fingers trace one of the flower patterns on the material of her skirt. "He would've given her the moon if she'd asked him for it. But even that wouldn't have saved her. Dancing is not an easy industry to break into." She pinned me with a stare. "As I am sure you know."

I nodded and she went on." Madison had gone for audition after audition, but they always found someone more experienced. Skinnier. Prettier. It took a toll on her, and she soon realized she couldn't sustain herself like that.

"Now the Youngs were—and still are—a proud bunch. The thought of going home and admitting she'd failed never even crossed her mind. So she started dancing in strip clubs. Turned tricks fairly soon after too."

My heart broke for my dad's sister. I knew how tough it was. Understood the need to succeed and the hurt that followed when you didn't. "Where was Dad when this was happening?"

"Back here in Clearwater Bay." My mom sighed. "His father had needed him at the store. He came back while his sister chased after her dreams in New York."

Man, that sounded eerily familiar.

" He used to visit her over the weekends," my mom continued. "Even took me with him a few times. I can't even tell you how many times I had wished I'd been with him on that fateful day." Tears were streaming down my mom's cheeks, and it was impossible to keep my own away any longer.

"When he'd gone to her apartment, her roommate informed him she hadn't been home in a few days. Your dad spent the entire day going from place to place, chasing down leads that led him to the motel room she was found in."

My mom's shoulders shook with every broken sob that left her body. I was out of my seat and had my arms wrapped around her within seconds. "Oh, Maddie." She wept into my shoulder. "She'd taken a bad batch of whatever she'd been injecting herself with. For two days she was in that room until your father found her. Lifeless."

My tears came hot and fast. I didn't even want to think about how I would feel if I found Jennah's lifeless body. I couldn't fathom how something like that affected your psyche. No wonder my dad was the way he was when it came to dancing.

Holding my mom tighter, I sniffled. "I hate what happened. I really just wish you or Dad had told me about this. It might not have changed how I felt about dancing, but it would've helped me understand better."

My mom pushed me back slightly so she could look me in the eye. "I know, Maddie. Heaven knows we've made so many mistakes when it comes to you girls. It's not an excuse, I understand, but we honestly didn't know any better. Your father's parents blamed him for Madison's death. He was the big brother; he should've protected her. I think in his own way he wanted to protect you and himself, that's why he couldn't fully support you."

What did I say to that? She was making sense, but I was still hurting. Maybe even a little more now that I had the entire story.

I wasn't sure where this left us, though. It was obvious my mom was trying.

But would my dad?

"He loves you, Maddie," Mom said softly. "He might go about showing it the wrong way, but you and Jennah and little Tommy are his world. It's not his fault life had made him hard, and it's not fair he took it out on you."

My mom's arms were around me, and even though I was halfway between sitting and standing and uncomfortable as hell, I wasn't letting go. Her hand smoothed up and down my back as the floodgates finally opened and years of hurt came spilling over my lids.

I ached with every wretched sob that left my body. I cried for the sister my dad lost. For the horror he faced. Wept for the little girl who craved her family's support and never received it.

My heart broke for all of us. Wrapped up in my mom's embrace, I cried until I lost track of time. Until all the pain and anger was purged from my broken soul.

When my mom walked me back to my car after who knew how long, our eyes were puffy, our cheeks mottled and red, and our lips smiling. She hugged me tight once more and begged me to give my dad a chance.

I couldn't promise her I would.

There were a lot of things my Dad and I still had to figure out, but if he was willing to try, I'd be too. Because family was important and even though mine had their faults—myself included—I loved them.

Driving away, I felt lighter. Not completely healed but definitely lighter. And the only person I wanted to see happened to live right next door to me.

29

ADAM

Ugly.
Hideous.
Monster.

Taking in the sight in the mirror, I swallowed hard. How would Maddie react if she saw the gnarly rifts marring my skin? If she knew what had happened to cause me to look like this?

My fingers trembled as I brought them to the raised smoothed skin that spread like an intricate spider web. Covering half of my left pec, sinewy veins bleeding over my ribs and hugging my side.

A frustrated growl tore from my lungs as I dropped my hand and balled it into a tight fist at my side. I bowed my head and swore. I didn't want to be like this, and yet I had no clue how to be different.

Dragging in a ragged breath through my nose, I screwed my eyes shut. Almost immediately, Maddie's face appeared behind my closed lids. Big, beautiful eyes and a smile so bright it could light up the darkest crevices of my tattered soul.

Somewhere between the arguments about Sheldon and the dinners, she'd crawled under my skin and burrowed her way straight into my heart. And if anything, she deserved my truth.

Thing was, I didn't even know what exactly that was anymore.

Opening my eyes, I turned away from the mirror and grabbed my phone from my nightstand. Ass perched on the edge of the bed, I scrolled through the numbers until I found what I was looking for.

I stabbed the green button and pressed the phone against my ear on a deep exhalation. The sound of my heart whooshing in my ears almost deafening. But I had to do this. I had to know the one thing I'd been too afraid to ask.

"I'm beginning to think you've got an alien probe stuck in your arse." If my nerves hadn't been as frayed as they were, I might've laughed at Griffin's greeting. Clearly, he could sense some of my emotional state because when he spoke again the playfulness had disappeared from his tone. "You all right, man?"

I dragged a palm through my hair before sliding it down the back of my head to grip my neck. "I don't know. Can you talk?"

"Aye, give me two secs." Almost immediately I heard muffled voices, one of them female. I felt a little guilty for intruding on his time with his girlfriend. That, of course, had me thinking about Maddie and the way we were interrupted earlier that morning.

Shit, I'd wanted to taste and devour every little inch of her. Still did. Right after I gave her a piece of me I hadn't given to a single person before.

"I'm here." Griffin's voice filtered through the line again. "What's on your mind?"

My right leg started to hop nervously. If I hadn't known any better, I would've sworn a million ants were crawling all over my skin. I needed to move. Jumping up, I started pacing in front of my bed.

"Adam? You still there?"

"I'm here," I croaked. "I...I need to know about the day of the fire."

There was a long pause of silence. Too long. "Shite. Are you sure you want to do this now? It's been years and—"

"Griff," I interrupted, too desperate to know. "Please?"

More silence followed, and I wanted to bang my fist into the nearest wall. But I knew my friend and he was carefully weighing his options, most likely wondering if I'd finally gone stark raving mad.

"What do you want to know?" he finally asked, his tone measured and calm.

This was it. I sucked in a breath through my nose. Held it for three seconds. Then slowly released it through my lips. "Would I have been able to get to her?" The words choked me on the way out. And now I'd voiced the one question that'd been haunting me over three years, I was deathly afraid of the answer.

Even more when a loaded sigh filtered through the line. It gave me pause. My stomach rolled violently, I felt sick. The self-loathing that Maddie had managed to chase away came crashing over me with a force so strong, my knees gave out and my ass connected with the floor.

"No. I tried to tell you, Adam, but you were so far gone. So busy hating yourself." He swallowed so hard, I heard it on my end. "Even if the beam hadn't immobilized you, you would have been too late."

I swiped a rough trembling hand over my face, pausing over my mouth. "But I still failed her." The words came out muffled. "I shouldn't have left in the first place."

"Adam, you can't think like that. You had a fight and you went to the bar to cool off. How the hell were you supposed to know there was a gas leak?" Griffin asked sincerely. "Sometimes bad things happen and we're helpless to stop them. It's messed up and cruel. But it's life."

My heart was slamming against my ribs something fierce. "I told her I wanted a divorce before I stormed out." Shame laced every single word I muttered.

"I'm sorry. But I know Angie knew you didn't mean it." He was quiet for a few moments. "Adam, I understand I could never fathom the pain you were faced with, and I say this with all the respect in the world, but you have to let go."

Every ragged breath I took felt like pulling in fire to my lungs. The back of my eyes stung. My jaw was clenched so tight, I felt the sting of pain in my ears.

Unaware of the battle I was facing, Griffin continued, "It's not right that it happened. And I don't wish this on me worst enemy, but you must know, your life isn't over.

And yes, you have lost a lot, yet you haven't lost everything."

His words echoed in my brain. So loud, I wanted to slap my hands over my ears to make it stop. He was right, I knew he was and that only managed to add more guilt to the heavy load on my shoulders.

"I blamed you," I rasped in a whisper.

"Aye," Griffin said on a slow exhale. "We do and say a lot of things in anger we don't mean to do."

"I'm sorry." The first apology of many I had to offer.

I was a bit stunned when Griffin chuckled on the other end. "There's nothing to apologize for. Not once did I hold it against you."

"But you left Sault Point without even saying goodbye to Mom and Dad."

"Aye, that I did." There was the smallest hint of embarrassment in his tone. "It was never about what you or anyone said or did. I had me own guilt to deal with. And me own mourning to do."

I leaned back against the bed and pulled my legs up, draping my free arm over the top of my knee. "I've been a pretty shitty friend, haven't I? It's three years too damn late, but I am sorry for the things I said to you."

"Already forgotten." The last part of his response tapered off before I heard a muffled female voice followed by Griffin's chuckle and then something that sounded like a smacking kiss.

It didn't really surprise me that Maddie's face popped into my mind. What did surprise me was how desperately

I needed to tell her about everything. Give her all my truth and pray like hell that she wouldn't walk away.

Because Griffin was right. I hadn't lost everything. In fact, I found something. Something so beautiful and precious. So unique. I'd do anything in my power to keep her. And her ugly rat.

"Sorry." Griffin's voice broke through my thoughts. "I haven't seen Rae in three days." He didn't explain and, honestly, he didn't need to. Maddie wasn't even mine and still, the days where I never got to see her or spend time with her were the longest.

"Go be with your woman," I told him. "We'll talk again."

There was a beat of silence and then, "I'm glad you called, Adam."

"Me too."

I wasn't entirely sure how it was possible, but I felt ten times lighter when I hung up. For years, the thought that my last words to Angie had not been the ones she needed to hear had slowly picked away at me. The guilt of not getting to her in time to drag her out of the fire, had consumed me.

I breathed easier knowing a flicker of light had now been cast over the darkness that'd haunted me for so long. I wasn't foolish enough not to realize the road to becoming the man I had been was suddenly going to be an easy one.

However, for the first time in a really long time, I was hopeful.

Even more so when I heard car doors slamming shut. A smile spread across my face. Maddie's visit was probably over which meant I finally got to see her. The few hours that'd passed since I'd had my hands and mouth on her had been a few hours too long.

Pushing to my feet, I snatched a t-shirt from my closet before bounding down the stairs and rushing to the door. I barely had time to pull the cotton over my head when the first knock sounded.

Something about it sounded different but I didn't give it too much thought. Hand on the handle, I took a steadying breath to calm my racing heart before pulling the door open. The calming breath I'd taken mere seconds before didn't do shit when it wasn't Maddie standing on my doorstep but rather my sister.

My very pregnant sister.

"Surpriiiise." Her palms were facing the sky and an uncomfortable smile played on her lips.

Words. I needed words if only they'd come. Seeing my sister—in the flesh—after all this time was somewhat unnerving. Not necessarily in a bad way. She just looked so different. So grown up. I hardly recognized her.

" I hope it's okay we're here?" She spoke so carefully, my heart twisted. I had made her like this around me. It was the walls around *my* heart that'd pushed everyone away and now I needed to lower them.

If only I knew how.

Movement in the street caught my attention. I flicked my gaze over my sister's head and it landed on the SUV parked curbside. Her husband and stepdaughter—she'd kill me if I used that term in front of her because for all intent and purposes the little girl whose name I couldn't remember was hers—were leaned back against it. Probably waiting to see if the monster would bite.

My focus shifted back to Zoe. "I was expecting you in two weeks." She winced, her face falling a moment later. I swore under my breath. Dealing with people face-to-face, even if they were family, was so unfamiliar to me.

Unless it was Maddie.

Everything with her was easy.

I cleared my throat and tried again, "Of course it's all right." The way her lips instantly stretched into a wide grin made my heart smile. Especially when it went all the way to her eyes.

"I'm so happy." She wrung her hands together. "Eli told me to call and check first, but I was so scared you'd say no. And the doctor told me he didn't want me traveling too much in my last trimester, so—"

I stepped forward and placed my hands on her shoulders. "Breathe, Zoe. It really is all right." I took a breath of my own. "I'm happy you're here."

Her husband must've thought something was wrong because he was next to her before I even had time to blink. His arm curled around her waist, and he protectively tucked her against him.

My hands fell to my sides. I took a step back just as he whispered, "You okay, sunshine?"

Zoe tilted her head back and looked at her husband with so much love and adoration. If I thought the smile she'd given me seconds ago was bright, the one she was giving him completely eclipsed it. "I told you he wouldn't mind."

He smiled down at her as if she was his entire world and I swear, I understood what it meant to look at someone like that. To know your life would never be the same again.

As if finally realizing where he was, Eli's gaze shifted to mine. The man didn't even try and hide his scowl and I respected him all the more for it. It was there because of the way I'd handled things with my sister—*his* wife—and I couldn't blame him for being angry on Zoe's behalf.

Wordlessly, he thrust his hand toward me. Holding his assessing gaze, I smacked my palm against his. "Good to see you again, Eli."

With a grunted acknowledgment, he squeezed my hand hard before letting go. It was an intimidation tactic that probably worked on a lot of people. Just not me. If my sister wasn't standing right there next to him looking at me with so much hope shining in her eyes, I would've laughed.

Out of the corner of my eye, I caught a flash of dark hair before the little girl stepped out from behind Zoe's back. My sister immediately wrapped an arm around her and beamed even more. No wonder her husband called her sunshine. She damn well rivaled it in brightness.

"And this is Molly." Zoe's chin tilted up with pride as she introduced her stepdaughter. "I don't know if you remember her?" she added cautiously.

I did.

I remembered how she stared at my scars like I was the big bad boogeyman. Kind of like she was doing right now. Uneasiness rolled over my skin, pulling it tight. A part of me—a very big part—wanted to step back and slam the door shut.

Wanted them to go back from where they came from and leave me the hell alone.

It was the other part, the one that a certain beach ballerina had unlocked, that calmed the beast and reminded me the healing process wasn't always easy or pain free.

With a tight nod, I forced my attention away from her stare and kept my hands tightly pressed against my thighs when all I wanted to do was use them to cover the ugliness on my neck.

"Why don't we go inside." My voice was hoarse, my throat thick. Motioning toward her rounded stomach, I added, "You probably want to sit down."

She was still smiling when she cradled her bump with both her hands. "Yeah, these two are *busy*."

We were silent as I led them through the house and into the living room. Well, all of us except my sister who kept commenting on the barren state of my walls. She even offered to ship me one of her pieces that would look *absolutely amazing* in my hallway.

Once they were settled on the couch, I escaped to the kitchen under the guise of getting refreshments. This was too much. After I'd gotten off the phone with Griffin, I'd felt ready to take a small step forward.

But this was a leap and I wasn't ready.

I couldn't breathe. With every rough inhalation, I desperately tried to force air into my lungs. Tried to find that little something to hold onto. To ground me. But, shit, the walls just kept closing in on me.

Closer and closer they came until I wanted to run.

A warm hand pressed against my shoulder. "Adam." Zoe's voice was so full of concern, I had to screw my eyes shut. "I'm sorry, we shouldn't have just shown up like this. I didn't think."

I snapped my eyes open and spun around to face my sister. Nervously, I scratched at a spot above my eyebrow as I searched for the right words. "It's a little unexpected." Slicking my tongue over my teeth, I blew out air through my nose. "I didn't have time to prepare," I tapped a finger against my forehead, "up here."

"Oh, Adam."

She looked so damn sad for me and I hated it. "I just need a minute."

"What if Eli and Molly take a walk on the beach? It'll just be you and me for a bit. Give us time to…catch up?" I was supposed to be the older one. The one who looked out for her. The protector of her feelings. And here she was doing it for me.

I swallowed thickly. "I don't want to chase them away."

"There will be no chasing," she vowed with a smile. "Molly could not stop talking about the beach for the entire drive up here. And Eli understands."

If she wasn't being so damn nice, I might've told her the only thing her husband understood was the fact that he'd like to ram his fist into my face. Instead, I went with, "That might help a bit."

What I couldn't bring myself to admit to her was how I didn't care about making conversation. Yes, I was completely shit at it and had the personality of a rock, but I knew how and when to sound interested.

The thing I didn't know was how to not feel like hiding when everyone's eyes were on me. When all they saw were the scars maiming my skin. Or how I felt judged and uncomfortable because how miserably I'd failed was stamped onto my skin. Branding me for life.

Sure, I now knew I never had a cold day's chance in hell of actually saving her. But one conversation didn't mean I was suddenly ready to let go of years 'worth of conditioning or that I was able to.

Zoe reached for my hand and squeezed it. "I'll go tell them." One more reassuring squeeze and she was off.

My mind raced while I went through the motions of preparing her tea. Every single frayed thought leading back to Maddie and how desperately I needed her to be there. It was utterly ridiculous, but somehow, I knew her mere presence would have been enough to steady me.

To keep the craziness away.

30

ADAM

What began as a shaky start turned out to be a not-so-bad afternoon. Eli and Molly were gone for most of it while my sister eagerly filled me in on her new life in Willow Creek and how much she adored being an art teacher.

It was impossible not to smile along with her. The happiness she exuded was infectious and honestly, I didn't mind it one bit. By the time her husband and daughter strolled back into the house, the tension in my body had gone from a ten to at least a five.

Molly's curious stares still made me want to go up to my room and close the door. Instead of hiding like I wanted to, I did a slow count to ten and forced my mind into a different direction.

It was a little more difficult to do when everyone piled into the kitchen with me when it was time to prepare dinner. I'd opted for a simple pasta dish that could quickly be slapped together with the hopes they'd give me the little space I needed.

Drawing strength from who knew where, I'd powered through their happy chattering and Zoe and Eli's public displays of affection. Even though those were a little harder to stomach. Not because it was my sister he was kissing like no one was watching, but rather because every time they shared a look, a touch, or a kiss, I thought of Maddie.

I hadn't heard from her all afternoon and it had me feeling restless. From her text that morning I'd believed she was going to stop by after she'd visited with her parents. Hell, a part of me was even looking forward to introducing her to Zoe.

But as the sun slowly started to make way for the moon and I still hadn't heard from her, I seriously doubted she was going to show up. My heart constricted at the thought of not seeing her.

Amazing how vital she'd become to my everyday life. How I needed to see her and talk to her to feel the peace I was always chasing. As I knew the case would be, my mind never wondered far from her. Not while we were eating or even when we collapsed onto the couches after that.

By the time my sister excused herself a little after eight with Molly bounding up the stairs after her, I kind of hoped Eli wanted an early evening too. Not only had I hit my cap on socializing for the next month, but I wanted to go see Maddie.

Because, shit, I missed her.

I wanted to touch her. Kiss her. Hold her. I needed it as desperately as I needed air to breathe. My thoughts were intruded upon when Eli cleared his throat from his perch on the couch opposite mine. I was fully expecting him to finally give me a piece of his mind. That was not what happened. He cleared his throat again, the sound almost uncomfortable. With a slight cock of his head, his gaze flicked to the staircase.

"Being here with you means a lot to her," he finally said when his gaze met mine again. "I don't need to know how things went down. It ain't my business, but *she* is." Pausing for a beat, he gave me another look I was certain was meant to intimidate me. "I'm not asking you to suddenly call her every day or come down for regular visits. I am reminding you she loves you, and hearing from you more than once in a while puts a giant smile on her face."

I held his stare as he pushed to his feet. Slowly, he walked across the room toward the stairs where he paused. "Thank you for making my wife smile today." With that, he pivoted and took the stairs two at a time until he too disappeared from view.

My brain was a jumbled mess I needed to clear. Normally when I felt like this, I'd escape to the garage and put my body through a strenuous workout. I didn't want that tonight. Straightening, I flicked off the television and quietly made my way to the glass door. Careful not to make too much noise, I slid it open and slipped outside before sliding it shut in the same manner.

Soft light spilled from Maddie's living room and my heart thudded excitedly. The anticipation of seeing her, possibly even holding her, propelled me forward. My legs moving faster with every step I took.

In less than a minute, I'd hopped over the fence and rushed toward her door and almost choked on a laugh when it was shut completely. The curtains were pulled back though, giving me the perfect view of her curled up on the couch, eyes focused on the television.

One look at her and already my body relaxed. My chest expanded, and the calmness that only she could give started crawling over my skin. Stepping up to the door, I gave the glass two sharp taps.

Her head snapped my way and her lips slowly lifted into a smile. I swear, my heart just about gave out. Knowing she was at least somewhat happy to see me did things to me. Strange, inexplicable things that I wanted so much more of.

Before she had time to get up, Sheldon was already standing on his hind legs, furiously scratching at the glass. That had me grinning because I had no clue why the little shit had latched on to me as he had. I just knew I owed him the biggest piece of steak for leading me to his human.

My person.

My Maddie.

Man, it was scary how far ahead of myself I was getting. There was no use in dancing around what I felt for her anymore. Without even trying, she'd slipped past every single one of my defenses and took up residence in my heart.

The door slid open with a low hiss. Sheldon immediately attacked my leg as if he hadn't seen me in days. As I always did, I stooped and gave him a quick rub behind the ears and on the belly before pushing to my feet again.

"Bewitched, I tell you." With her shoulder propped against the doorframe and arms tucked under her breasts, she nibbled on her lip. "He isn't the only one."

One look at her and my insides turned over. I was in front of her, cradling her cheeks in my palms before she had time to blink. "You were crying again." The words came out low and angry. Not at Maddie, but the person who'd caused her to hurt.

In contrast to her red-rimmed eyes and blotchy cheeks, her lips spread into a smile. One that didn't look remotely forced. "They're not all sad tears." Her gaze held mine. "Wanna come in?"

"Yeah."

She took my hand and led me to the couch she'd just vacated. Once we were seated, Sheldon hopped on and made himself comfortable on my lap. Maddie gave her dog one look and immediately shook her head as she reached for the remote and turned off the television.

One of my hands dug into the fur on Sheldon's head while the other wrapped around Maddie's fingers. Her gaze immediately dropped to our connected hands. When she looked up at me again, I swear, I felt my heart split in half.

She looked broken and vulnerable but also strangely at peace.

"Remember how I told you about Lucetta and the dance studio?" I nodded and she swallowed before continuing. "Well, I have the opportunity to make it mine. So, this morning when I said I was going to see my parents, it was to ask them to help me."

I didn't even think about the words, they just spilled from my lips without hesitation. "If they can't help you, I can. I have more than enough savings. Whatever you—"

"Adam," Maddie gently interrupted my rambling. She let go of my hand and scooted closer to press her palm against my cheek. Eyes flicking between mine, she whispered, "You sweet, sweet man."

"Is that why you're sad," I pressed. "Because they said no?"

Her hand found mine again. "No, not really. My mom and I had a heart to heart today—our first one ever—and I learned things. Big things that will take a while to process but have already given me some sense of understanding." She shook her head, an embarrassed laugh blowing over her lips. "Am I even making sense?"

"So much." I reached forward to cup the back of her neck and Sheldon moaned in protest. Chuckling at the way too comfortable dog, I tugged Maddie's face to mine. "When you're ready, will you tell me about it?"

She shut her eyes and ran her nose along mine before pulling away. With those beautiful eyes trained on me, she smiled and said, "I'm ready." The story she told me after those two words was devastating. And even though, I could maybe understand why her dad acted the way he had, my heart shattered into a million pieces for the little girl who never understood why.

When she was done, I immediately took her face in my hands. "Oh, baby. I hate you had to go through all of that." My thumb brushed over her cheek before sliding down to follow the line of her cupid's bow. "That why you didn't come over today?"

"Mostly, yes." She licked her lips, the tip of her slick tongue catching the pad of my thumb. "I saw an SUV I haven't seen on the block before parked in front of your house. I didn't want to disturb in case you had company."

" It's my brother-in-law's."

Her eyes went wide, eyebrows shooting up. "Your sister was visiting you?"

"Still is. They're asleep in my guest room. But I wanted to see you, so I snuck out."

Maddie's gaze roamed over my face for what felt like an eternity. "Why?"

I'd been so focused on the hurt in her eyes when I'd arrived, I'd forgotten I'd come over to lay my ugly truth at her feet. To confess my failures and pray like hell she'd want me. Only now I wasn't so sure I had the courage to go through with it. Because if Maddie walked away from me today, I wouldn't survive it.

I let go of her face and bowed my head, working my clammy palms up and down my thighs.

" Adam." Maddie's hand landed on my shoulder. "What's going on?"

Chin still pressed to my chest; my gaze flicked to hers. "There are things about me I need you to know."

"Okay," she said softly. "You can tell me anything."

Shit! Could I do this? Could I really cut open these wounds and show her how nasty they were? I didn't know. But damn if I wasn't going to try.

I lifted Sheldon off my lap and set him on the floor. Shifting in my seat, I faced Maddie. Our gazes connected and held while I poked my tongue against my cheek and blew out a loaded breath.

"Today was the first time in over eight months where Zoe, my sister, and I were in the same room. And before that, it'd been years." Stubbornly, the rest of my words refused to come out. Closing my eyes, I begged for the strength to give her this broken part of me.

The fingers brushing over my hand closed around it in a tight, reassuring hold. I opened my eyes and was immediately met with Maddie's beautifully patient stare.

Deep breath in.

Slow breath out.

"A little over three years ago, I left my home to go have a few drinks, When I came back, the building was engulfed. Giant orange flames viciously licked up the walls and capped the roof."

Her eyes grew a little, but she remained silent. I was thankful for that. The hard part, the hardest part, was about to come. "Angie, my wife, had been trapped inside. I was a trained firefighter, I knew better than to run into a burning building without gear or backup, but when you're on the other end of it, you don't think straight.

"I never made it very far before one of the beams tore from the roof. It slammed against my shoulder and pinned me to the floor. There was too much heat, too much smoke. My body fought and fought but eventually, I passed out. Woke up in the hospital looking like…." I swallowed roughly, and Maddie pressed her trembling fingers to her lips. "Well, like this."

My leg was doing that hoppy thing again. Jumping up, I speared my fingers through my hair and started pacing. "I had so much guilt over not being able to save Angie and then every time I looked into a mirror, I saw this hideous beast looking back at me. I pushed everyone away. My parents. My sister. My best friend."

I stopped in front of her and dropped my hands to my hips. Maddie tilted her head back; our gazes met and held. Licking my lips, I forced the words from my tongue, "At first I couldn't leave the house, then I refused to leave my room. My mom tried everything. She hired nurses and housekeepers, but I chased them all away. Because they'd always stare. No one looked at *me*, they only saw this," I ground out, flicking my hand toward my neck.

Slowly, torturously slow, Maddie climbed off the couch. "I see *you*," she whispered. Just like they had on the beach the other morning, those three words held so much conviction.

Closing my eyes, I nodded once before reaching over my head to grip my shirt between my fingers. One rough tug and the material was up and over. Releasing an unsteady breath, I opened my eyes just as I dropped my tee to the floor.

I had run into burning buildings more times than I could count. Walls had crumbled around me, roofs had caved in. But not once had I been as nervous as I was right then. My heart pounded so hard, so fast, I feared it might give out. I wanted to look at her, to see the expression on her face but I was afraid to.

Taking the coward's way, I screwed my eyes shut again and waited for the sound of her disgust to reach my ears. I waited and waited and fucking waited but it never came. When I opened my eyes, Maddie wasn't looking at my scars; her gaze was on me.

No disgust.

No pity.

But rather something that looked a hell of a lot like amazement.

I didn't deserve it.

Averting my gaze, I tried to turn my face away. Maddie pressed her palm against my cheek and guided me back. "Don't hide, Adam. Not from me."

Emotion pushed up my throat and I gritted my teeth to keep it down. A task made more difficult by the gentle way she was touching me. Her fingers moved along my jaw in a slow caress, brushing over my stubbly scruff before smoothing down my neck.

I knew where she was going and, so help me, I wanted to stop her.

The tips of her fingers traced over my collarbone and down over my pec. She was an inch away from the ugliness that covered most of my left side.

When her questioning gaze lifted to meet mine, my heart slammed against my ribs like a wild animal desperately trying to break free. Still, with a stiff nod, I gave her permission to proceed.

Because I wasn't expecting it, a sharp breath hissed from my lungs when instead of her fingers, she touched her lips against my mangled skin. Palms pressed to my side, she dragged her mouth over my scars. The touch registered in the deepest darkest part of my being. The part only she could reach.

I speared my fingers into her hair, grabbing a fist full of the silky tresses. One small tug and she lifted her head and met my gaze.

"No one has ever touched me like this." The words came out hoarse and broken. My chest squeezed tight, verging on the edge of being painful.

This gorgeous woman pushed onto the balls of her feet and pressed her lips to the side of my jaw. "There's not a single part of you I don't want, Adam." Another kiss. "Your broken parts fit with mine." She pulled back and studied me. "Tell me I'm not alone in this."

My hand slipped from her hair to cradle her cheek. I damn near lost it when her lids fluttered closed as she pressed into my touch. Did she even have any idea how fast and hard I was falling for her?

Dropping my forehead to hers, our mouths hovered just a whisper apart. Precariously dangling on the edge of what would be an amazing kiss. Tilting my head slightly, my bottom lip brushed over hers.

"I'm right there with you, baby."

I crashed my mouth to hers, our tongues immediately slipping, sliding, tasting. Our movements urgent. Frantic. Maddie's hands were all over me while I buried one of mine in her hair and swept the other down to fill my palm with her ass.

Curling my fingers, I squeezed hard and pressed her soft body even more flush against mine. She moaned into my mouth. The sound so incredibly sexy, it had me twitching with need.

I used the hand fisted in her hair to tilt her head; deepening an already impossibly deep kiss. One that wasn't just physical. Every bold stroke of her tongue against mine reached further and further into the darkness that'd controlled me for so long; breaking the chains link for link.

"Bed," she mumbled breathlessly against my lips. A bed would have definitely made it a hell of a lot easier for me to do all the things I'd only imagined doing to her hot little body.

"Mhm." I sucked her bottom lip between my teeth before giving it a little bite, earning me a sinful sound somewhere between a gasp and a sigh. "Take me to bed, Maddie."

Sliding her fingers through mine, she made her way up the stairs. With my gaze firmly fixed on her swaying hips, I followed. Once we slipped into her bedroom, I hardly had a chance of taking in the décor.

The instant the door clicked shut—I didn't want Sheldon watching us—she was on me. Legs wrapped around my waist, hands spearing through my hair. She kissed me like she'd been starving for this. For us. And damn, if I didn't feel it too.

Her mouth was hungry as it sought out skin to latch onto. Nipping, sucking, licking. She was driving me insane and we hadn't even started yet. I began moving with haste, only stopping when we tumbled to her bed in a mess of tangled limbs.

I palmed her ass and hissed out an unholy sound when she shoved her hand down the front of my sweatpants and held me tight as her tentative little fingers moved in a way that felt like pleasure and torture combined.

So good.

It felt so damn good.

Maybe a little too good.

And if she kept on stroking me like she was, it was definitely going be over before I even had time to properly take my fill of her. Gripping her wrist, I moved fast, flipping us over so I could straddle her.

Maddie tilted her head back and looked up at me; lids heavy, eyes filled with filthy, filthy promises. I wanted her to make good on every single one of them as soon as I delivered a few of my own.

Lifting her lips into a downright sinful smile, she trailed her free hand up my thigh, I quickly grabbed it and pinned both hands high above her head.

"Don't move those."

Sucking in her bottom lip, she slowly worked it back and forth over her teeth. "And if I do?" she asked, voice all sugary sweet. "What will happen then?"

Tightening my hold on her wrists, I leaned down and grinned wickedly. The tip of my nose brushed along the length of hers. My mouth teasing her with a promise of a kiss before pulling away.

"You really want to find out?" I rasped against her parted lips, earning me another one of those body shivers. I got a strange kick out of knowing I could affect her the exact same way she affected me.

"Maybe."

Holding her gaze, I slowly slid my palms down her outstretched arms, her eyes burning hot with desire. For *me*.

It was some fucking high knowing the woman I ached for felt the same way about me.

My hands kept moving. Down and down they went, brushing the sides of her breasts as I made my way to the hem of her shirt.

In one fluid motion, I lifted the flimsy piece of cotton over her head and tossed it aside. I sucked in a sharp breath when I found her breasts bare and absolutely perfect. Unable to resist, I bent down and drew a tip into my mouth.

Flicking my tongue before rolling her sensitive skin between my teeth.

The moment I applied more pressure, Maddie's back arched off the bed, a low "*mmm*" echoing from the back of her throat.

Smiling against her skin, I trailed my fingers down her body, circling the stud in her naval before toying with the waistband of her shorts. "Feel good?"

"Yesss." Eyes screwed shut, her head rolled back and pushed deeper into the pillow.

Shifting my body, I tugged and pulled until my hand was trapped between the fabric of her underwear and her warm skin. "How 'bout this?" My ego not the only thing swelling when I found her hot and ready.

So damn ready.

Closing my mouth over her breast, I pushed my fingers inside her. Her hips bucked, and I sucked harder as she shamelessly writhed against me.

Pushing her over the edge would've been so damn easy, but selfishly I wanted to be right there with her when she slipped into ecstasy. Wanted to feel her tighten around me before her world exploded.

I pulled my hand away and sat up on my knees, Maddie's loud moan of protest shortly on my heels. She looked about three seconds away from cussing me out until I hooked my fingers in her waistband and pulled off her shorts and underwear.

Slipping from the bed, I shoved my pants and briefs down my legs and kicked them to the side. Maddie nibbled on her lips, eyes slowly tracking down the length of my body, pausing at the important parts with a salacious grin tugging on her mouth.

Shit! I was man enough to admit she was knocking me on my damn ass.

Rooted to the spot, I held her gaze as she crawled toward the edge of the bed and pushed onto her knees to drape her arms over my shoulders. Tilting her head, she pressed her lips against my jaw, slowly working her way to the shell of my ear.

My arms banded tight around her waist, pulling her naked body flush against mine. I was assaulted with all things Maddie at once. Her warmth. Her sweetness. Her delicate strawberry scent. And when she sucked my lobe into her mouth and rolled it between her teeth, a deep, deep groan tore from my lungs.

Working her fingers through the hair at my nape, she dug the tips into my scalp. "I want you inside me, Adam. Right. Now." To reiterate her words, she rubbed against me, pulling a string of curses from my lips.

That was also the time I realized something very important that could potentially kill the mood. With another muttered curse, I dropped my head to her shoulder. "Shit, Maddie. I didn't come here thinking this would happen." Lifting my head, I chuckled ruefully. "I don't have protection."

Maddie's cheek popped out like she was sticking her tongue against it. Her gaze roamed over my face; eyes so serious it made my heart stop. My breath remained trapped in my lungs as she slowly brought her hand to my cheek.

"I have some in the drawer, but..." She closed her eyes and swallowed. When she opened them again, the vulnerability shining her irises nearly killed me. "I'm on the pill, and... I trust you."

My heart stuttered inside my chest. "Are you sure? I haven't been—"

"I trust you, Adam," she repeated her words in a whisper. "Wholeheartedly."

Cradling her face between my palms, I touched my mouth to hers. Kissing her with fervor. Each swipe of my tongue fueled by something deep within me. Feelings I couldn't or wouldn't name.

Feelings that had the power to not only burn but destroy me.

Gently pushing her onto her back, I hovered over her. I wanted to tell her how beautiful she was. How by just being her she'd brought so much light and happiness to my life.

Before I could utter a single word, Maddie hooked her legs around me and dug her heels into my ass. The action pulled my hips down, aligning us perfectly. All it took was one sure thrust forward and I was lost in her warmth.

"Fuck," I groaned. "You feel so damn good."

But I couldn't move. Not yet. Not when it took every last bit of willpower I had to keep my self-control in check. To not ravage her like the starved beast I was.

Unaware of what was going on inside me, Maddie arched her back and swept her palms over my shoulders. Digging her fingers into my skin, she tried to rock against me. And still I couldn't bring myself to move an inch.

"You have to move," she hiccupped against my skin.

Knowing she was right, I pulled back before gently easing into her again.

As much as I craved to screw her senseless, the last thing I ever wanted to do was hurt her in any way. Sucking in a breath through my nose, I rolled my hips once, twice; desperately trying to keep my sanity.

My self-control.

It was stupid of me to think that Maddie wouldn't notice. Lifting her head, she drew my lip into her mouth and bit, hard. "I want it all, Adam. All. Of. It."

With a curse, I sucked in a sharp breath and began to move. It wasn't sweet and slow like I'd wanted it to be. It was me losing all control, like a shot of pure ecstasy straight into the veins.

Addictive.

All-consuming.

My hands shot to her hips, fingers digging into her soft skin as I continued drive into her over and over again. I soon realized my fears of hurting her were completely unnecessary when Maddie matched me thrust for brutal thrust.

"Just like that." She moaned, clawing at my back, the sharp edges of her nails scraping over my skin.

I wanted more.

I wanted everything.

Hooking my hand behind her knee, I pushed her leg to her chest. I sucked her breast into my mouth, our hips finding a faster, wilder rhythm.

"So close," she whimpered as we continued to chase our release like to two rabid animals. The sound of skin slapping against skin, her moans, my grunts bouncing off the walls the closer we got to that sweet state of bliss.

It was Maddie who fell first. Throwing her head back, she cried out my name and then pulled me into an abyss of ecstasy with her. I swear, it hit me so hard, I saw stars. Fucking stars. It shouldn't have surprised me, though, because nothing with this woman was ever normal.

Chest heaving, breaths coming fast, I pressed my forehead against hers. "Holy shit, baby."

"Yeah." She smiled lazily." That." Her hand came up, fingers trailing over the scars on my neck. "You okay?"

Behind my ribcage, my heart turned over. This woman was nothing short of amazing and I hoped like hell for all the shit I'd done, I'd still get to keep her. Holding her gaze, I dropped a kiss to the corner of her mouth, and then another to the opposite side.

For the first time in an impossibly long time, there was truth in my words when I said, "Yeah… In fact." I grinned and turned us over so she was straddling me. Her eyes went wide when I lifted my hips.

"Again?" she asked incredulously. "Didn't you just…" Laughing, she shook her head. "How?"

My hands smoothed up over her chest. "I've had way too much time to imagine all the things I want to do to you. Did you really think once would be enough?"

I had a sneaky suspicion if I had her for the rest of my days, it still wouldn't be enough.

31

MADDIE

Feather-light kisses brushed over my forehead, down my nose, and at each corner of my mouth. Popping my eyes open, I smiled happily. Next to all the deliciously wicked things Adam had done to my body through the night, waking up to his lop-sided grin had to be my favorite.

It made my heart sing and gave the butterflies in my stomach their wings. "I like waking up with you in my bed," I told him honestly.

The grin on his lips stretched into something wide and beautiful that went all the way up to his eyes. "I like being in your bed."

My gaze flicked down his torso, expecting to see muscles stacked on top of delicious muscles to trace with my fingers and my tongue. That was not what I found. He was already dressed in his sweatpants and t-shirt. Pushing into a seated position, I pulled the sheets over my chest and leaned back against the headboard. "Already leaving?" I tried not to pout, I really did, but it was impossible to hide my disappointment. Especially since I was hoping for another round of bed gymnastics.

Adam dragged his thumb over my lips and chuckled. "I still have guests, remember?"

Nope, I didn't remember. The only thing I recalled about the previous night was how completely open and honest he'd been with me and the feeling of those massive muscles shifting beneath my touch as he moved over me.

Under me.

Behind me.

Just thinking about it sent wonderful shivers down my spine that had me rubbing my thighs together. Adam laughed even louder, the sound of it coating my insides with warmth. "You're even worse than I am," he exclaimed.

"What?"

He gripped my chin between his fingers and drew my face to his. "I know exactly where your mind had gone just then, and trust me when I say I want nothing more than to crawl back under the covers with you and love on your body until you can't walk."

Oh, holy hell. The things that came out of this man's mouth. "But it would look very strange if my houseguests wake up and the host is missing," he continued, unaware of how he was turning me on.

He smoothed his hand up over my cheeks, his gaze turning serious. "Come with me?"

"What?" Apparently, that was the only word my brain now knew.

Those dark eyes roamed over my face. "Meet my sister. Have breakfast with us or just stay for coffee."

Inside my chest, my heart started on its wild gallop. Taking a deep breath, I tried not to overthink, not to read too much into what he was asking of me. Yes, last night he'd told me he was right there with me, but he had no idea how far gone I was.

Mistaking my silence for something else, Adam frowned and started pulling away. "It's okay if you don't want to."

"No." I hooked my fingers around his neck and drew him back to me. "I want to." I pressed a small kiss against his lips, but he quickly moved to deepen it. Turning my face, I muttered shyly, "Morning breath."

Again, my chin was trapped between Adam's strong fingers. "You think I give a shit about that?" He didn't give me a second to respond before he smashed his mouth against mine; kissing me until my toes curled.

When he was satisfied he'd kissed me good and stupid, he pulled back and grinned victoriously. "Get dressed, I'll wait downstairs."

Adam dropped one more quick kiss to the tip of my nose before he casually strode out of my bedroom. Considering I was about two nanoseconds away from jumping his bones, downstairs was a good place for him to be.

Less than twenty minutes later, showered and dressed, I came bouncing down the stairs. A smile immediately lifting my lips when I found Adam sitting on the couch with his arms stretched across the top and Sheldon curled up on his lap like a cat.

"I think my dog likes you more than me."

At the sound of my voice, his head whipped up in my direction. I tried not to fidget when his gaze steadily swept over the light pink blouse I'd knotted at my naval and down over the white skinny jeans covering my legs.

In one quick, gentle move, Adam lifted Sheldon off his lap and set him on the empty space beside him. Eyes trained on me, he rose and walked over to where I was standing, his powerful legs eating up the distance between us in no time.

The instant he stopped in front of me, he pushed his fingers into my hair and lowered his mouth to mine. His inked arm snaked around my waist, hand sliding down until he could squeeze my butt.

And then his mouth was on mine, effectively robbing of every sane thought I had. Because, holy freaking hell, this man kissed like he was put on this earth with the sole purpose to do just that. Every greedy swipe of his tongue making me crave more.

More kisses.

More Adam.

He pulled my lip between his teeth; giving it a gentle bite before pulling away. "You look gorgeous."

I'd never in my life blushed at a compliment from a man. Not once. Yet, there I was glowing like a damn tomato because of his words. Dragging my fingers through my hair, I scoffed, "You mean I look thoroughly kissed."

With a way too sexy grin, he swiped his thumb over my lips. "That too." Reaching for my hand, he laced our fingers together. "You ready?"

I nodded and after we fed Sheldon and let him do his business, the three of us made our way to Adam's place. Since I had no intention of jumping over the fence, we left through my front door and walked the long way around.

I laughed when he led me around back. Apparently, like me, he used the sliding door that led to his back yard a lot more than the front one. Squeezing one eye shut and sinking his teeth into his bottom lip, he tried his hardest to slide the door open with as little sound as possible.

Once we stepped inside, he immediately sought out my hand again. I could hardly believe how giddy that simple action made me feel. Like he needed me as much as I needed him to anchor me.

Walking slowly, we rounded the corner and almost got run over by a woman with an enormous belly.

"Are you nuts?" she screeched, hands clutching her chest and eyes taking up half of her face. "You could have scared me into early labor."

I was fairly certain that wasn't a thing, but I also knew better than to correct a heavily pregnant woman. Besides, I definitely didn't want to make a bad first impression on his sister.

Adam's hold on my hand tightened. "Sorry. Didn't mean to scare you." His shoulders lifted in a quick shrug. "I thought you guys would still be asleep."

A loaded sigh blew over her lips and her hands moved in slow circles over her belly. "I wish. These two are preparing me for all the sleepless nights I'll have to endure once they arrive." Her voice was soft, her smile content. I didn't think she was going to mind having those sleepless nights too much.

As if just realizing her brother wasn't alone, her gaze bounced between me and Sheldon before settling on me. My skin prickled with an awareness I hadn't experienced before. It wasn't necessarily discomfort but rather a need for her to like me for no other reason than she was Adam's sister.

That right there spoke volumes to how much this man meant to me. And it scared me a lot more than I was willing to admit.

Adam squeezed my hand once more. "Zoe, I'd like you to meet Maddie." He hefted the dog under his arm a bit higher." And Sheldon."

She had no interest in my dog at all. Her gaze swept over me in a quick once-over before she thrust her hand out and smiled." Nice to meet you, Maddie."

To shake her hand, I had to let go of Adam's. I missed the security of it almost immediately. Touching my palm to hers, I gave her a smile of my own. "Likewise." We stood like that for a few seconds longer than what was deemed normal. I had no doubts she was sizing me up, making sure I was good enough for her brother. Or something like that.

I had to suppress my sigh of relief when she finally released me. Her curious stare never left me, though. Of course, Adam chose that moment to stoop and whisper in my ear, "I need to take a shower. Will you be okay here for a couple of minutes?"

My eyes flicked to the man beside me and I wasn't entirely sure if I'd ever get used to the way he looked at me. "I'll be fine." One corner of his mouth curved upward and for a second it looked like he wanted to kiss me but then thought better of it.

"I'll be right back." He bent and set Sheldon on the floor, who instantly trotted after him. Seemed like my heart wasn't the only one Adam had taken up residence in.

I was still staring after them like a lovesick fool when a soft touch to my arm snatched my attention away from the stairs. "I was going to make some tea; would you like a cup?"

"Please."

Wordlessly, I trailed behind Zoe as we made our way to the kitchen. I slipped onto one of the chairs at the dinette while she busied herself with preparing our drinks. When she was done, she set a steaming cup with a string dangling off the edge in front of me. With a few grunts, she took the seat opposite me.

"I have to be honest," Zoe said, steadily lifting the teabag in and out of the boiling water. "I wasn't expecting my brother to have a friend who is a girl." I liked how carefully she had phrased that. Not jumping to conclusions even though her brother and I had snuck into his house hand in hand at the crack of dawn.

"I don't think he expected it either," I told her honestly.

Nodding, she let out a little laugh laced with concern. Her gaze flicked to the entryway for a beat before coming back to me. "Do you know what happened?"

It didn't feel right telling her that her brother had given me his truth or at least a big chunk of it. Shifting in my seat, I sat up straighter. "I know he's been through a lot."

Her eyes narrowed like she was trying to get a read on me. "He has, and unfortunately he hasn't come out unscathed."

"I know," I admitted quietly.

Zoe looked me dead in the eye. "Whatever is going on between you and Adam isn't my business. But if it is what I think it is, I am begging you not to hurt him." Her eyes turned glassy. "I just got my brother back."

My mouth opened and closed so many times, I probably looked like a fish out of water desperately gasping for air. I wanted to tell her I'd never do anything to hurt him intentionally, but before a single sound escaped my lips, a streak of black came whirling past me.

A little girl with the longest dark hair launched herself at Zoe and hugged her tight. The expression on both their faces tugged on something deep inside me.

I'd never really given thought to the whole married with kids thing. But here I was, sitting in Adam's kitchen wondering what that might look like. Imagining a little boy with Adam's dark hair and dark eyes running around, squealing happily.

I could see it so easily, it scared the crap out of me.

"Are you okay?" I blinked and found two gazes on me. One worried and the other curious. "You look a little pale," Zoe added.

Swiping my hand over my mouth, I nodded, "Yeah." But I wasn't and I didn't know how to handle these new feelings. They felt big. Almost too big and the risk of my heart being broken all too real.

My legs felt restless. The need to jump up and run so incredibly strong. But would I really be able to outrun my feelings? To beg my heart to slow down. To not fall so hard.

Before I even realized what I was doing, I slowly pushed to my feet.

"Will you please tell Adam I'm not feeling well and I'll get Sheldon from him a bit later?" I didn't wait for her response, simply spun on my heels, and started walking toward the door.

A few steps into my escape, Zoe called after me, her hurried footfalls closing in. I stopped; screwed my eyes shut for a beat before opening them and pivoting. The poor woman looked white as a ghost when she grabbed my hand. "Please don't go. I'm sorry if I made you uncomfortable or said—"

"You didn't do anything, I promise." Patting her hand, I gave her a pleading look, hoping she'd let me go. Give me the space I needed to sort through the mess inside of me.

My shoulders sagged with relief when she released her grip on my hand. "It was nice meeting you, Maddie." Zoe took a step backward. "I hope I get to see you again soon."

"Me too." I spun around and rushed out of the house as if the hounds of hell were giving chase. With every step

I took, my legs moved faster and faster. The tension coiled so tightly around me eased somewhat when I set my hand on the little gate. Until…

"Maddie?"

No.

Taking a steadying breath, I turned to face Adam. He was dressed in dark jeans and a white t-shirt that clung to his muscles like a second skin. Hair still wet from his shower and brows tightly knitted together.

"Where are you running off too?" Adam asked in a low gruff voice.

I opened my mouth and lied through my teeth. "I'm not running."

Eyebrow arching, Adam gave me a pointed stare. "Really? You call this not running?"

Every fiber of my being begged me to step forward right into that massive chest and have those thick arms wrapped around me. I needed it like I needed my next breath. And because of that, I hugged myself instead.

"You scare me, Adam." The words came out barely above a whisper, but he heard me all the same.

I saw hurt flash in his eyes before he blinked it away. "I do?"

"Yes." Closing my eyes, I sucked in a deep breath and decided to dive into the deep end. To serve up my heart on a silver platter. His for the taking…or the breaking. My lids parted and the words rushed out of my mouth. "I'm terrified. I shouldn't be feeling what I'm feeling. It's too soon."

Behind my ribcage, the sacrificial organ thundered about wildly. Adam's eyes, dark so very dark, bore into me but I couldn't read a single emotion in them. Suddenly, I felt vulnerable and exposed. Swallowing roughly, I twisted my head away from him.

Not even a second later, Adam gripped my chin and guided my gaze back to his. "Didn't I tell you I was right there with you?" he rasped, his voice cracking on the last word. Adam moved to cup my cheek, his thumb brushing back and forth over my skin. "It scares me too, but not finding out where this can lead scares me even more."

His gaze roamed over my face. Serious. Searching. It made my skin feel about two sizes too small and had every hair on my body standing on end.

"Be mine, Maddie? Just mine."

Instead of voicing my answer, I lifted onto the balls of my feet; winding my arms around his neck and pushed my fingers into his hair. I kissed him with everything I had in me. And I knew without an ounce of doubt that I was never getting my heart back.

32

ADAM

"I like her." My sister nudged my arm with her shoulder as we walked along the beach. Maddie had left not too long ago after she received a message from her sister about some party. It didn't take Zoe long to drag my ass out for a walk.

She had questions, probably a million of them. Since her inquisition had been cut short by her husband not long after Maddie and I had walked back into the house, I knew she'd find a way to get her answers.

My gaze skittered over the ocean. There was no wind, no crashing waves. Only calmness. Exactly what I felt deep in my bones. "So do I," I said to Zoe as we stopped walking and turned to face the big blue.

In the quiet that followed the past three years played out like a movie in front of me. In it, I was the antagonist. Selfishly putting up walls around myself and shooting hurtful arrows at the people who cared for me even when I didn't deserve it.

Twisting, I looked at my sister. She'd gone to hell and back all by herself and not once did she shift the blame onto anyone else. "Zoe, I'm so sorry. I should've been there for you. Protected you."

Shaking her head, she tucked a few of her blonde strands behind her ear. "You know I don't hold it against you, right? You had your own battles to fight."

"But maybe if I had pulled my head out of my ass, I would've been able to see that you needed me."

More head shaking. "Don't do that. The past is the past. No amount of anything can change it." Zoe reached for my hand and squeezed. "Honestly, if I had to go through it all again just so I could have Eli, Molly, and these babies inside me, I would. Sometimes we have to walk through the pits of hell to find our own slice of heaven."

Shit if I didn't understand exactly what she meant. I had been in my own version of hell when Maddie had found me. Looking back, it was those horrible events that led me to her.

My second chance.

My salvation.

My everything.

Wrapping my arms around Zoe's shoulder, I pulled her to my chest. "I'm so proud of you, Zo. You're one hell of a woman, and these babies are so damn lucky to have a badass mom like you."

She sniffled against my shirt. "Don't forget Molly."

I chuckled and smoothed my hand down her back. "And Molly too."

Gently pulling back, she wiped under her eyes, lips lifting into a wide teasing smile. "I can't wait to tell Mom and Dad you have a *girlfriend.*"

I threw my head back and laughed, surprised at how easy it came. "Maybe I should do it…I do not want to give either of them a heart attack."

She laughed too. "Definitely not." Over her shoulder, she looked down the path we'd just walked. "We should probably head back. We still have a few hours on the road ahead of us."

"I hope I didn't chase you away."

"You didn't," she promised. "Eli has to be at the station early tomorrow morning and I still have a few things to take care of at school. After I spoke to the doctor and realized I'd have to cancel our planned trip, it made me so sad I forced Eli to drive here without really thinking it through." Her expression turned solemn. "I wish we could stay longer."

"Me too," I told her honestly. "Maybe next time?"

That beautiful wide smile was back. "Definitely."

***

I was standing on the curb waving my sister and her family off when Maddie's little blue car pulled into her driveway. The wheels had barely stopped turning before she jumped out and rushed over.

"Oh no," she cried. "I wanted to say goodbye before they left."

Stepping behind her, I wrapped my arms around her waist. "Don't worry, I'm sure once the twins make their appearance they'll be back."

Maddie twisted her head. "Really? It was a good visit then?"

With a deep breath, I took her sweet strawberry scent straight to my lungs before nuzzling her neck. "It was."

Turning in my embrace, her fingers immediately went to the hairs at my nape. Eyes searching mine, the corners of her mouth lifted. "I'm so happy for you."

"Yeah." I dragged my hands down her body until I could cup her ass and pull her flush against me. "I'm happy too."

Maddie laughed heartily. "Oh my goodness, you're terrible."

"I'll show you terrible." As I said the words, I bent my knees and hoisted her over my shoulder in a fireman's hold. She squealed and swatted my ass over and over again, but I didn't stop walking until I was standing in front of my bed.

One flick and she was flat on her back with me hovering over her. Lowering my mouth to hers, I claimed the kiss I'd been craving the little time she'd been away. It started out sweet and slow and quickly turned to frantic and sloppy.

We were ripping at each other's clothes like we couldn't get to what was underneath fast enough. Which we probably couldn't. Fueled by nothing but the need to be connected in the most intimate way possible, there was no slow seduction or teasing touches.

Our bodies moved to the same rhythm. Grunts and moans bouncing off the walls. It was no wonder it didn't take us long to topple over the edge into sweet, sweet ecstasy. Chests heaving and our breaths coming fast and hard, we fell to the mattress. I brushed along her jaw with my thumb before dropping my hand to my stomach. Banding my arm tighter around her, I tugged her to my side and didn't miss how well she fit.

It was as if for all this time I'd been trying to rebuild the puzzle that was my life with the wrong pieces. And lying in my bed with Maddie draped over me, it felt as if the right ones had finally clicked into place.

Her finger slowly started tracing the lines of my tattoo. Starting at my wrist, she carefully followed the ink up and over my shoulder, and across the expanse of my right pec. She lifted those beautiful eyes to mine, and I knew without an ounce of doubt I was done for.

"This means something, doesn't it?"

Lazily, I ran the tips of my fingers down her back and over her hip bone. Grinning when her eyes fluttered closed and a shiver ran through her body. "Why do you think that?"

Her lids parted, revealing golden irises at the same time the slightest pink color stole her cheeks. I wasn't sure whether it was her answer or my fingers brushing her skin that'd brought it on.

She slicked her tongue over her lips. "I might be wrong, but you don't strike me as the kind of person who would do something so elaborate and permanent if it didn't mean something to *you*."

I blinked and blinked again. Then once more. Because how could she know me like this? She saw something that most people had never even given a second thought to. She saw me.

And shit, if that didn't do all sorts of things to my heart.

My fingers kept trailing up and down her skin; tiny bumps popping up beneath my touch. "You're right." I cleared my throat and shifted my gaze to the ceiling. It wasn't hard to recall the events that played such an important part in molding the man I used to be.

"There are certain things that you can never be prepared for no matter how much training you've undergone. For me, that was my first loss to a fire." My eyes flicked to hers; she was watching me so intently. "I'll never forget how cocky we were when we rolled up to the bakery and saw the small amount of smoke billowing out the building."

Young and stupid, that's what we were. "We weren't prepared for what was waiting for us inside. Not even close. Smoke so thick, we couldn't see. Still, we managed to pull almost all of the people out until the owner informed us that one of his employees was unaccounted for."

I closed my eyes against the flash of memories. "I found him in the storeroom. He was pinned beneath a fallen shelf, already breathing heavily due to all the smoke inhalation." My eyes opened and locked onto Maddie's gaze. "I'd promised him I'd get him home to his family."

The words stung as they worked their way up my throat. "I lied," I said thickly. "It was my first loss as a firefighter. I took it hard. For days, I couldn't eat or sleep until I decided to pay my respects to the family. They had pictures of him everywhere, and when I saw his tattoo in one them, I knew straight away I wanted one just like it. I never wanted to forget."

Maddie was staring at me with big, shiny eyes so full of wonder. I wanted to remember that look for the rest of my life. I swallowed hard; I'd never shared this with anyone mostly because no one had ever asked about it.

She wiggled until she was close enough to press her lips to mine. "Thank you for telling me that." Her gaze flicked between my eyes like she was trying to work something out in her head. "You miss firefighting, don't you?"

" I do."

"Something changes in you when you talk about it. Even when the story you're relaying is as tragic as this one." Her fingers brushed over the left side of my chest. "It's a part of you as much as dance is a part of me."

"I suppose it is," I agreed quietly.

Maddie's fingers slowly moved over my scarred skin. "Have you considered going back?"

I had. More times than I could count but for all the steps I'd taken forward, being around people, especially ones I didn't know, still freaked me out. I wasn't entirely sure if I'd be able to get over this particular hurdle if I were being honest.

For whatever reason, I couldn't admit this to the woman who meant the world to me. Maybe it was because I was terrified of her looking at me differently or possibly seeing that there was a coward still living inside me.

Even though there wasn't space for a breath between us, I hugged her body closer to mine. My fingers worked their way into her hair, reveling in the feel of her silky strands brushing against my knuckles. "I don't know," I answered her honestly.

"That's okay." Maddie shifted until she was straddling me. Bending down, her hair fell around us like a thick curtain. Her lips brushed over mine once. "One step at a time and you'll get where you need to be."

I cupped the back of her head and pulled her mouth back to mine to keep the words that burned up my insides from spilling out. Because, yes, it was fast. Yes, it was completely beyond understanding but it didn't change the fact that I loved this woman.

33

MADDIE

I trailed my fingers over the barre that stretched the length of the studio. Unable to contain it, I smiled at my reflection in the wall-to-wall mirror. Soon this would all be mine. I could hardly believe how fast everything had happened over the last couple of days.

Following Frankie's advice, I'd gone to the bank to secure a loan for the amount I needed to acquire Soulbeat. Even though I didn't have bad credit, I was still stress-sweating until the manager had called me with the news that it had been approved.

My excitement could barely be contained.

Lucetta and I had spent quite a bit of time on the phone too. She wanted to make sure I was satisfied with the contract her attorney had sent over and to reassure me that I could change anything I wanted.

Not that I did.

Soulbeat held too many great memories for me. There wasn't a thing I'd change about it. My hope was to build upon what Lucetta had created here. To encourage little girls and boys to follow their dreams and give them the tools to do so.

I was still lost in my own thoughts when the studio door flew open; Jennah and Frankie rushing inside soon after. Digging my heels in, I braced for impact as they hurried toward me.

Sandwiched between my sister and friend, both wrapped their arms around me and hugged me tight.

"Has it sunk in yet?" Jennah asked when I got some of my personal space back.

I grinned at her. "Nope. Not one bit."

Frankie bumped my shoulder with hers. "As soon as the dust settles, we're celebrating."

"Speaking of celebrations," my sister chimed in. "Mom still has no clue about the party, and everything is set and ready to go for tomorrow."

Jennah and Frankie started filling me in on the few things I'd missed during the week as we walked to the— *my*—office together. Even though I was looking forward to celebrating my mom's birthday, I was nervous too.

My mom and I were trying to mend fences as best we could—she'd been to the studio and had asked me about dancing and my plans for the future—but I hadn't seen or spoken to my dad since the day I'd told them about wanting to make Soulbeat mine. I'd called the house and gone to the store a couple of times only to have my mom apologize and beg me to give him more time.

At least my mom was trying. Yes, I knew it was hard for her, but she was doing her best. But my dad? No, he needed time. How much time did he—the man whose blood ran through my veins—need to accept my dream or at least pretend to be happy about it for me?

"Yoo Hoo, Maddie!" I blinked and then blinked again until Frankie's snapping fingers in front of my face came into focus. "The lights are on but nobody's home." Shaking her head, she crossed her arms in front of her.

Scratching the corner of my eye, I scrunched up my nose. "Sorry. What were you saying?"

Frankie rolled her eyes and sighed heavily. "Are we finally going to meet this man of yours, or are you going to keep him locked up in the house forever?"

Jennah nodded like she'd been dying to ask the same question. "I hope he's coming to the party at least. You know, meet the family and all that jazz."

A little tingle started at the base of my neck before it worked its way down my spine and filled my stomach with dread. There was no doubt I wanted Adam at the party with me. But I knew about his aversion to people and being in public places, so I hadn't asked him yet.

I couldn't tell that to my sister or even my best friend. I didn't think they'd understand. Or they'd ask me the one question I really didn't want an answer to.

Was it always going to be like this?

Me flying solo because my boyfriend's demons refused to let him go. I couldn't think about what it would mean if the answer was yes.

"There you go again." Frankie sounded as exasperated as she looked when she threw her hands in the air.

"I'll ask him if he wants to come along." There was a slight trip in my voice, and I hoped like hell they didn't hear it. Judging by the annoyed look on Frankie's face, I highly doubted she heard anything other than her teeth grinding together.

For the first time since we'd been friends, she was in the dark about what was going on with me. Of course, I'd told her Adam and I were seeing more of each other but that's where it stopped. No matter how many times she asked about him, I kept steering the conversation in a different direction.

And it wasn't because of shame or anything like that. Adam's story simply wasn't mine to tell. In some weird way, I felt like I was protecting him if I told them nothing.

Jennah touched her palm to my elbow, effectively pulling me from my thoughts. "I have to go pick up Tommy at Mom and Dad's. I'll see you tomorrow." Her hand tightened around my arm and she pulled me in for another hug. "I'm so proud of you, Maddie. You've already done so many great things and you're going to do so many more."

"Thank you, Jen." I had no idea how I managed to get the words past the enormous lump in my throat. Sure, all my ducks weren't in a row. A lot of unanswered questions still floated above my head like big fat blinking lights but at least my relationship with Jennah was better than it had ever been.

"I have to get going too," Frankie said as Jennah and I pulled out of our embrace. "Those fifty cupcakes aren't going to bake themselves." She might have been slightly irritated with me earlier, but she still hugged me close and once again told me how happy she was for me.

We said our goodbyes and after I walked the two of them out, it was just me and my thoughts left in the studio. Retrieving my phone from my pocket, I connected it to the speaker via Bluetooth and cued up one of my favorite *Amy Lee* songs.

I toed off my shoes and hurried to the middle of the floor. Once the song started, I let go of everything. I allowed the music and lyrics to guide my movements. Kicking my leg high before quickly pulling it back and wrapping my arms around my waist while still swaying to the beat.

I jumped, twirled, and allowed gravity to drag me to the floor while the song reminded me how unexpected love was and how it could grow from nothing. My body moved to every slow beat, drawing out emotions from deep inside me.

Only this time, it wasn't freeing. It hurt. So much that I collapsed into a heap on the floor, my body shaking with every heart-crushing sob that left it. I wasn't even sure why I was crying just that I couldn't stop.

Curled into a ball, I dropped my forehead against the floor and gave in when a pair of arms suddenly wrapped around me and pulled me into a familiar chest. One hand cradled my head as the other smoothed down my back.

I curled my fists into my dad's shirt as my body produced even more tears and snot. This was full-on ugly crying that showed sign of letting up. In fact, the more my dad comforted me, the harder my sobs became.

"That's it. Let it all out," he said softly.

Somehow the gentle tone in his voice coupled with the way he was he was holding me just made me wail even harder. Everything about the moment felt foreign and yet desperately needed.

I wanted to pull away and yell out my frustrations but at the same time, I couldn't bear to let go in case this was the one and only time I'd get to be like this with my dad.

"Please forgive me, Madison," he begged. "I've done so wrong by you; I don't even know how to start making it right."

I shook my head slightly. Not because I didn't want to give him forgiveness, I was trying my hardest to form actual words instead of the unholy whimpering sounds coming from the back of my throat.

" So many mistakes," he whispered against the top of my head, his voice trembling with emotion. "I've made so many mistakes. I wish I could take them all back and start over. But life doesn't work that way, now does it?"

Pausing for a beat, my dad pushed me away slightly, instantly cupping my cheeks. "I'm an idiot, Madison. An idiot who doesn't deserve the gifts life has given me." His thumb swiped at the tears still rolling down my cheeks. "I'm so very sorry, my child. I'm sorry for not supporting your dreams. For not recognizing your talent. For making it all about me when it should've been about *you*."

I took a deep stuttering breath as I tried to regain some of my composure. "You…" *sniff*." Should have…" *sniff*." Told me about…" *sniff*." Your sister."

Dad's eyes were shimmering with tears just waiting to fall. He nodded furiously. "Yes, yes, I should have been honest with you."

My throat felt so thick, it hurt. "So many secrets. So much hurt." Wetting my dry lips, I forged on, "You hurt me, Dad. Made me feel like I wasn't enough. That my dreams were nothing more than silly notions."

"I know, Madison." Two thick tears rolled down my dad's leathery cheeks. "I wish I could go back. Heaven knows how desperately I want to go back and do things differently. It was never you...And it wasn't fair of me to pass my demons on to you."

At this point, I was a sniffling, blubbering mess. I didn't need my dad to go through the whole ugly ordeal for me. It was enough to understand the reasons why he'd acted the way he had.

"But I'm here now and I promise you, no more," he vowed, earnestly. "No more. You hear me? I swear to you, from now on, I'm here. One hundred percent. Whatever you need. I love you so much." My dad crushed me to his chest again, holding me as if he was afraid I'd run away.

I hugged him right back. "Love you too, Dad," I croaked out between sobs.

We probably looked a picture. Both of us sitting in the middle of the floor, crying our eyes out. I didn't care, though. Because there was absolutely nothing in the world that could bring me down after this.

34

ADAM

Who knew seeing a little blue Prius rolling to a stop could put a big smile on my face? It was also entirely possible that the sappy-ass grin I was sporting had nothing to do with the car but rather the woman driving it.

Until the door swung open and she stepped out.

I set Sheldon down and got up from where I was sitting on her front porch step and hurried over to Maddie. Her eyes were somewhat swollen, her nose red, her cheeks blotchy. She'd been crying. And so help me, if I found the person who'd hurt her, *they* were going to hurt.

She didn't have time to shut the door before I held her face in my hands. "Baby, what happened?"

My brow furrowed when Maddie's mouth curved upward, her eyes sparkling with unfiltered happiness. "Something wonderful." When I just kept staring at her, she laughed. "Let's go inside and I'll tell you all about it."

Hand in hand, we headed into the house while Maddie fervently tried to fill me in on how her father had finally given her something she'd craved since she'd been a little girl. The more she talked, the more her features lit up. Warmth seeped into my pores and coated my insides with happiness…for her.

Because of her.

I didn't know the entire story when it came to her parents, but from the little I did know, I understood how important the moment with her father had been. And hell, if she didn't deserve it.

We were standing in the kitchen where Maddie was scooping dog food into Sheldon's bowl. I waited until she set it in front of him before I took her in my arms and held her close. Resting my chin on top of her head, I marveled at how well we fit together. Like she was made just for me.

Maddie tilted her head back, training those whiskey eyes straight at my soul. "Today has been amazing," she admitted quietly, "and it just got better."

There were some pretty powerful words stuck in my throat. But instead of voicing them, I touched my lips to hers. Every brush of my mouth, swipe of my tongue, filled with everything I felt for this woman.

She'd found me at my lowest low when all hope had been abandoned and there was nothing left. Without even realizing, she'd reached in and pulled me from the darkness that had swallowed me whole.

She'd saved me when I'd believed I was unsavable. Taught me to love not only someone else but myself too. There weren't enough words to even attempt to confess to her what she meant to me.

So I kissed her harder instead.

Her hands swept up over my shoulders, fingers spearing into my hair. With a tilt of my head, I deepened the kiss, greedily taking everything she gave me. Down and down I dragged my hands, hoisting her up the instant my fingers dug into her waist.

I lifted her onto the counter and stepped forward as she wrapped her legs around me. Trading her mouth for her throat, I nipped and licked my way along her satiny skin while my fingers found the hem of her shirt.

In one quick move, I tugged it over her head and tossed it to the floor, my lips immediately latching onto the newly exposed skin. I kissed a hot path along her collarbone and down over the swell of her breast. Following the line of her bra with my nose, I took a deep breath and smiled against her skin.

I loved how she always smelled like fucking strawberries.

My tongue touched a lace-covered tip; swirling, licking, teasing at the same time as I worked my fingers up the inside of her thigh. But instead of arching into me, Maddie flattened her palms against my chest and shoved me backward.

"Not so fast," she purred, hopping off the counter. Standing right in front of me, she curled her fingers around the waistband of my jeans and tugged my hips closer. "Why do you always get to have all the fun?"

Holding my gaze, Maddie slowly dropped to her knees while her nimble little fingers worked on my button and zipper. Gripping the material in her fists, she peered up at me, smile all sugary sweet.

But it was the look of pure sin shining bright in her eyes that nearly did me in. In one quick move, she yanked my pants to my ankles and skimmed her palms up my legs. With her hands resting on my thighs, she slicked her tongue over her lips before curling her fingers around my twitching hard-on.

Nothing, not a single thing on this planet could have prepared me for the moment she sucked me into her hot little mouth.

"Shiiiit," I groaned, my hand immediately sliding into her hair, fingertips digging into her scalp. "That feels so damn good, baby."

Maddie hummed, the vibrations of that erotic little sound pushing my hips forward. My grip on her hair tightened, desperately needing her to stay right there a little longer. And Maddie, well, she didn't let up. Using her hand and mouth, she pushed me further and further until I was about two seconds away from exploding. But as always, I wanted to be buried deep inside her when I came.

Hooking my fingers under her arms, I yanked her up with a hard tug. My hand found hair again, wrapping it tightly around my fist. I pulled her face to mine, our lips barely a breath apart.

"You drive me crazy," I rasped against her mouth, "batshit-I-can't-get-enough-crazy."

Her tongue darted out, the tip slicking over *my* lips. "Is that a bad thing?"

"No."

I claimed her mouth in a punishing kiss then. One that had my blood boiling hot with need and my heart threatening to explode from the sheer pressure of what it was keeping inside.

Without breaking the kiss, I stepped out of the pants bunched at my ankles, hoisted her up and walked us over to the couch. Maddie was flat on her back with me grinding into her not even a minute later. It didn't matter that there were still layers of fabric separating us, my skin buzzed as if it was alive and on fire.

White-hot heat blazed through my veins giving my racing pulse a higher gear. As fantastic as that felt though, I still needed to feel her skin against mine. Reaching between us, I'd just slipped my fingers into the waistband of her leggings when she gently pushed at my shoulder.

"Let me do that."

I sat back on my heels; gaze fixed on her as she slipped of the couch. Steadily swaying side to side, Maddie shimmied out of her pants and underwear. Her eyes never left mine. Then she reached behind her to undo her lacy bra before tossing it at me.

I caught it easily. Lifting the material to my nose, I inhaled deeply and groaned. "Strawberries."

With quick movements, I lifted my shirt and tossed it aside before positioning myself at the edge of the couch. Hands parked behind me; I jerked my chin in her direction. "Hop on, baby."

Nibbling on her lip, she let her gaze slowly track down my body and as always with Maddie, there was no shame coating my skin. One heated look from her and it felt as if I could conquer the damn world.

Maddie moved closer. Placing her hands on my shoulders, she set her knees on either side of me and steadily lowered herself. Her warmth wrapping around me with every inch she took.

I wanted to yell. To scream. To curse.

To beg every deity I could think of to give me more of her. Because I needed Maddie. And I needed her to need me as desperately as I did her. Needed her heart to match the crazy rhythm of mine.

For her to love me even if it was just a fraction of the depth of my feelings for her.

Slowly, steadily she began to move. Trailing my hands up her back, I curled my fingers over her shoulders. The tips digging hard into her impossibly soft skin.

Maddie's fingers speared through my hair. Tilting my head slightly, our eyes met. I would've needed to be blind to not recognize the emotion swirling around in those depths. And, shit, if that didn't have my heart expanding and flooding with hope.

Holding my gaze, she rocked her hips, up and down she went, at an impossibly slow pace. Movements that were meant to torture. To steadily drive me toward the brink before pulling back and doing it all over again.

I ducked my head and sucked her breast into my mouth. Eagerly. Hungrily. Clawing at her skin as I took my fill. In the space of a breath, our movements turned frantic. My hands shot to her hips, fingers digging into the skin below her hip bone. Faster and faster she rocked, the grunts and moans of our pleasure bouncing off the walls in a loud echo.

Every thrust, kiss, and lick felt like brutal strikes to my heart, forever branding me with the memory of this.

Her. Us. The words I'd fought so hard to keep inside wanted out. But I wasn't sure if she was even remotely ready to hear them.

So instead of telling her how deeply I had fallen for her, I sank my teeth into her shoulder just as her world exploded. Lightning-fast I lifted my head and seeing her with her eyes closed, mouth agape riding the waves of ecstasy was what broke the dam for me.

I breathed out her name in a harsh whisper over and over again. The intensity of the moment, my feelings, so strong it felt as if it might split me in two.

There was no denying my life would forever, irrevocably be changed because of this woman.

Chests heaving, we fell back against the couch. When our breathing had leveled somewhat, Maddie turned sideways and pushed onto her elbow.

Unable to resist, I wrapped a few of her silky strands around my fingers. "You've brought so much joy back into my life, Maddie."

With a gentle touch, she splayed her fingers over my chest. Her gaze serious as it roamed over my face. "Can I ask you something?"

"Anything, baby. You can ask me anything."

She smiled at me then; big, bright, and beautiful. "It's my mom's fiftieth birthday party tomorrow. We're going all out." A little laugh bubbled over her lips. "Well, as much as we can at the community center. It's not going to be anything massive. Just the family and a few of Mom's friends." The hopeful smile tugging on her lips felt like a sucker punch to the balls.

In the silence that followed, tension knotted my gut. Before she even uttered the words, I knew what was coming. Knew I was about to break my girl's heart.

"Come with me? I want you to meet my family." She nibbled on her lips. "To introduce them to the man I—"

"No."

With one hoarse word my newfound happiness turned to nothing but smoke and ash.

35

MADDIE

"No," he gritted out again. Jaw furiously working back and forth, he glared at me. "How can you even ask me that?" He looked angry and so incredibly hurt. I made a move to reach for him, but he jumped up and grabbed his pants, roughly shoving his legs into the material. "You know why I can't go."

Without zipping up his jeans, he planted his fists on his hips and pinned me with a hard stare. The expression on his face reminded me so much of the Adam I met that very first day. The one who wasn't approachable.

A little crack formed in my heart right then.

My hands trembled when I slipped off the couch and pulled the throw with me, wrapping it around my body like a life jacket. Keeping some distance between us, I desperately searched those dark eyes for any sign of the man who had just made love to me. The one who owned me so completely.

When nothing but coldness stared back at me, I felt another crack behind my breastbone.

Funny how it only took one moment, one minuscule moment in time for things to change so drastically. Suddenly all those niggling little questions that I never really paid too much attention to, fought their way to the surface and demanded answers.

"Is this how it's always going to be?" I asked, my voice shaky. "Will I constantly have to do things by myself? Go to the movies alone? Go to dinner and be seated at a table for one?" Once I started down this path, I couldn't stop. "Will I have to make up some excuse when my friends and family beg to meet you. Or even worse, are you always going to flee when they show up unannounced?"

"That's not fair, Maddie." The way he was looking at me, I couldn't tell if he was hurt or furious.

My throat burned with the effort it took to keep my tears from falling. "I know and I'm sorry." I pushed my hair behind my ear. "But it's not fair to me either, Adam. I want us to be together. To go out and do things…you and me…*together*."

Nostrils flaring, he shifted his gaze away from me. "I can't."

Two words. That was all it took for my heart to finally break. To shatter into so many pieces, I wasn't sure I'd be able to put it back together. This time I didn't fight the tears, they rolled down my cheeks unchecked.

"No," I said softly. "You won't." My voice sounded wobbly and broken when I needed it to be strong.

"I can't do this right now," I heard him mumble under his breath.

I swiped at my eyes and tried to take a steadying breath. "What?"

Adam's gaze snapped to mine. Eyes wide, jaw popping, he looked like a bull ready to charge. "I have to go. I can't be here." He shook his head and repeated his words, "I can't do this right now."

"Then when, Adam?"

Gritting his teeth, he set one foot in front of the other, closing the distance between us with measured strides. My broken heart picked up speed, painfully slamming against my ribs. "Why are you doing this? I thought you understood—accepted—me."

Lifting his hand, Adam took a few strands of my hair between his fingers but quickly let go again as if being burned. "Clearly, this was a mistake." With a sharp shake of his head, he took a step back. "It's been fun, Maddie."

If my heart was the intended target, then those four words so callously thrown out certainly hit their mark. A slap across the face would probably have hurt less. My chin trembled as I watched him snatch up the rest of his clothes from the floor. When his legs started moving, I closed my eyes because I didn't want to see him walk out of the room.

Out of my life.

Adam's footfalls grew softer and softer until the front door closed with a loud slam. I jerked, the action violently ripping what little strength I had left from my body. My knees wobbled and then gave out, leaving me to slide to the floor in a miserable heap while staring at the empty doorway.

Sheldon chose that moment to come scurrying toward me, his little tongue furiously trying to catch the tears spilling over my lids. I cradled him to my chest and greedily took the comfort he was offering.

How did we even get to this in the blink of an eye? Did I push too hard? Was I being unfair? Expecting too much of him too soon? Was it better that it ended now before I got in too deep?

Was it even over?

My head was spinning. All these unanswered questions bouncing around and around.

The only other time I'd felt this lost and confused had been right before I'd decided to leave New York to come back to Clearwater Bay.

At that time there'd been only one person to give me perspective, so it was only natural that I sought her advice again. Which was why I found myself knocking on Sugar Booger's door almost thirty minutes later.

Through the large panel of glass, I could see Frankie heading toward the door, she'd barely pulled it open when I started rambling, "I know you're busy with my mom's birthday cupcakes, but would you mind if I kept you company for a bit?"

Almost immediately Frankie threw her arms around me and hugged me tight.

" What's wrong, Maddie Cakes?"

"Everything."

Before I had time to fully process what was happening, she shuffled us to the kitchen and started preparing tea. While she was busy, I took in the rows of cupcakes on the bench. Sitting in silver foil cups, the tops were adorned with frilly lilac and white frosting with the smallest sprinkling of glitter.

"Mom's going to love these," I said to her.

Frankie smiled wide as she walked over and handed me a steaming cup of comfort. "They're earl grey and lavender flavored, and I used cream cheese frosting to make it less sweet."

"They're perfect." I had no doubts that my mom's face would be lighting up the instant she tasted Frankie's creation. Of course, just thinking about the party had my mind going straight back to Adam. Or more specifically how I handled things.

Frankie patted my arm before slipping around the bench. I didn't miss the fact that my usually chatty friend was being uncharacteristically quiet. I knew it was because she was giving me breathing room to work through the mess in my head. But all this time to think was only filling me with doubts and regrets.

Carefully, Frankie set a cupcake on the turntable in front of her and while she spun it in a circle, she steadily moved the piping bag back and forth. Smooth ripples of frosting peeled from the nozzle to create the beautiful ruffled design.

"Talk to me, Maddie," Frankie hedged without taking her eyes off her hands. "What happened?"

My gaze flicked to the cup resting on the countertop in front of me. "I think I messed up—" Once I started talking there was no stopping the words from spilling out. I told her everything from how Adam and I grew closer up until the fight—was it even that?—we had earlier.

The entire time while I was pouring my heart out, she quietly decorated the cupcakes. It was that eerie stillness from her that had panic clawing at my chest. "I overreacted, didn't I?"

Frankie's shoulders rose and fell with the deep breath she took. Setting the piping bag on the counter, she reached across and patted my laced fingers. "This is a tricky one." Pulling her hand back, she lowered herself onto a stool. "You're not wrong for wanting the things you do—"

"But?"

"Can you imagine how Adam feels? The things that run through his head when people look at him?" Leaning forward, she drummed her fingers against the surface of the workbench. "Take me for instance, I don't have scars or deformities but there are times when I get uncomfortable when someone stares too long. It makes me feel icky and self-conscious. I'd bet anything it's a hundred times worse for Adam."

I narrowed my eyes. "So you're saying I was wrong?"

"No one is in the wrong here, Maddie Cakes." Pushing to her feet, Frankie rounded the bench and gripped me by the shoulders. "Like I said, you have every right to feel the way you do just as he has that same right. There's also a very real possibility that he might never be comfortable with being in public. You're going to have to decide if that's something you can live with."

Could I do it? Be in a relationship and still go out and do things by myself—all the time?

36

ADAM

The weights in my hands fell against the concrete floor with a loud clank. I chuckled bitterly when the hollow sound disturbingly matched the hole inside my chest. The stupid space behind my breastbone that suddenly had feeling after years of being numb.

As much as I hated the dull ache inside my heart that seemed to find new heights with every thump against my ribs, I didn't wish it away. Because buried beneath the hurt and confusion was everything I felt for Maddie.

And I could never wish her away.

It'd taken me a good few hours to accept the possibility that I might've overreacted. Make no mistake, being around people scared the shit out of me. The way their eyes always lingered had a direct line to the part of my brain where my confidence stemmed from.

What I had failed to let sink in was the fact that these weren't just any people Maddie wanted to introduce me to. It was her family and friends. The people closest to her. Her inner circle.

And she wanted to include me in that.

Shit! I wasn't just screwed up; I was a gigantic ass too. I fell back on the bench and threw a sweaty arm over my equally sweaty forehead. With a heavy sigh, my eyes roamed over the ceiling.

I needed to see her, talk to her. Make this right between us because there was no way I could let her go. Not without a fight. And definitely not when I knew she felt the same way about me.

Maddie's mouth might say one thing, but those whiskey eyes that could see into the very bottom of my soul? They could never lie. Buried deep inside her and loving on her body, I'd not only felt her love, I'd seen it too.

Dropping my arm, I pushed to my feet and grabbed the towel dangling over the barbell. With jerky movements, I dragged it over my face and damp hair. My arm screamed in protest at the simple task, an indication that I'd spent way too long brooding, throwing around weights when I should've dragged my ass next door.

Not even two minutes later, I hopped over the fence and all but ran up to Maddie's glass door. When I noticed that the curtains were drawn and the door pulled shut, I threw my head back and barked out a laugh.

How damn ironic. The one day I needed to see her, she made sure no one was getting in. I knocked and knocked some more, my heart sinking to my feet with every agonizing minute that passed.

After what felt like an eternity, I stepped back and swiped my hand over my mouth. Reaching behind me, I pulled my phone from my pocket and swiped the screen to life. My heart's nervous rhythm almost deafening while I scrolled to her number and pressed the device against my ear. Instead of Maddie's sweet voice filtering through the line, a generic one informed me she was unavailable and to leave a message.

If my fingers hadn't been curled so tightly around the device, I might've given in to the need to toss it across her yard. I didn't want to leave a damn message. I wanted to talk to Maddie.

Rubbing my thumb and index finger over my eyebrows, I dropped my chin to my chest and let out a heavy breath. Knots twisted and turned in my stomach, hopelessness crashing over me like a big angry wave.

Where was she?

Out of the corner of my eye, I caught movement by the curtains. My head snapped up, heart furiously trying to hammer its way out of my chest. The curtain moved again, I held my breath and waited to see her beautiful face appear at the other side of the glass.

Unfortunately, when the curtain shifted once more, it wasn't Maddie standing there but rather Sheldon. On his hind legs, he was pawing at the glass with super speed. His normal yapping replaced with a melancholic howl I'd never heard before.

Even the damn dog knew how I'd screwed up.

Crouching down, I pressed my hand against the glass and felt my heart make a funny dip when Sheldon's wet nose immediately squished against it on his side. Apparently, I loved the little shit almost as much as I loved his owner.

"I'll make it right, buddy, I promise."

There was a plan forming in my head as I slowly straightened. The mere thought of what I was contemplating doing had my stomach rolling with nausea and my heart beating ten times too fast.

I'd push past all of it for the opportunity to tell the woman I loved how much she meant to me.

MADDIE

"Oh! You look gorgeous."

I closed my eyes and sucked in a breath when Jennah's arms wrapped around me. I'd promised myself I would be one-hundred percent present today. I owed my mom that much. Even though my heart was constantly yelling at me to go home so I could talk to Adam.

Like the hot mess I'd been the previous day, I'd left my phone at home when I'd hurried over to Sugar Booger. Then after Frankie and I had talked, she'd insisted I spend the night at her place, using the time to really think about what I wanted and what it would mean for my future.

And I had.

I'd thought long and hard about everything and every time I came to one simple conclusion: I loved Adam.

Of course, I felt like an even bigger fool over the way I'd reacted. Instead of my woe is me act, I should've understood and respected his decision. And I was going to tell him that as soon as this party was over.

"So do you," I said to my sister when we finally pulled apart. The flowy white dress she was wearing hit her just above her knees. It was soft and feminine with a scalloped hem and lace detail to the collar completing her look.

Jennah touched the curls tumbling over her shoulder, cheeks turning rosy. "I can't even remember the last time I wore a dress, let alone something as pretty as this one." She scrunched up her nose, a soft laugh blowing over her lips. "Kinda pathetic, right?"

Cupping her shoulders, I gave them a gentle squeeze. "Well, you've been busy being a badass mom to an amazing little boy." Another squeeze. "Once you get your party planning business up and running, you can wear pretty dresses every day."

Probably thinking it was a joke, Jennah waved me off with a giggle. Only, I wasn't joking. The moment I stepped foot inside the community center, I knew this was my sister's calling.

She'd taken the boring space and transformed it into a white and lilac paradise. Beautiful balls of flowers suspended from the ceiling at different heights with delicate fairy lights draped in between. The tables were adorned with a small arrangement of three flowers with a candle sitting in the middle. A space that could've easily been overpowering looked soft and inviting.

Yeah, I was pretty damn impressed with what Jennah had pulled off. This was without a doubt something she needed to pursue, but today wasn't the day to talk to her about it. So instead, I gave her another hug and told her I was proud of her.

With a smile, she headed off in the direction of the kitchen. Turning the opposite way, I went in search of

Frankie and walked straight into my mom's friends, Mrs. Peterson and Mrs. Hendrickson.

I'd known them all my life, so it was no surprise they already knew I was taking over Soulbeat. What did manage to knock me on my butt was how excited they were.

I smiled and nodded as they enthusiastically told me I should consider doing something for the seniors as well. The idea wasn't bad at all, and I was going to give it serious consideration…as soon as the Adam-sized anvil was lifted off my chest.

Mrs. Peterson parked her hands on her hips before slowly rotating them. "See? Age ain't nothing but a number," she said on a laugh. "I can still keep up with the young ones."

Naturally, while she was talking about *her* hips, my mind shot to Adam and our first kiss. Hadn't it been stiff hips that'd started it all? My heart squeezed tight. So painfully tight I wanted to press my palm to the spot for relief.

Instead of doing that, I grinned at the ladies in front of me. "Mrs. Peterson, you're not only keeping up, I think you're even out-dancing some of them."

Both women threw their silver heads back and laughed heartily. The sound was so happy and infectious, I couldn't help but join in.

"This looks cheerful." My mom sidled in beside me and immediately slipped her arm around my shoulders. That one small action had such a big effect on my heart.

There'd been a time, not so long ago, where something as simple as this had seemed completely out of my reach.

Mrs. Hendrickson was the first to regain her composure. "Maddie is going to teach us old ladies how to properly wiggle our hips."

"Speak for yourself." Mrs. Peterson looked appalled. "*I* already know how to wiggle and jiggle. I just want Maddie to do the classes so I can keep all of *this* in shape."

"Yes, Glenda, we know." With a small shake of her head, Mrs. Hendrickson rolled her eyes. Smiling at my mom and I, she hooked her arm through Mrs. Peterson's and together they strolled away.

Twisting sideways, I wrapped my mom up in a hug. "Happy Birthday, Mom."

Her arms banded tight around me. "Yes, it really is a happy one today." Pulling back, she held on to my shoulders as her eyes roamed over my face. "I can't believe you and your sister planned all of this for me."

"It was all Jennah," I said. "She's pretty amazing."

Her hands moved from my shoulders to my cheeks. "You both are." I heard the truth in her words, felt it all the way to my heart. She pulled me in for another crushing embrace before taking a step backward. "You know, I think this might be my best birthday yet."

I grinned. "That makes me so happy."

Mom nibbled on her lip before asking, "Tell me more about this dance class Glenda was talking about?"

I didn't even think it was possible but inside my chest, my heart swelled. I was positive it was going to take me a long while to get used to my mom and me chatting away about dancing.

Which was exactly what we did for the following ten minutes until I spotted my dad ambling toward us. I held my breath as my pulse ticked to an uneasy beat until he stepped up next to my mom. We hadn't talked since my *wonderful* meltdown in the studio, and even though I knew we were rebuilding the burnt-to-a-crisp bridge between us, I was still somewhat nervous to see him.

Time healed all wounds, right?

Funny how time was the one thing I didn't give Adam. I'd stood before him, assured him I saw him, and then when he really needed me to be understanding, I pushed him away.

I was such a freaking idiot.

"You look lovely, Madison." At the sound of my dad's voice, my attention shifted back to my parents.

Smoothing my hands down the lilac material of my dress—one that looked similar to Jennah's—I tried my best to give them a genuine smile, but I just couldn't. Everything weighing inside me was simply too heavy. "Thanks, Dad."

Both my parents 'brows drew together in tandem. If I wasn't feeling as crap as I did, I probably would have laughed at how freaky it was. Holding my gaze, my dad slung his arm around my mom's waist and pulled her to him. "Everything all right?"

I wasn't entirely sure if he was asking whether things were good between us or if I was doing okay. "Of course,

Dad." If I heard the lack of conviction in my own voice, certainly they did too.

Dad's eyes narrowed. "You're not having man troubles, are you?"

My eyes bugged out of my skull. "What? W-why would you think that?" Even though he was pretty spot-on, I couldn't fathom how the hell he came to that conclusion in the first place. Sure, Jennah knew about Adam, but she wasn't clued in on the latest development. And I highly doubted Frankie would've said anything.

While I tried to work it out in my head, my dad's gaze flicked to something over my shoulder before it returned to me. "Well, there's a six-foot-something man standing right there—" he jerked his chin toward my shoulder "—looking at you as if you might just be his world."

My eyebrows shot up. "There's a what now?" It took my brain two full seconds to properly take in my dad's words. The instant they registered, I spun around so fast, I almost fell over. My heart stopped dead at the same time as my trembling hands flew to my mouth. "Adam."

38

ADAM

I drew in a deep breath. Held it for a few seconds. Then slowly released it through my nose. My heart was pounding wildly, furiously trying to escape the confines of my chest. Even my palms were sweaty.

About a million ants crawled over my skin while I was acutely aware of all the eyes on me. It'd taken every ounce of willpower I had to walk through the doors and search the crowd for Maddie.

There were a thousand things I'd wanted to say to her. Hell, I'd even rehearsed this wonderful speech on the way over. But now that she was standing in front of me, looking like my every dream come true, the words remained trapped on my tongue.

Not that she was doing any moving or talking either. With her eyes taking up half of her face and her hands covering the rest, she was staring at me like she couldn't decide whether I was real or not.

My throat felt impossibly thick as I tried to work down a swallow. Slowly, I parted my lips to speak but before I could utter a single word, an older man with thick gray brows pulled tightly appeared at Maddie's side.

I didn't need to ask how I'd missed him in the first place. The instant I'd spotted her, Maddie had been the only person in the room to have my full attention. Shifting my gaze to the man, it only took a few moments to see the resemblance.

Eyes that looked so much like his daughter's looked me up and down before he thrust his hand toward me. "Fraser Young. And this here is my lovely wife, Carolynn."

Straightening my spine, I pressed my palm against his. "Adam Carlisle. A pleasure to meet you, sir." I traded his hand for his wife's. "Happy Birthday, Mrs. Young. It's good to meet you."

Touching her free hand to the edges of her shoulder-length hair, Maddie's mom graced me with a sweet smile. "Thank you." Gently pulling her hand from mine, she turned to her husband. "Come on, dear, I want to show you the lovely cupcakes Franchesca made."

Mr. Young looked at his wife like she had a third eye. "Didn't you just—"

"Fraser," Mrs. Young said sternly, eyes not-so-subtly bouncing between Maddie and me. "Come look at the cupcakes with me."

She didn't really give him the chance to respond before she slipped her hand in his. "So lovely to meet you, Adam." And then she was off, dragging a grumbling Mr. Young behind her.

My gaze followed them for a bit before slowly shifting back to Maddie. Eyes wide, she was still staring at me. So damn beautiful. All I wanted to do was take her in my arms and never let go.

But I probably needed to say something first. "Hi."

Pulling her hands away from her lips, she slowly started shaking her head. "You're here." It was barely above a whisper. "I can't believe you're here." Her hand was trembling slightly when she lifted it to tuck a few strands behind her ear.

Fighting the need to reach for her, to slip my fingers through hers, was almost impossible. It was like my body knew it needed her to stay sane.

"Neither can I."

Although, from the moment I'd figured out what I had to do to make it right between us, not coming hadn't even been an option. Even if it was the last thing I ever did. Yes, it felt like the scariest, most daunting thing I could possibly do, but I'd happily do it ten times over for *her*.

I took a small step forward. "You look stunning." At my compliment, she bowed her head and smoothed her hands over the front of her pretty dress. I couldn't hold back anymore, I needed to touch her. To feel some part of her. I tucked my fingers beneath her chin and gently guided her gaze back to mine. "I'm sorry, Maddie. So damn sorry."

My hand moved to cup her satiny cheek and her eyes immediately fell shut as she pressed into my touch. When her lids slowly parted again, the sadness shining in her eyes felt like a slap to the balls.

I'd put it there and I sure as shit was going to do whatever the hell I could to take it away again. Before I could tell her that, she pulled my hand from her face and stepped closer. The space between us was so little, I could've easily bent down and touched my lips to hers.

And damn it, that's exactly what I wanted to do.

"There's a gazebo outside," she said softly." It's not completely private, but it's a lot less crowded than in here."

My heart almost couldn't handle her words, the thoughtfulness behind them. Stooping, I looked straight into her beautiful eyes. "I'm good exactly where I am."

With her gaze frantically searching mine, Maddie's tongue darted out and slicked over her bottom lip. "I shouldn't have put you on the spot like that. It was very unfair of me." Her breathing picked up and she shook her head. "I don't care, Adam. Not about dinners or movies or whatever the hell else I said. I just care about you. About us."

The grin lifting my lips couldn't be helped. Wasn't that the exact same thing I'd come here to tell her? That our relationship was the only thing that mattered to me, too. Instead of saying any of those words, I closed the distance between us and touched my mouth to hers.

Never before had a kiss tasted as sweet as this. Like a soothing salve to a gaping wound. Food for a dying man's soul.

Like coming home.

Not even considering we were in the middle of a fairly crowded room, I licked at the seam of her lips;

begging for entry. She parted them on a sigh, her hands sweeping up the back of my neck and pushing into my hair. A deep groan vibrated through my chest the moment my tongue touched hers. I tasted, savored like I was a starved man.

Because I was.

I wanted more. More of her kisses. More of the way she was holding on to me like she couldn't stand to let me go. More of the life I'd gotten a glimpse of since Maddie showed up.

I wanted it all.

When we finally broke apart—with great reluctance—Maddie's cheeks were flushed and her lips my favorite shade of thoroughly-kissed. Her gaze flicked to the side before settling back on mine. "I think we've attracted an audience."

Curling my fingers into her waist, I brushed my nose along hers. "I don't care." I pulled back and pinned her with a stare. "Do you?"

Her answering smile was big, bright, and wonderful. "I still can't believe you came here...for me."

"Believe it, baby. I'd walk to the ends of the earth for you." I laced our fingers together and turned my head to scan the crowd. "Now, we better go find your parents. I don't want them thinking I only came here to devour their daughter."

Maddie dropped my hand and threw her arms around my neck. "I love you, Adam."

My arms banded tight around her. Angling my head, I spoke low against the shell of her ear. "I feel everything for you, Maddie, *everything*."

And then just because I could, I pulled her in for another kiss. My tongue had barely slipped into her mouth when we were interrupted by a woman, an unmistakable hint of amusement in every word she spoke.

"I'm all for public displays of affection, but the two of you seriously need to cut it out."

Drawing back, I groaned. Maddie laughed. Because I couldn't stand to let her go, I slipped my arm around her shoulders and tugged her close to me as we turned. The moment my eyes landed on the raven-haired woman, I immediately recognized her from the pictures hanging on Maddie's wall.

"Frankie, I presume."

One corner of her red-stained mouth curved upward. "And you must be Adam." Her eyes narrowed into thin slits as she looked me up and down and then flicked her gaze to Maddie. Whatever Frankie saw on my girl's face had her features softening in an instant.

Then her attention was back on me. Smile wide, she took a step forward and held out her hand. "It's great to finally meet you." Before I could take her offered hand, I noticed her eyes on my scars. In a blink, my heart found a new gear. The collar of my dress shirt wrapping around my neck like a noose.

Who the hell was I kidding? I couldn't do this.

My nerves were hanging on by a thin thread, and just when I thought I was going to crack, I felt Maddie's arm tighten around my waist. My eyes found hers. So much love and understanding shining in those whiskey irises. And that was all it took to calm the restless beast.

Grinning, I took Frankie's hand. "Likewise. I'm looking forward to—"

"Mister Adam!"

I barely had time to look to my right when a little person skidded to a stop in front of me. I remembered him. He'd been at Maddie's place a while ago, talking a mile a minute about airplanes.

"Hey, buddy."

His face lit up, lips parting like he was about to speak. Before he could utter a single word, our little gathering grew. Maddie's sister—I recognized her from the other night—came to a stop behind her son.

With her hands perched on his shoulders, she bent forward and whisper-shouted next to his ear, "When I tell you to stop running, you stop running, mister."

She was still hunched over when Frankie elbow-jabbed her in the side. "This is *Adam*."

I heard Maddie's soft laugh as her sister's eyes shot to me.

Even though I didn't feel remotely comfortable, I smiled and held out my hand. "Nice to meet you."

"Jennah." Shaking my hand furiously, she turned her attention to her sister. "This is him, huh?"

Leaning in closer, Maddie's hold on me tightened even more. "Yes, this is Adam. My Adam. And he was about to kiss me stupid before all of you rudely interrupted."

It was a bit comical how quickly Jennah slapped her hands over her son's ears and muttered, "Little ears."

Even more funny than that was the boy's dramatic eye roll and his whiny, "Mooooom."

A laugh rumbled from my chest, surprising me for a moment before I realized how good it felt to be around people.

Or maybe it was good because the woman I loved, loved me back.

"Now that's the sound of folks enjoying a party." Mr. Young and his wife sidled in beside me. I felt a sharp clap against my shoulder blade before he turned toward me. "You and I need to have a beer, son. Discuss your intentions with my daughter and all that."

"Oh my gosh, Dad," Maddie groaned.

"Fraser!" her mom reprimanded.

I just grinned. "I'm ready when you are, sir."

He must've liked my answer because his wrinkly lips stretched into a pleased smile as he squeezed my shoulder.

Another wall came crumbling down at that moment. Sure, I still had a hell of a long way to go, but I wasn't going to walk it alone.

***

"Finally," I groaned against her mouth before diving back in for another kiss. We'd stayed and mingled at her mom's party for another two hours before Maddie and I finally slipped away.

As great as it had been to meet and spend time with the people who meant the most to her, it was still new and very daunting to me.

There were moments where the room had felt too small. Where eyes would linger too long and anxiety would rear its ugly head and claw at my skin. In those moments I'd wanted to flee. To hide myself from their assessments, their judgments.

But then Maddie would squeeze my hand or touch her palm to my chest like she knew what I was feeling. And then by some miracle, my thoughts would settle. My heart would calm.

She grounded me, kept me sane. I was incredibly grateful for that.

For her.

So grateful, in fact, that we'd barely stepped through her front door before I pinned her against it and devoured her mouth like a ravenous beast.

Judging by the way she was fumbling with the buttons on my shirt, I didn't think she minded our current position too much.

My lips moved along her delicate jawline to the sensitive spot below her ear. Latching on, I grazed her skin with my teeth before nibbling my way down her throat.

"Mhm." Maddie's back arched, her beasts pushing into my chest. There were at least three layers of material separating us, but I still felt the warmth of her as if her bare skin was touching mine.

But that's how everything was with this woman. Always heightened to the max.

Maddie threaded her fingers through my hair. Lifting her knee, she dragged it up along my leg. My hand went to her thigh, slowly skimming up her satiny skin until I could fill my palm with her ass.

At that first touch, an animalistic growl tore my lungs. Because shit, she was either wearing a thong or absolutely nothing at all.

It was the deep-rooted need to find out that had me sinking to my knees and ducking my head under her dress. Grinning, I traced the lacy triangle with my finger before shoving it aside and putting my mouth on her.

With a not so gentle touch, I gripped her leg and guided it over my shoulder. My mouth never left her, eagerly, hungrily lapping everything she had to give.

"Oh yes." Maddie bucked her hips, frantically writhing the more I licked and sucked.

When she got closer and closer to that blissful edge of ecstasy, I doubled my efforts. Because I lived to make this woman feel good.

"So close," Maddie moaned, her needy whimpers growing louder and louder by the second. The moment I gently bit into her sensitive flesh, her thighs shook, and my name blew over her lips in a reverent prayer.

With my hands gripping her hips, she rode the final waves of her pleasure. "You're so good at that," she finally breathed out as she slouched and slid down against the door.

Before her ass hit the ground, I gathered her in my arms and cradled her against my chest. Tilting her head back, she beamed at me with a lazy smile spreading across her gorgeous face.

It was also the moment Sheldon chose to join us. Hopping on to my stretched-out legs, he showered both Maddie and me with wet doggy kisses. Loud peals of laughter spilled from her lips, bathing me in so much happiness I feared my heart might explode.

She lowered her face and smacked a kiss to the top of Sheldon's head before guiding him down to her lap.

Then her beautiful gaze was back on me.

My eyes followed the movement of my hands brushing a few wayward strands from her forehead. "I don't even want to think where I'd be if you hadn't come into my life when you did."

With a feather-light touch, Maddie trailed her fingers over my scarred neck. Peering up at me from beneath those impossibly thick lashes, the corners of her mouth lifted into a mischievous grin. "You'd probably be scowling at the world."

I threw my head back and laughed. "You're right. I had a hell of a chip on my shoulders."

Her face turned serious within the space of a breath. "You know I wouldn't change a thing about you, right?" Maddie smoothed her hand over the left side of my chest. "Your broken parts were made to fit mine."

"I know."

Slipping my fingers beneath her chin, I pressed my lips to hers. My heart so impossibly full because it didn't matter how broken I was, the universe still gave me her.

My person.

My Maddie.

And I was going to spend the rest of my life being the man she deserved.

EPILOGUE

MADDIE

My heart fluttered as the first notes of the wedding march filled the small church and wrapped around me like a big, happy hug. With my grin stretching wider, I slowly pushed to my feet. But instead of watching the bride walking down the aisle, my gaze traveled to the man standing next to the groom.

The one who looked way too damn sexy for his own good. And who apparently found me more interesting than the vision floating toward them. You'd think after being on the receiving end of that dark intense stare for over a year, I'd be used it.

I wasn't.

Not even close.

Honestly, I couldn't imagine a day where one look from Adam wouldn't have heat rushing through my veins or the butterflies in my stomach taking flight. And I was completely okay with that.

Like it had done a million times before we'd arrived at the church, his gaze leisurely swept up and down the length of my body before he subtly patted his pants ' pocket. The one he'd stuffed my panties into after not-so-delicately removing them before we left the hotel room.

His lips twitched before curving upward in one of those I-can't-hide-how-happy-I-am smiles. He'd been doing a lot of that lately. Especially after he took a position at Clearwater Bay Fire Department. I loved seeing him like this. Loved how comfortable he'd gotten in his own skin.

I just loved him.

I was still getting lost in Adam's eyes when the beautiful bride reached her destination and we were prompted to sit down. As wonderful as the ceremony was, it was always the best man who stole my attention.

And when Mr. and Mrs. Gallagher finally said their I do's and rushed toward the exit, *I* hurried toward Adam.

"Hi." His strong arms wrapped around me, tugging me closer.

I tilted my head back to look into his eyes. "Hi, yourself."

The way he smiled down at me filled me with so much happiness, I thought I might burst from sheer pressure of it. Adam's dark head stooped to run his nose along mine. "Wanna take a walk with me?"

"Aren't you supposed to be taking photos with the wedding party."

"Mmm mmm." His lips touched the corner of my mouth sending a delicious shiver down my spine. "We took a ton before the ceremony. I'm all photoed out." He pulled back and pinned me with a stare that had my blood turning to lava. "Besides I want to steal a few moments alone with you."

My brow arched. "To return my underwear?"

"Oh no. The only thing covering that part of you will be my mouth." Before I even had time to say anything to that, he grabbed my hand and started walking toward the side exit.

Once outside an endless stretched of green hills greeted us. The moment we'd arrived in the small Irish town two nights ago, I'd fallen in love. I couldn't wait to come back and explore.

Still holding onto my hand, Adam turned left, taking us away from the overexcited guests gushing over the bride and groom. It wasn't long before we reached the edge of the cliff overlooking the town.

With a happy sigh, I wrapped my free hand around Adam's tick bicep and leaned my head against his shoulder. As beautiful and peaceful as the landscape was, it had nothing on the feeling I felt standing there next to the man I loved.

The man that would catch me every single time I fell.

Adam pressed a soft kiss to the top of my head before he detangled himself from my hold and wordlessly dropped down on one knee.

My heart picked up speed, furiously slamming against my ribs. Was he…? I got my answer when he reached into his back pocket and pulled out a little velvet box.

Instantly, my hands flew to my face and yelled out, "Yes!" before he could utter a single word.

Those dark eyes narrowed in my direction, lips curving upward as he dryly remarked, "I haven't asked yet."

Unable to contain my excitement, I hopped from one foot to the other. "I know. Sorry." Scrunching up my nose, I squeaked out, "You can ask now."

With a soft chuckle, he shook his head. "The moment is kind of gone." Bracing one hand on his knee, he pushed to his feet. I was wrapped up in his strong arms barely a second later. "So you wanna spend the rest of your life with me?"

My hands smoothed up his chest and over those massive shoulders. "I thought you'd never ask."

He graced me with the most brilliant smile right before he crashed his mouth to mine and stole the breath from my lungs.

Yeah, I had no doubt I was going to be living my best damn life.

ALSO BY A.K. MACBRIDE

ALL BOOKS ARE FREE IN KINDLE UNLIMITED

Willow Creek:
Shattered
Wrecked
Ruined

Breathing Hearts:
Instant Heat
Wild Fire (preorder)

Cocky Hero Club:
Egotistical Jerk

Montana Dudes:
Broken Roads

Standalone Titles:
An Inconvenient Marriage

Novellas:
Stuck on you
The Other Brother

Please visist www.akmacbride.com for more information.

Printed in Great Britain
by Amazon